PRIME SUSPECT

SYD SULLIVAN

ARCHWAY
PUBLISHING

This is a work of fiction. All of the characters, names, incidents,
organizations, and dialogue in this novel are either the products
of the author's imagination or are used fictitiously.

Archway Publishing books may be ordered through booksellers or by contacting:

Archway Publishing
1663 Liberty Drive
Bloomington, IN 47403
www.archwaypublishing.com
1 (888) 242-5904

Because of the dynamic nature of the Internet, any web addresses or
links contained in this book may have changed since publication and
may no longer be valid. The views expressed in this work are solely those
of the author and do not necessarily reflect the views of the publisher,
and the publisher hereby disclaims any responsibility for them.

Any people depicted in stock imagery provided by Getty Images are
models, and such images are being used for illustrative purposes only.
Certain stock imagery © Getty Images.

ISBN: 978-1-4808-7919-5 (sc)
ISBN: 978-1-4808-7918-8 (e)

Library of Congress Control Number: 2019907591

Print information available on the last page.

Archway Publishing rev. date: 6/24/2019

1

PROM-TO-BE

On May 22, 1995, Nick, a high-school senior, was excitedly getting ready for his senior prom. The whole year had been amazing with his girlfriend, Amy; he wouldn't want to go to prom with anyone else. She was perfect in his eyes, and he loved her more than anything in the entire world.

Although Nick did not know it, Amy was not feeling entirely the same way about him. The truth was that she was in love with another classmate. She wanted to tell Nick, but she couldn't bear to confess to him. Amy couldn't force herself to make a clean break with Nick because of all the history they had together. So she ended up keeping her relationship with Sean a secret.

Nick was a typical boyfriend. He did everything Amy expected on dates. He showered her with small gifts throughout the day on the first of every month.

But when Sean had moved to the city, Amy had found him to be irresistible. He was a striking, fit guy who had just moved from New York to Boston, and he had a big reputation to uphold. Sean's father was a very successful businessman, and his mother was a well-put-together housewife who was a talented gourmet cook. They moved into a first-class gated neighborhood just outside of Boston, and Sean arrived at school every day driving a silver 1995 Porsche. He always had the windows cranked down and the music blasting as he drove by jealous classmates. The whole parking lot could hear his radio as he pulled into a spot.

It appeared that the new kid had his life all put together. Nick had also heard through the school that Sean had already been accepted to Harvard University. He would be leaving for early orientation right after graduation.

Sean's flashy car and clothes seemed to impress everyone at school but Nick. He could see that Sean had a chip on his shoulder the size of a boulder, along with a cocky attitude. Nick wasn't going to get drawn in by his fake personality. For a New Yorker he represented well, but now Nick had decided he would never want to visit the state.

Nick was in his bedroom, putting on his tux for prom. His room was plastered with Gwen Stefani and Shakira posters. You could barely see any of the paint on the walls. His record player was playing "Billie Jean" by Michael Jackson. To the right of his record player, he had albums by every artist imaginable, from the Beatles to Michael Jackson, Queen, and Elvis Presley. Under that section of albums were dozens of Nick's favorite novels; everything was stacked alphabetically, and there was not a speck of dust on the wooden bookcase. Nick loved music, and whatever mood he was in, one of his favorite songs could make his day.

In his suit and tie, with his dark hair slicked back, Nick was all cleaned up for the night. As he was about to leave his room, he remembered the corsage for Amy that was sitting on his desk. He raced to grab it and then looked in the mirror again on his way out of his bedroom. He made sure his tie was perfectly straight and grabbed a bottle of cologne from his dresser. He put a small dab on each side of his neck. He was ready to go. He rushed down the stairs, his shoes shining like mirrors.

His mom, Veronica, was waiting for him at the bottom of the stairs, pleased to see her son dressed very dashingly. She smiled at how handsome he looked as he reached the bottom of the stairs. Nick's dad had left his mom high and dry when he found out she was pregnant with Nick. She'd raised Nick all on her own and was so proud of the man he had become over the years. He was a strong individual, he was smart, and he had a very bright future ahead of him.

"Sweetheart, you look very striking in that suit." She brushed slightly at some lint on his jacket.

"Thanks, Ma. Do you think Amy will like this one?" He showed his mom the corsage. It had a pink rose in the middle surrounded by white lace and smaller blue flowers weaving around the rose and throughout the lace. It sat in a small, clear box that Nick struggled to hold as his hands became jittery.

"She's gonna love it, baby."

Nick smiled nervously as he went to grab his camera in the living room. He looked around at the yellow walls, brown couch, coffee table, rocking chair, and TV by the fireplace. Nick and his mother were considered to be lower-middle class, and Nick was jealous of Sean's lifestyle. Sean had done absolutely nothing to get the luxuries in his life—his parents had made sacrifices for everything that he had. That was the only reason Sean enjoyed living his extravagant lifestyle; he hadn't worked a day in his life.

"Honey, don't be nervous. Just go and have fun."

Nick turned back to his mom while putting his camera in his pocket. "Yeah, I'm trying not to be nervous. I just want everything to go right. You know?"

With a kind smile, Nick's mother pulled her long, dark hair behind her ears. Some strands of hair were just starting to come in gray. She came close to her son and gave him a hug. Veronica was much shorter than her son, so her head rested right at his chest. He returned the hug by resting his chin on her head while his arms wrapped around her. Then he heard her say, "You've never looked more handsome, Nicholas." She was happy that Nick was able to afford the rental tux in the first place. Nick had had to take on another job to save up enough money for prom. With him being their only source of income, he'd had no choice but to get a steady job to help with all the expenses.

Since his mom had been diagnosed with cancer three years ago, she hadn't been able to go back to her job. Her energy levels were not the same, and she was unable to perform at her job as she had before she got sick. Nick had to carry all the weight on his shoulders; he was the one who took care of everything. He had seen his mother fight through surgery and treatment, and he looked at her now as a strong woman who had beat cancer. She had been cancer free for some time now, but Nick feared for her every year she went for a checkup.

"Okay, go have fun!"

Nick raced out the door to the porch. He said goodbye through the screen door and then hurried to his car. The sun was just starting to go down, and he was very eager to get to Amy. He couldn't wait to see how beautiful she looked in her dress.

He started the car and pulled out of the driveway. His mom watched from the window as he drove away. She then remembered his very first day of kindergarten, when he'd had a tantrum about not wanting to leave her side. It seemed like yesterday to her.

Meanwhile, Amy was also getting ready for prom, along with her best friend, Allison. Allison lived right down the street from Amy, and they had been best friends for a long time.

"I can't believe tonight's the night," Allison said as she sat in front of a mirror, putting on mascara.

"I know—I'm so excited," Amy replied as she finished curling her blonde hair.

Amy had an adorable personality. People described her as sweet and kind, and she always made others laugh. The only problem was, she wasn't as excited as she should be on prom night.

Tonight she was going to do something cruel and hurtful, and she was afraid of what Nick would think of her afterward. She was anxious about how the night would end, but she knew she would never be happy with the man she loved if she didn't break up with Nick once and for all.

"So, have you told Nick about your dress?" Allison playfully jumped on her bed and then rested her chin atop her crossed arms while lying on her stomach.

Amy looked at the black garment bag that held her dress. She skimmed the zipper on the side with her hand. "I'm not going to prom with Nick." Amy closed her eyes, praying that Allison would be understanding. Then she turned around to face her.

Allison sat up, a look of disbelief on her face. "What are you talking about? What do you mean you're not going to prom with Nick?" Allison said in confusion.

"You know that new boy at school? Sean?"

Allison's eyes widened. "Hold on a minute. Have you been seeing Sean behind Nick's back? So the rumors of you fooling around with Sean are true? How could you?"

"Look, Allison, Nick and I—we don't have the same spark as we used to. I hate that I've been stringing him along, but I couldn't bear to let him go! A part of me still loves Nick, but Sean is the right person for me." No words could describe how terrible Amy was feeling at that moment. Her heart was being tugged in two different directions, but she knew she belonged with Sean.

"Sean isn't going to pick me up until later. We have this connection that I've never felt before, and I can't keep lying to Nick anymore. I just can't!" A single tear swam down the side of her face, and she quickly wiped it away, thinking that she would ruin her makeup. She started to tremble as she lay down on the bed next to Allison.

"Calm down, Amy. Do you know how Nick is going to react? He's going to have his heart broken. This is going to end up being bad—I can feel it."

Amy sat up on the bed and looked down at her feet and then

back up again. "But I don't know when else I can do it. I have to end things with Nick. He can still go to prom without me and have a good time. All his friends will be there."

Allison was enraged. "Seriously, Amy? You think that Nick will still want to go to prom after you break up with him! He's gonna be crushed! You should've broken things off with Nick before you started seeing Sean!"

"I can't go to prom with Sean unless I do this now! I'm not a monster! I just want to be happy." All of a sudden, they heard the doorbell ring from downstairs. "Oh my God, that must be Nick!"

Allison had no more to say on the matter. She stayed in the room while Amy went downstairs to go talk to Nick. Allison was disgusted that Amy had led Nick on for so long. Her heart ached for Nick, as she knew what was about to come.

Allison's mother and Amy's mother were having a quiet conversation and a glass of red wine in the kitchen when she came down the stairs. "Is that Sean, honey?" her mother asked.

"Ugh. He's not coming until later, Mom; it's probably no one."

Amy's mother was a woman who lived an affluent lifestyle. She wore diamonds for earrings and a delicate string of pearls around her neck. She always thought she was better than everyone else she met, thumbing her nose down at people who were less fortunate. She was telling Allison's mom how she was so glad she'd dumped that nobody of a boyfriend months ago. She was talking about Nick and how he was a poor individual who would never amount to anything in life. He would never be able to support her daughter if they ever got married. She worried all the time about them growing more fond of each other. When Amy had said she'd met a new boy from school, she'd been happy. Amy had lied to her mom about breaking it off with Nick, because she couldn't stand her constant taunting about Nick not being good enough to date a gem like her daughter. But now she was going to break it off with Nick for real.

Amy still hadn't put on her dress yet, so she was just wearing sweatpants and a T-shirt. She had a full face of makeup, and her hair still slightly hot from the curling iron. She had to go and face Nick. She took a deep breath before opening the door.

Nick's brown eyes grew wide as Amy opened the door. He held the corsage in hand and smiled at her gorgeousness. He took into account that she was not yet dressed yet. She was wearing comfortable clothes, for that matter, but she still looked beautiful.

"Hi, babe. This is for you." He took the corsage out of the box and knelt down on one knee.

Just as he was about to slip it on her wrist, she said, "Nick we need to talk." She then crossed her arms, not letting him into her personal space.

He sensed that something was wrong when she didn't even reach out to him and give him a hug or kiss as she normally would. He put the corsage back in the box for a moment to hear what she had to say.

She stepped out of the house completely, onto the porch, ready to tell Nick the truth. She couldn't bear to look into his eyes, because Nick would try to meet her gaze. Leaning up against the house, she continued to look down at the porch, trying to not get emotional. She hadn't even said a word yet. This was going to be a heavy conversation for Nick to understand. She closed her eyes before speaking, trying to come up with the words to say to Nick.

"Amy, what's wrong? You're scaring me."

Amy sniffed as she tried to hold in the tears. She knew the main reason why she had to go through with this. Her mother had never approved of Nick, and she would never let her only daughter marry someone who was not a part of her circle—her circle meaning the higher-up community, those that lived in her ritzy neighborhood. Sean lived about five miles down the road in his gated community.

Amy's heart was breaking, but on the outside she was trying to stay calm. She was so nervous about how he would react. He had no clue what was coming, and Amy hated herself for stringing him along when she knew she could've ended it earlier.

"Can you please tell me what's going on with you?" Amy had not looked at him since she had opened the door. Nick tried to grab her hand, but she put her hands behind her back. Now he was worried. Not even a minute ago he'd thought everything was going to go as planned, but now it was as if she were afraid of Nick as she flinched away at his open hand.

"Nick, I don't know how to tell you this, but …" She paused, still trying not to look up at him. If she did, then she couldn't stay on track with what she had to say.

Nick was concerned that it was something important, like she had to move, or something about her family, or she was sick and couldn't go to prom. But her hair and makeup were perfectly done. It never crossed his mind that she would want to break up with him. He thought that they were tight and they were going to be together at college.

In a stuttering tone she said, "There's someone else." When Nick heard the words come out of her mouth, he took a few steps back, almost thinking he'd misheard what she had just said. He couldn't believe it—but there was one person who ran through his mind. There was only one person at school who was more powerful.

"It's Sean, isn't it?" His eyes were piercing as he waited to hear her answer, and she nodded in agreement as she finally looked at him.

"Sean, really?"

Her mouth opened, but no words fell out. She couldn't move from that spot on the porch. It was almost as if she were frozen.

"I wanted to tell you, but—"

Nick cut her off before she could finish. "Tell me what, Amy! Tell me that you want to be with Sean now? No, you just don't do that to people!"

"I'm so sorry. I didn't want to hurt you!"

Nick threw his hands up in the air. "So you've been seeing Sean behind my back, and then you lie to me about him?"

"No, it's not like that! We became friends, and he didn't really know anybody around here when he just moved here, and we started to realize that there was a spark."

"Wait a minute! Since he moved here! So you've been lying to me for months!" Nick bit his lip, and he started to sweat. "There was a time that we had a spark, but it only became less and less. So, you're just throwing us away, then!"

Amy trembled and didn't want to answer that question, even though it was quite clear. She was just hoping that her mother didn't hear Nick yelling. If she came out onto the porch, she would only make the situation worse. Also, Amy would get into trouble for pretending that she had already broken up with Nick months ago, while in reality she'd been seeing two men at the same time.

"Is it because he's filthy rich?"

"Absolutely not, Nick! That's not the reason!"

Nick felt as if he'd just put the whole betrayal together. *No wonder she's breaking up with me, because I can't support her like Sean can*, he thought. "Ya know, I always felt strange about coming here to your house. When your mom would eye me up and down like I didn't belong here. I was never good enough for your mother, and of course I was never good enough for her standards—and now I'm not good enough for you anymore!"

"Nick, don't see it that way. This has nothing to do with her! This is my choice, and I'm following my heart."

He rolled his eyes and said, "Yes, it does. I wasn't good enough for her spoiled little brat!"

She gasped at what Nick had just called her. No way in the world was she going to let that slide.

Nick regretted it the minute he'd said it. "Amy, I didn't mean to say that."

"Ya know what, Nick? You can just go now."

There was about five feet in between them, and Nick didn't want to leave Amy. She was his world, his everything.

"Leave!" Amy screamed loudly enough for Allison to hear her

from upstairs. Allison decided to run downstairs to listen in on the rest of the conversation.

"Fine!" Nick threw the corsage down on the grass. Then he walked angrily over to his car, turned back around, and said, "So, all the time we spent together, you just went along for the ride. When you said you loved me, did you even mean it?"

Amy couldn't answer him. It had been true before she'd met Sean.

Nick stared at Amy, not believing she had kept this from him all this time. "I just want you to know that *I* meant every word *I* said, because I'm a man of my word." He felt that he said everything he needed to say before slamming his car door.

As he peeled out of the driveway, Amy went back inside to be comforted by Allison, who was right at the doorway, to give her a hug.

On the edge of tears, Nick drove away in a rage. His knuckles were white from gripping the steering wheel. *She's just been stringing me along this whole time,* he thought. *No wonder she has been so distant the last couple days. I should've seen this coming when she didn't return my call last night. She couldn't just tell me—no, she had to do it on prom night!*

Racing over the speed limit, he could barely see; his vision was becoming cloudy with tears. He didn't know where he was going; he was just driving. His first thought was to get as far away from the city as possible and go somewhere quiet, somewhere he could just think. His future had just changed in a matter of minutes.

He had everything planned with Amy for the next four years. They were going to go to the same university, and after they got settled in, he was going to give her a promise ring as a symbol of their love. But now he had to change his plans.

Nick didn't want to go home, because his mother would see that he'd wasted money on the tux. But there was no way he could've known, and now he wasn't going to the prom at all. So he just drove on. Amy clearly didn't want to affiliate herself with someone who didn't have gobs of money. Nick's opinion of Amy changed that night; she wasn't the girl he'd thought she was anymore.

Suddenly, he came to an intersection with streets lights, and his light had just turned red. No other cars were in front of him in this suburban area. He was traveling well over the speed limit, and he didn't want to stop at the intersection, so he was careless about looking to see if anyone was coming from the other directions.

As he reached the middle of the intersection, a recreational vehicle rammed into the passenger's side of Nick's car. At the speed he was going and with the power of the RV hitting him, Nick's car tumbled repeatedly, after the initial impact at the intersection.

Several other cars dodged him, honking their horns. He traveled off the road, still tumbling, and eventually came to the top of a hill near someone's front yard. The car then plunged down that hill before finally being stopped by a tree that was down under the road.

The owner of the nearby residence saw the car roll down the hill as he was sitting in his recliner by the window, and he immediately ran out of his house. The man saw the car tipped on its side with the wheels facing him. All the windows were shattered, and he could see that the airbags had deployed. The body of the car was all dented and smashed.

He raced back inside to call 911 and tell the operator what he had just observed. All he could think of was whether the person driving the vehicle was okay. No human could withstand that kind of impact, he thought. He remembered the loud crashing he'd heard from inside his house before he saw the car rambling down his hill.

His driveway was also on a hill, and he could see the main road when looking up it. Several people started getting out of their cars to see whether the driver was okay. They all watched over the car while they waited for help to arrive. There was no sign of movement from the driver's side, and they could see the hands of the driver just resting on top of the air bag, because the windshield was completely shattered and they could see right into the car.

Broken glass from all the windows surrounded the entire car. Nick was unconscious and bleeding from his head. Cuts and bruises covered his arms. He had not strapped on his seat belt, and he'd used his arms to brace for impact when the car had tumbled over so many times.

Nick's legs had also been crushed; when the roof had smashed into the pavement the car had eventually concaved onto Nick's legs. Still unconscious, Nick was on the verge of death, losing a lot of blood. The morning of that day he never would've imagined an ending like this to his prom night. He had dreamed of slow dancing with Amy and how perfect everything would be. This was the total opposite of what he'd wanted; it was far from perfect. But since leaving Amy's porch, his plan had been ruined and his thoughts had changed entirely.

2

FORGOTTEN

Meanwhile, at the high school, the glorious prom night was just getting started. Every person was dressed in style, and the school was decorated flawlessly. The theme of prom night was an elegant masquerade ball.

There was a stand at the entrance of the school filled with different masks you could choose from. They had been handmade by the decorating committee, and everyone grabbed a mask before heading into the gym.

The decorating committee had gone all out for this occasion. Gold and silver balloons filled the hallways, along with drapes and streamers hanging from the ceilings.

Everyone was wearing a mask to go along with the prom theme. Even though Amy and Sean walked into the gymnasium wearing their masks, the whole school still recognized Sean and the girl by his side.

Amy could hardly focus on spending time with Sean, because her mind was constantly on Nick and wondering if he was okay. Sean had his ways of showing her a fun time to get her mind off what she had just done; they danced all night to one song after the next.

When the DJ put on a slow song, Amy knew as she rested her head on Sean's shoulder that she had made the right decision.

Since everyone was wearing a mask, she had no idea whether Nick had decided to still go to the prom. He could've easily just gone home, or he could have stayed strong and hung out with his friends. Her eyes wandered around the gym looking at guys who wore similar suits to Nick's and had his hair color. She eventually figured out that it wasn't Nick, though, and it was difficult to spot him out of a large crowd, especially when the guys were all dressed very similar.

With all the school knowing that Sean was going to be elected prom king, Amy was worried that her name would be called for prom queen, and she didn't want the eyes of the school to be all on her. Eventually Nick would tell everybody what she had done and how she was a heartless person for going with Sean behind his back.

Sean and Amy's names *were* announced for king and queen, and they stood on stage wearing their color-coordinated outfits. Amy was wearing her light-blue high-low dress, and Sean wore a black tuxedo with a light-blue tie to match. The tiara rested on Amy's head, while she looked out into the crowd, still searching for Nick. Although she didn't want to talk to him, she just wanted to know that he was okay.

The next Monday, Amy was at school, going about her business in between classes. She had to stop at her locker to get her science book first. Friday, she'd put on a facade that she'd had an amazing time with Sean, even though her mind had constantly been thinking about Nick. Guilt was eating her up inside, and she'd barely gotten any sleep the nights before. She'd thought about calling Nick in the middle of the night but decided it would only make the situation worse if she tried to explain herself.

Her heartless mother, on the other hand, was absolutely ecstatic that her daughter had found someone who came from money. Amy and her mother had come from nothing. She'd had Amy when she was nineteen and homeless. When she later became an exotic dancer, she'd met a very wealthy man. He'd given Amy and her mother a grand life full of luxurious cars, expensive clothes, and fine dining.

Amy still remembered to this day when she and her mom had begged for money on the streets. At night her mother would go to work while Amy stayed at a homeless shelter. She had been only ten when her mother had met James. Soon after they got married, James had died of a heart attack. That had been three years ago. He was the closest person to a father figure for Amy.

For years Amy had asked her mother who her real father was, but her mom would never tell her. After James's passing her mother had collected all his life insurance money; she started spending it as soon as he was cold in the ground.

Amy still thought that her mother had married James only because he'd been much better off than they had. James had promised a fresh start in life for her and her daughter. She remembered vividly that her mother would say, "Don't worry, Amy. We're never going to live on the streets ever again."

As Amy opened her locker, she grabbed her science book from the top shelf, and replaced the section with her math book. She was worried about seeing Nick in science class that day. She desperately wanted to be anywhere else in the world but there. Her mother had made it abundantly clear that she had to attend, even though Amy thought skipping one day wouldn't be the end of the world. Graduation day was only two weeks away, she kept telling herself.

Just as she shut her locker, Sean glided toward her, catching her by surprise. "Hey, babe." Amy gave him a modest smile before he laid a kiss on her forehead.

"Hi," she replied, shoving her book in her backpack.

"Hey, come meet me at my car after school. I have a surprise for you." Sean smiled. He looked very dashing with his twinkling eyes and his dark hair slicked back neatly.

"Sean, we've only been on one official date, and Friday night was enough of a treat."

He snickered and said, "Trust me, you'll love it! You feeling okay today?" Sean had noticed Amy's tiredness and how dark the circles under her eyes were.

"Yeah, I'm just a little tired from studying last night." Amy agreed to meet him, before they departed to their separate classes.

Sean was unpredictable and very irresistible. Every day they would meet, he would always say, "Let's go somewhere and do something fun," but most of the time they would actually just stay inside and watch a movie or stay up late talking. Sean Howard was one of a kind, full of mystery and excitement, and Amy couldn't bear to stay away from him.

When she was walking to her class, for a moment she completely forgot for the first time about Nick. For the moment her mind wasn't cloudy from the guilt anymore, but then she entered class.

Several other students were in the classroom, while her science teacher was sitting at his desk. Amy noticed the familiar desk where Nick usually sat; the desk was empty. She was relieved that she didn't have to see Nick but also worried about where he was.

As the class began, Amy paid no attention to her teacher. She just stared out the window, thinking about how she could've handled the situation better. She thought about the very first date she and Sean had gone on a month before prom; they'd been connected at the hip ever since. With stresses of school and family, they hadn't been able to really go on another date since, but prom night had been extra special.

They were both like magnets. Wherever she went, he followed. Sean was constantly checking up on her, calling her every other day. She knew in her mind that she would be well provided for if she ever married Sean, but in her heart she wanted to be with Nick. That's why she hadn't been able to make herself break up with Nick. But on prom night she'd had no choice but to draw the line in the sand and say she was picking Sean.

Through the rest of the week, Amy remained racked with guilt.

Every day she went to school, and Nick wasn't there. Every morning she would either hope he was at class, or she would pray that he wasn't there, to avoid confrontation. Every day his desk was empty, and each day she thought less and less of Nick.

Growing more fond of Sean every day, Amy was happy when he greeted her every morning before her first class with a kiss. Cheeks turning red, Amy would always tell him, "Sean, people are staring."

He would look behind him and say, "Well, I'll give 'em something to look at." He didn't care, and he would kiss her once more before hurrying off to class, leaving Amy in the hallway, smitten, as he ran away smiling.

Weeks passed, and Nick's face was fading from Amy's mind. Spending more hours with Sean and friends, she would only think of Nick as she was falling asleep at night. His phone number even was erased from her mind. She would try to make herself remember it, but she couldn't just recall those last two numbers.

Back when she and Nick had first been dating and Sean hadn't moved to the city yet, her mother had thrown out the small piece of paper with Nick's phone number; she had been trying to break them apart. She never told Amy she'd thrown it out; she told her that it had fallen on the floor and she had vacuumed it up by accident.

One night Amy ended up getting out of bed and calling her friend Allison after she'd had a very peculiar dream about Nick. She had to find out for herself, and for her conscience, whether anyone had heard about or talked to Nick since the night of the prom. It wasn't that she wanted to talk to him or anything; she just wanted to know that he was okay. It was well past three, but she decided to call and see if Allison knew anything. She also wanted to get the subject off her mind.

She switched her lamp on and picked up the phone from her nightstand. She dialed the number as she looked at the clock on her wall. It read 3:09. She hoped that Allison wouldn't be angry with her for calling at that hour.

It rang four times on the other end before a mumbling Allison answered the phone. "Hello. Hey, Ally, it's me. I have to ask you something."

Allison sighed and said, "You couldn't have just asked me in class instead? Do you know what time it is?"

"I know it's late, Ally, but I gotta talk to ya about something. It's important; I can't wait until tomorrow."

"Well, sista, by my clock it's three in the morning, so it really is tomorrow already, so shoot. Tell me what's wrong before I fall back to sleep."

"No, nothing is wrong. I just wondered if you or anyone has heard from Nick these past couple weeks. He hasn't been at school at all since I broke up with him, and I'm really worried. Do you think he'll even graduate?"

It was silent for a few moments before Allison said, "Haven't you seen the news lately?"

"No, I never watch the news. Why?"

"No one told you, did they?"

Amy frowned. It seemed some people at school had news about Nick, and no one bothered to tell her, not even Allison.

"What? Tell me what?"

"Amy, before I tell you this, what happened is not your fault. You can't think that this happened because of you. I look at you in class, and I can tell you're all stressed, and I'm sure you still feel guilty."

"Ally, you're starting to scare me. Just tell me!" she shouted a little too loudly.

Across the hall, her mom woke up and screamed, "Amy, get off the damn phone! It's late!"

"I will in a minute!" she called back. She returned to Allison. "Sorry about that. You were saying?"

Allison was worried about how Amy would react to this news, but she couldn't hide it anymore. She hated to be the one to tell her. "Amy ... Nick got in a car accident the night of the prom."

"Wait—what!" Amy covered her mouth, gasping.

Allison said, "The police said there were witnesses who saw him speeding, and the 911 call came in only a short time after he left your house. He's at Mass General."

This was the worst possible news that Amy could hear. One hand flew to her neck while the other still held the phone to her ear. She slowly slid onto her back, looking up at the ceiling.

"And Amy, he's in a coma. Now please, just don't be upset with me for not telling you, but I didn't want to see you upset anymore. You're in a good place with Sean, and I didn't want you to start pedaling backward."

Amy tried to speak but couldn't think of what to say. She was so blindsided by what she'd heard. She immediately thought that this was her fault. If she hadn't fought with Nick, then he wouldn't have been so mad, and he wouldn't have crashed his car.

"I have to go see him." Amy was about to say more, but Allison cut her off.

"No way! You can't go visit him. It's gonna make things more painful. Besides, he can't even talk to you."

"Then what I am supposed to do, Ally!" she asked with a sob. "If it wasn't for me, he wouldn't be in a coma! Oh my God, and his poor mom! I can't just not say goodbye or explain myself." She rested her hand on her forehead, trying to think what to do.

"Why don't you write him a farewell letter? He'll read it when he wakes up. It's the least you could do. This last week is supposed to be fun, Amy! Last week of high school, and then you and Sean will be off going to Harvard together."

Amy thought about writing a letter; it wasn't a bad idea at all. Besides, she wasn't going to be staying in Boston much longer anyway. "Yeah, I know. I'm gonna miss you."

A new level of emotion set in when she thought of leaving her best friend. Allison was going to attend college in California.

"Don't worry. Boston will always be my home. I just need to go to a warmer climate for a while." She laughed about the different temperatures in Massachusetts and California.

"As long as you promise me that you'll come back."

Allison laughed and then said, "Of course we will. David and I want to go somewhere new."

Two hours passed by, and Amy was still on the phone with Allison. Her mother yelled again. "Will you hang up that damn phone, for God's sake!" Allison laughed because she could hear Amy's mom in the back ground.

"Okay, I think it's time to for me to hang up now. The sun will be starting to come up soon." Amy tried to look past her curtains and saw that it was indeed starting to get light out.

"Yeah, that's probably a good idea. I'll see you in a couple hours."

Just as Allison was about to hang up the phone, she heard Amy say, "Wait a second." She returned the phone to her ear.

"Can I ask you something?" Amy asked.

Allison rolled her eyes and said, "Now what!" All she wanted to do was get some more sleep before she had to get up for school.

Amy said, "If anything ever happens to me, when I have kids, well, I want you to be their godmother."

"Now are ya sure you want me to be responsible for your kids? I mean, you've seen me with kids. I can't always tame them," she said sarcastically.

Amy chuckled at her joke, but she was actually serious. "No, I'm not kidding. There's no one else I would rather have take care of my kids if something happened to me."

"Okay, well then, I'd be honored. You're not going anywhere anytime soon, though, not with me around."

They both shared one last laugh, and Amy said, "Well, all right then. Bye." Allison didn't even say goodbye. Amy thought she probably had gone back to sleep already; she was surprised she'd talked to her that long.

Amy hung up the phone and turned her lamp off. Just as she

got comfortable under her blankets, she looked at the clock. It said 5:04. She thought to herself, *Well, I guess I'm already up.* There was no trying to go back to sleep now that her mind was racing.

Amy flipped her covers off her bed and sat down at her desk. She pulled up her blinds to see the small sign of sun. She took out a pen and a paper from her drawer to write her letter to Nick. She thought for a moment about what she was going to say, and then she began the letter, writing, "Dearest Nick."

Once she finished writing the letter, she let out a breath and let go of Nick. She looked at her clock and saw that it was nearly six. She'd accomplished what she'd set out to do, and she put the letter in an envelope. She wrote her address and put the hospital's address with his full name on it. She hoped that it wouldn't get lost in the mail, but she didn't want to bring it to him herself. It would be just too uncomfortable and hard to see him in such a state.

I guess I should start getting ready for the day, she thought. *One more day closer to graduating, and then I can put high school behind me.*

As she walked out the door to go to school, she almost forgot to put the letter in the mailbox. Before getting in her car, she unzipped the small compartment on the top of her backpack, pulled the letter out, and walked over to the stone mailbox at the end of the driveway.

She put the letter in the mailbox with a sense of relief. She felt that she could move on now. She was saying her final goodbye to Nick and looking forward to her life with Sean.

Amy got in her car and drove to school. She didn't know it, but her mom was watching her from the front window, peeking through the blinds, and she saw her put the letter in the mailbox. Her eyes squinted and her nose crinkled. She then waited until Amy had driven away.

Her curiosity made her go outside and see what Amy was trying to mail. She walked out to the mailbox in her bathrobe, feeling the cold morning air on her bare calves. Her blue slippers matched her bathrobe, and she was concerned that the neighbors might catch sight of her with her curlers in her hair, but this she had to see.

She opened the mailbox and snatched the letter with force. She saw Nick's name on it and frowned. She'd thought that Amy had ditched that loser months ago. Why would she be writing to him now?

Her coral pink nails had just been done yesterday and were long enough to be mistaken for claws. She took the letter and ripped it into several little pieces before going back inside. She went into her work room, which was hardly a work room. She simply called it her work room because she claimed that she would write a book some-day. But the years and years have gone by, and she had yet to come up with one page. Now the room mainly consisted of old artifacts of her late husband. There were dozens of boxes, almost skimming the ceiling, they were piled so high. She walked over to her desk, beneath which was a paper shredder.

She put each tiny piece of the letter through the shredder. *She's going to forget that loser if I have anything to do about it*, she thought. *No way in hell will she write to him ever again!* She cackled, knowing that she was doing the right thing, but she didn't know the whole story. She couldn't help recall that Amy had been on the phone for a long period of time during the night. Maybe it had been Nick, she thought.

After slipping all the little pieces of the letter into the shredder, she bit her lip as she looked out the window. *That better not be who she was talking to last night*, she thought. She sighed, shaking her head back and forth, thinking, *Why would she be writing to Nick when she has Sean in her life?*

But it wasn't Nick Amy had talked to on the phone. All Amy wanted to do was say goodbye to Nick and have the guilt be lifted off her shoulders, the guilt she had been carrying around since prom night.

Amy drove to school feeling that she could finally breathe. It was almost as if she had been holding in her breath for the longest time and now she had finally let it out. She pulled into a parking spot in front of the school and saw Sean waiting for her by his car, only a few spots up from where she was parking.

She got out of her car and grabbed her backpack from the back seat. She shut the car door and locked it. She made her way over to Sean; he greeted her with a warm hug and an aroma of strong-scented cologne.

In that moment, she felt his strong back through his leather jacket. She smiled and looked up at him as he pulled away. Then they walked across the parking lot, holding hands, to get to class. In her mind she simply said to herself, *Now I can move forward.*

3

REWIRED

Nick felt that he was lying down on something—something very soft and made out of cotton. He could hear an odd noise right next to where he was lying. It kept making the same sound over and over again, until he finally opened his eyes.

Squinting, he was blinded by a bright light. The figures in the room started to become clearer. He soon realized he was in a hospital room. Then the brightness dialed down, and he felt very tired. Everything was white, including the white covers on my bed.

He looked down at his arm and saw that he was wired up to this machine, the machine that continued to make that annoying beeping sound. He felt itchy around his nose, and he could see something clear and plastic on his face. Raising his hand to his face, he felt the oxygen mask that was covering the majority of it. He immediately took it off, pulling it away from his face and placing it on the small table to his left.

His mouth was incredibly parched, and he licked his lips; they were dry and cracked as hell. He looked down at his arm again and saw that he was somehow attached to another annoying machine by square black patches that were stuck to his skin.

As he pulled them off, they took some of his arm hair with them, but it only made the irritating machine beep louder and faster. *Why am I in a hospital, anyways? Where's mom, and why won't this machine shut up? What happened to me?*

After a few moments, the familiar face of his mother appeared. But she seemed to be back down to the weight she'd been while battling cancer. She entered with a kind smile, and her eyes widened as she saw him looking at her. "Sweetheart, you're awake!" She made her way over to him to give him a joyous hug. He wondered how long he had been asleep.

Nick noticed that she was wearing a bright-purple bandanna around her head, and it appeared she'd lost over fifty pounds. Could it be that his mom was sick again?

"Mom, what happened to me?" he asked as she wrapped her arms around him. As he hugged her, he could feel her spine. They held onto each other for what seemed like forever; she just couldn't seem to let go. It was as if he'd been gone for a while and had just returned. *Where, exactly, have I been?*

Finally letting go, she sat down in a chair beside his bed and cupped his hand in both of hers. He was starting to get worried, as she seemed hesitant to speak. She kissed the top of his hand and said, "I thought you were never going to wake up, but my prayers were finally answered."

Nick swallowed, thinking, *How is it possible that I've fallen asleep for so long? What got me here in the first place?* He couldn't remember why he was there or what he had done last. His memory was blank.

"What are you talking about, Ma? How long was I asleep?" Looking at his mom, he could tell that she was afraid to tell him the truth. He didn't understand any of this.

"Four years! You were in a coma for four years!" The rest of what his mom said sounded like she was under water, and he could only catch small parts of what she was saying. He could hear her words, but he was primarily focused on Amy. She'd broken up with him on prom night! She'd been seeing Sean behind his back! She'd done it all to please her mother, stringing him along for months! He suddenly started to heat up at the memory of how poorly prom night had ended for him.

"You were found in your car off the side of the road, and witnesses said that an RV rammed into the side of the car. When I got the call from the hospital, I drove here as quickly as I could. You've been in a coma until now. You woke up on your own! Thank goodness Amy wasn't with you."

Nick became enraged when he heard Amy's name. He looked out the window of his hospital room and saw the blazing sun shining in. He clenched his hands as he wondered whether Sean and Amy were still together.

Veronica smiled. She'd finally got her son back—the angel that had been given to her from God himself. The first time she'd gotten cancer, Nick had been there to help her through it, but now it had come back worse, and she was all on her own. She'd been waiting desperately for her son to wake up, and he finally had.

Nick looked at the calendar on the wall. It read January 6, 1999. He guessed it was true; he'd been in a coma for four years! He couldn't believe that he'd missed four years of his life—and it was all because of Sean! If he had never moved here and met Amy, she would still be with him. Mama wouldn't have had to go through treatment alone while he was asleep. She had gone through cancer treatment before, but not this severe. Her hair had never fallen out before; that must be why she was wearing a bandanna.

He looked at her again as he said, "I'm so sorry I wasn't here for you."

"No no no, honey, don't be sorry. You're here now, and that's all that matters. You were in rough shape when I saw you come out of surgery after that accident. I thought I'd never see your smile again."

"What's going on with you, Mama? Are you sick again?"

She closed her eyes, shook her head, and said, "You don't have to worry about me. You need to focus on getting better, all right? You're a strong boy, and you need to win this fight." Veronica's empowering words wove into Nick's mind. He felt awake and ready to leave the hospital now. But it wasn't going to be that easy. Doctors had to make sure that he was 100 percent ready to leave on his own; they would have to keep him until they thought he was strong enough.

Veronica tapped the top of her son's hand, remembering the night she had seen him come out of surgery. Then she looked at his face; it appeared that his youthful glow had come back not long after his eyes had opened.

The night of the accident, Veronica had rushed to get to the hospital. She'd driven like a maniac to get to her son as quickly as possible. At first she couldn't believe what had happened, thinking of how excited Nick had been to go to the prom.

Swerving left and right, she'd passed dozens of other drivers, finally arriving at the hospital. She'd been relieved that she wasn't pulled over by a cop, but in case she was, she had her speech in mind to explain why she was speeding. She had accelerated over the speed limit in her rush to get to the hospital.

At the hospital, there were ambulances from another incident blocking the front entrance. There was no way to get through. So, she banged a U-turn and drove around the back of the hospital.

"I'm coming, Nick! I'm coming!" Reaching the south entrance of the hospital, she decided to just park on the curb of the hospital. There was no time to find a spot. She came to a halt that made her tires screech.

She jumped out of the car and ran into the hospital. The revolving doors spun as she ran inside. She rushed to the front desk, out of breath, and frantically she said, "Where is he? Where is my son?"

The nurse at the front desk was on the phone at the time, and put up her hand to say she would be with her in a moment. Furious,

Veronica said, "My son was just in a car accident, and I don't know if he's dead, alive, or in surgery! Put down the damn phone!"

Screaming loud enough that the whole hospital could hear her, she stomped her foot up and down. The nurse clearly saw her frustration and still continued to talk on the phone. She was the only one at the desk. As people sitting in the waiting room witnessed Veronica's hysterical act, they continued to stare at her, curious to see how this was going to play out.

The nurse saw that this woman was agitated about someone who had just been admitted to the hospital, and she hung up the phone. "Yes, hi. How can I help you?"

Veronica's ears started to turn a bright red as she brushed her hair behind them. "A police officer called me from the side of the road where the crash took place. My son was taken to this hospital after a car accident. The officer didn't say how he was or how badly he was hurt! Can you help me?" Veronica spoke so fast and was crying so uncontrollably that her words were very hard to understand.

The nurse only understood some parts of her sentences and was a little concerned about this woman's mental state. "Okay, I'm going to need a little more information than that. What's his name?"

"His name is Nick Williams, and I'm his mother!"

The nurse turned to her keyboard, still sitting in her chair. She typed his name in, and his information came up. "Okay, Nick Williams. He was just admitted to his room; he just got out of the OR."

"Okay, what's his room number?"

"I'm sorry, ma'am; I'm going to have to see some ID to give you his room number."

Veronica slammed her hand on the front desk so hard the nurse was scared she would become violent. "I don't need to give you my ID! I am Veronica Williams, and I am his mother! Now give me his room number before I have to jump over that desk and see for myself!" She was so worked up because she'd forgotten her purse in the car.

The nurse wanted proof that this woman was his mother. People should have identification for the little things such as this, she thought. Still frightened of this women's outburst, she willingly read off the room number, mainly because she was afraid of what the woman was capable of. "Room 312." That nurse had gotten her first dose of locals in Boston. She had just transferred there from Alabama and was shocked at how things weren't as relaxed as back home.

"Thank you! Now, was that so hard?" Veronica said sarcastically and gave her a fierce stare as she started walking away from the desk. As she made her way over to the elevators, she raised her hand and pressed the Up button. The task was hard to achieve, as her hand was incredibly shaky, and she waited impatiently for the doors to open.

She paced back and forth, waiting for the elevator to come back down to the bottom floor. She tapped her foot while she stood silently thinking. She tried to calm herself and regain her composure.

Her patience wore out quickly, so she made her way to the stairs. She bolted up those stairs like a gazelle, running up three flights of stairs in a matter of seconds. Once she reached the third floor, she burst through the door, making a loud entrance and forcing everyone on the floor to look in her direction.

Standing up tall again, she walked away from the stairs along the cold hospital floor. She walked at a fast pace down the hallway, looking at the numbers of each hospital room. She remembered the nurse downstairs saying, "Room 312," in her southern accent. The faster she walked, the faster the numbers on the rooms increased.

At the end of room 310 came a corner. As she turned that corner, she realized there were two men standing outside room 312. They both turned as they heard her footsteps coming. One man was a cop, and the other was a doctor. She knew that they wanted to talk to her about Nick.

"Excuse me, are you Miss Williams?" the doctor asked. He was still in his surgery scrubs.

"Yes, I'm Nick's mom. How is he? Can I see him?" As she was about to brush open the curtain of the hospital room, the doctor put his arm in the way of the door.

"Prepare yourself, Miss Williams. I must discuss some things with you before you see your son."

Veronica understood but was still extremely annoyed that she had rushed all the way to get there and now she was not allowed to see her son yet. But she wanted to hear what the doctor had to say.

"Now, your son suffered major injuries in the crash. Both of his legs were severely fractured; the deep wounds on his arms and the scratches on his face I was able to repair, but he might have some rather prominent scars after they heal. Apart from his body, his skull was fractured, but on the whole the surgery was a success. He suffered a lot of trauma to the head, which is what I wanted to warn you about. With that kind of trauma to the head, the person can have a lot of side effects even after surgery."

Veronica was overwhelmed with hearing all that had happened to Nick. She tried to keep everything together, and she said, "What kind of side effects?"

"Well, it all depends on the patient; everyone heals at their own pace when it comes to a surgery this complex. Certain side effects can occur, like migraines, very intense headaches, strong personality changes, and strong hallucinations. No one can tell how hard his head was hit or how fast the impact came onto his skull."

Processing everything the doctor had told her, Veronica said, "Okay, can I talk to him now?"

"Not quite, Miss Williams. You see, Nick went into a heavily induced coma. He won't be awake for a very long time. It's up to his body to wake up when he's ready and is fully healed. Plus, Officer Brown would like to ask you a couple questions."

Veronica looked over at Officer Brown. She remembered his

name because he had been the one who'd phoned to tell her what had happened to Nick. He stayed stationary, waiting patiently to talk to Veronica after the doctor had left.

"Thank you, doc."

The doctor rested his hand on her shoulder, seeing the level of pain she was in. "Stay strong. All right. I have another patient waiting for me in the OR." He left, his Crocs squeaking slightly down the hallway.

Veronica could barely breathe. It felt like a load of bricks was weighing on her chest. She couldn't speak, she was so devastated for Nick. He had been so excited for this night, and this was how he'd ended up. But she turned to the cop and met his gaze as he asked his questions.

"Hi, Miss Williams. I know you're in a very stressful place right now, but if you don't mind, can I ask you some questions?" Veronica nodded, and he got out his notepad to write down her answers.

"Now, due to the clothes Nick was wearing when we found him, it appeared he was going to an event of some sort?"

"Yes, he was heading to his high school prom." She wondered whether Amy knew about the accident. She would be devastated.

"And witnesses told us that he was flying way over the speed limit. Was he in any way intoxicated? Did he use any substances before he left your house?"

Veronica was disgusted with what she was being asked. It had never crossed her mind that Nick would ever use drugs or drink. He cared too much about his body. "No, absolutely not! Something must of went wrong, because he never drives five miles over the speed limit. There must have been a reason."

The cop concentrated on writing everything down, and she kept defending Nick, saying how he would never drink and drive. "Did your son say anything to you before he left?"

She couldn't hold in her tears any longer. That question literally broke her, and she couldn't help but get emotional. She closed her eyes for a moment before she took a deep breath and answered. "Nothing really out of the ordinary. He was so excited to get to prom." She spoke in a very raspy tone at first but soon became a blubbering mess. She used the sleeve of her sweater to wipe the tears from her face. "He looked so handsome, my beautiful baby boy." She trembled, covering her face as she leaned up against the wall. She soon began to sob, as she thought, *How could this happen? Why did this have to happen to Nick?*

"Thank you, Miss Williams, for your cooperation. I'll leave you to spend some time with your son now." He closed his notepad and walked back down the hallway before taking the turn around the corner.

Veronica looked up, seeing that the cop had vanished and she was all alone in the hallway. She sniffled and tried to get herself back together. She had thought that her worst fear was about her cancer coming back—but this was ten times worse. One's child getting hurt is every parent's nightmare.

As she turned to Nick's room, she hesitated to pull open the floral hospital curtain. She remembered what the doctor had told her, how much trauma he'd endured. She couldn't imagine how much pain he was in. She took another deep breath and opened the curtain.

Nick was completely unrecognizable to his mother. He was connected to a machine that was keep him breathing; there was a breathing tube down his throat. His eyes were closed shut, with stitches and bruises around his entire face.

When she got closer, she noticed the six-inch cut above his eyebrow; also, he had what looked like a white cast wrapped around his whole head. With deep sadness and agony, she slumped into the chair next to his bed.

She went to grab his hand, and she noticed that his hands were covered in very deep scratches. His pointer finger and thumb on his left hand were in splints, and she could see the colorful casts on both of his legs through the thin white covers. Veronica gently took hold of his hand, carefully minding his two broken fingers. She was trying to send him a message to let him know that she was here and she would never leave his room.

Between that night and now, Nick has made a full recovery, Veronica thought to herself. She had so often imagined that he would wake up from his coma, but this day he finally had.

"I'm gonna go find a nurse to turn off the stupid machine. I'll be right back." Veronica left the room, leaving Nick by himself.

When Nick had woken up that day, he had not woken up as himself. He appeared normal on the outside, and he acted normal. But something had changed inside Nick, something had snapped. For four years, while Nick laid in his hospital bed, millions of other people had continued their day-to-day lives. He felt that he had been left out of everything that had happened in the world while he slept.

Nick looked out his window, and there was a devilish look in his eye. He wanted revenge. He was eager to get out of the hospital. He continued to stare out the window. His neck was sore from lying down for four years, so he quickly turned his neck left and right to ease the stiffness. Then he turned back to the window and began plotting his wicked plan.

4

UNUSUAL

A few days after Nick had woken from his coma, his mother took him home to get reacquainted with life. The doctors had cleared him to go home and resume his life as it had been. But in his mind his life had fallen apart before the car crash. He had to go on living as if everything was okay, but Nick wasn't okay. He'd turned into someone who was going to become a monster.

The very first day he went home, he felt the joy of being back in his own room again. Nothing had changed, and nothing had been touched. It was almost as if he'd never left.

Immediately, he went online to try and find some information about Amy and Sean. His mother was convinced that he was just going up to his room to take a quick nap. Even though he had been in a deep sleep for four years, his body was still in recovery mode. Nick went on his high school website to look at the class of 1995. Four years of his life he had missed, and he wanted to snoop at pictures simply to catch up on what had happened at graduation.

On the website he saw hundreds of pictures from graduation day. It suddenly hit him—he hadn't even graduated high school! He hadn't gotten a high school diploma, as his classmates had. It started to set in how much he'd actually missed out on. What fueled him more was what he saw on the Fun page on the website.

Sean, now his natural enemy, had been voted most likely to succeed in his senior class. Nick clenched his fists, thinking about how Sean had only spent one year at his school and become the most popular in school without even trying.

Nick had often been the most active person, helping out in the community, along with being on the principal's list almost every semester of his high school years.

Nick then looked at a list of where all the graduating students were going to attend college; they would be at college now. He scrolled and scrolled until he found Amy's name.

Amy Fitzgerald had enrolled at Harvard University. Nick was shocked to learn how close Amy had been to him all this time; Harvard wasn't too far from his house. He immediately jetted out of his room, down the stairs, and into the living room.

His mom was making lunch in the kitchen. "Why, you're in a big hurry. Where ya goin', hun?" she asked him.

"I'm goin' out to see an old friend. I'll be back." He slung his winter jacket over his shoulder before putting on his shoes. Without any more words, he walked out the door.

When Nick had left, Veronica was again alone in her home. Now that Nick had woken up, she was happy to have him home again, but she understood that he was eager to go out, to get back into the world again and meet up with old friends. She just wished that he would spend some time with his mother first.

Nick got into his mom's new car. He felt uneasy to think he would ever get behind the wheel again. He could still hear the glass cracking in the windows and the horns honking as he tumbled by the other cars. It made his spine tingle just thinking about it. The flashbacks made Nick's stomach turn, and he became dizzy as he sat and looked at the steering wheel.

There was one memory of him being pulled from the vehicle

after the accident. He remembered how his arms had been draped over the wheel and blood had dripped down onto the shattered glass below him on the car mat as he went in and out of consciousness.

Nick had to get to Amy, to confront her once and for all. Then, something caught his eye. He saw his old bike leaning up against the metal fence near the side of the house. He walked over to it and saw that it was all rusty, and the tires were flat, but he knew he couldn't very well walk the whole way.

It only took him a few minutes. He grabbed the bike pump from the shed in the backyard and brought it back to pump the tires up. Once the tires were firm enough, he decided to give it a try. He was a little wobbly at first, but eventually he found his balance and started pedaling down the street. He guessed his mother was right: once you learn how to ride a bike, you'll never forget.

Wearing her bandana, his mom watched him from the window as he pedaled away from the house. She did not know that Nick was going to see Amy. She thought how lucky she was to have her son back in her life. It had certainly been lonely while he'd slept for that long, long time. Every night she had prayed before going to bed, asking for her son to return to her. That was probably the only time that Veronica had doubted God. Why would he let something like this happen to such a well-rounded individual, her perfect son? Her faith had been strengthened when Nick had woken up.

Nick did not know what he would do if he saw Amy. In his mind, he just wanted to watch her from a distance if he got the chance. He was enjoying the cool air as he made his way to Harvard campus. Believe it or not, Nick had missed the cold winter air brushing against his face. He felt alive again, completely different than when he'd been in the hospital. The sky was white, and sheets of ice covered the sidewalks as hundreds of tiny snowflakes fell to the ground. Trying to navigate around the sheets of ice, Nick almost wiped out a few times on his way to campus.

Out of breath, he finally made it to the campus. He'd had no idea how out of shape he was until he'd tried riding his bike. It was good for him to break himself in to physical activity again after doing absolutely nothing and staying in a lying position for so long. When he stopped pedaling, his legs felt like jelly, and he could feel the sweat dripping off his forehead. Even though it was cold out, it hadn't taken much for him to break a sweat.

Nick got off his bike and started to walk, still holding the handlebars. He looked around and saw hundreds of other students walking from class to class. He thought, *How on earth can I spot Amy out of a crowd like this?* It was around lunchtime, and the majority of people were heading up to eat at the dining hall in between classes.

He spotted a metal bike rack and decided to put his bike in a slot. He put his hands in his pockets while he simply walked around campus looking for a woman with long blonde hair. Several women he spotted with blonde hair, but each time he got close it turned out not to be Amy.

His legs got tired from walking, so he found a bench on the outskirts of what seemed to be a dormitory. People passed by him for hours as he sat on that cold bench, and he was debating whether to give up and head home. Nick could feel that his butt was freezing to the bench. He feared that he wouldn't be able to stand back up.

Just as he was about to try and get up, a familiar face caught his eye. She came out of the main entrance, not looking Nick's way but heading toward the middle of campus. Nick would recognize that walk anywhere. She walked with her feet slightly turned out and at a very fast pace.

Without Amy knowing, Nick followed closely behind her. She was wearing a black hat and a long black coat. Her back was to Nick, but he was far enough away that if she turned around, she wouldn't recognize him.

Wondering where she was headed, Nick admired her long blonde hair emerging from under her black hat. He didn't know what he would say to her if she caught a glimpse of him, so he chose to stay far back while still being able to see her from a distance.

After a while, Amy stopped in front of another building, waiting in the cold. She was still in Nick's view, and she was jumping up and down, trying to stay warm. Nick found a spot behind a tree where he could watch. He wanted to be able to hear whoever she was going to talk to. From Nick's point of view, she was waiting for someone to come out of the east dormitory.

Finally someone emerged from the building—someone Nick loathed and desperately wanted to drop-kick off the face of the earth. It was Sean, and he greeted Amy with a warm hug and landed a kiss on her forehead. They talked, and Nick heard Amy laugh. Sean gladly rested his hand on her lower back while they walked away from his dorm.

Nick couldn't believe that Amy had stayed with Sean all this time while he'd been in the hospital. It was as if he had held his blink for a really long time and everything had stayed exactly the same in his life. Well, everyone had aged slightly, and his mom had gotten sick again. Nick was still completely and utterly in love with Amy, and when he saw her with Sean, he was revolted. His heart ached at the sight of their happiness.

Even though it was freezing cold outside, Nick started to heat up when he saw how in love they looked as they walked away. He'd thought Amy was a different person, that she would of at least come and visited him in the hospital. But his mom had said that no one from school had called or visited. *She didn't even send me a card*, he thought.

Nick didn't know that Amy had tried to send him a letter four years ago, when she found out what had happened to him, but her mother had destroyed the letter. He watched as she and Sean walked together at the end of the street. They faded as the snow started to come down harder. He looked again down the street, to see Amy once more, but her figure had already disappeared.

Worried that he would get caught in the storm, he hurried back across campus to find his bike to head home. As he ran, it started getting slick, with the snow coming down more thickly and the wind blowing against his face.

When he reached his bike, he pedaled out of campus. Furious at what he'd seen, he felt his chest getting very tight. He could see his breath in the cool air; breathing in the wintery air was not helping. He just wanted to get home and snuggle up near his fireplace with a warm blanket for the rest of the day.

All of a sudden his tire hit a pothole on the sidewalk, sending him flying off his bike onto the icy concrete. He used his hands to brace his fall. The ice cut into his skin, and both of his palms started to bleed; it stung like hell.

He felt stupid for not seeing the pothole before hitting it. He could've swerved, but he didn't want to ride on the street with cars coming toward him. After his accident he no longer wanted to drive or be near cars. They terrified him, and it had even been a struggle to get into his mom's car for the drive home. They had fought for a long time, but she'd eventually convinced him to get into her car.

As the snow kept coming down, he decided to walk his bike home. He left a trail of blood on the snowy sidewalks. Nick grabbed onto his handlebars tighter when a strong breeze blew his way, making the stinging worse. He hated himself for going out in this weather, but it only made him more eager to execute his murderous plan. When he'd left the house, the sky had shown no signs of snow. When he looked up now, the sky was dark gray.

Back at the house, Veronica was resting in her rocking chair near the window. Her eyes were closed, and feeling warm from the fire, she was waiting for Nick to return. Then she returned her attention to the newspaper she was holding in her hands. Flipping page to page, she glanced up from the paper, and that's when she saw Nick on the porch, making his way in.

The front door slammed and Nick stood before her, holding his hands close to his chest and trying to keep the blood from dripping onto the carpet. She stood up from her chair, dropped her newspaper, and rushed over to him in concern. She glanced at his hands and saw that he was holding a puddle of blood. After guiding him to the couch, she dashed to the kitchen, saying, "Oh, my boy, what happened?"

Nick slumped on the couch near the fire, trying to warm up. "I hit a pothole on the street," he told her.

Veronica grabbed a towel from the kitchen and ran it under the faucet. Nick was still on the couch, shivering. The warmth from the fire began to thaw the snow on his boots. His hands could no longer hold the pool of blood; drops of blood spilled out and started dripping down his forearms.

Veronica walked back over to him with the towel, placing it on his palms to get the bleeding to stop. He gasped as he felt the cold water touch his open wounds. The white towel soon turned red as the blood seeped through. Veronica shook her head, thinking this wasn't going to be enough to stop the bleeding. "I'm gonna go get some more towels. Keep pressure on it." She got up from the couch and dashed upstairs to get more towels.

Still freezing cold, Nick wrapped the towels around his left hand to stop it from bleeding. His right hand was only bleeding a little, but his left hand was more severely injured, and he had lost so much blood that he was starting to become woozy.

Veronica returned with the towels, holding them in her arms while she ran down the stairs. What Nick didn't know was that she also had hydrogen peroxide with her. She knew that it would sting, but the only way he would let her put it on was if she did it by surprise. It would certainly stop the bleeding and help the cuts not become infected. It was an old-school remedy, but she swore by it to clear up any cut.

She put the towels on the couch next to Nick, grabbing the hydrogen peroxide and putting it behind her back so Nick wouldn't see it. As she removed the blood-soaked towel, she could see the open cuts on his palms. The skin had been scraped away, and there were some spots that still hadn't stopped bleeding.

Without his permission, she dabbed his palms with the hydrogen peroxide that she had poured onto the fresh towels. Nick screamed as the hydrogen peroxide seeped into his wounds. It felt like a burning sensation. He banged his feet up and down while he still sat. He squeezed his eyes closed, as his fingers began to feel tingly.

"I'm sorry, honey—it's going to heal them." Then she took two towels from her pile and wrapped them tightly around his hands. Nick held the towels with his thumbs to keep them in place, and the stinging sensation started to subside.

He opened his eyes to look down at his hands, and he could tell that these scrapes were going to leave scars on his palms forever. The cuts felt so deep, and he kept replaying in his mind the moment when he'd hit the pothole with his bike. He'd known after that hit that there was going to be blood. He was just glad he hadn't hit his head.

"Nick, honey, I don't understand why you didn't just take my car—"

Nick cut his mom off before she could say anything else, screaming, "No! No more cars!" His eyes turned bloodshot, and he gritted his teeth as he stared at this mom.

She backed away from him when he snapped at her. He just needed some space, she thought. "Sweetheart, you don't have to go back in the car."

"Good, because I'm never getting in a car ever again!" Nick then turned away from his mother to face the warming fire.

Veronica felt that she'd been talking to a completely different person when Nick had lashed out at her. He had not done that since he was little, one day when she couldn't take him out for ice cream. Since then he hadn't ever raised his voice at her, and she was taken aback for a moment.

As Nick looked into the fireplace, he stared at the burning fire as if inspired to burn down everyone and everything all around. He had gone mad and completely blank. He was set on one task and one task only, and that was to seek revenge on Sean.

When Veronica was talking to him, she noticed that Nick wasn't listening or responding to her. She repeated herself twice, telling him that she was going upstairs to put everything away. She came back downstairs to find Nick still staring at the fireplace. It was almost as if she wasn't even here, as if she were invisible. Veronica didn't know whether he was just ignoring her or somehow didn't hear her. It was possible his ears were ringing.

But Nick was really listening to the voices in his head. This was the first time he had ever heard these strange voices, and he had no idea where they were coming from.

Veronica saw that he was fixated on something, so she said again, "Nick, who did you go and visit?" Now she was annoyed for him not answering her, so she sat down next to him on the couch and placed her hand on his knee.

That touch took Nick out of the trance he was in, and he heard his mother's words. He had not heard a word she said until she'd put her hand on his knee. It was as if he were underwater and could only hear the voices in his mind. He then came out of the trance and faced his mom.

"Are you okay, honey?" she asked him.

He smirked as he said, "Oh, I'm wonderful." His tone of voice changed as he spoke.

Veronica felt that something in Nick had changed, that she didn't have the same son since he'd woken up from his coma. The Nick she knew was soft-spoken and always took notice when someone was talking to him. Now he barely responded to her. It was as if his mind was occupied by something else.

When she took her hand away, he turned back to the fire. She looked down at his hands and the towels still wrapped around them to stop the bleeding. Veronica felt that maybe it would be best if she just gave him some space. But it was hard for her, because she had missed him so much and wanted to help Nick if there was something wrong.

He was acting strange. His voice often sounded dark, and he would go places without an explanation. Nick had shown that his personality had changed, just as the doctor had warned her it might. It was clear to her Nick was not the same person he'd been before the car crash.

Going back, she wished she had stopped Nick from going out the door that night. If he hadn't left, then she would still have the son that she'd raised. Nick was more of a stranger to Veronica now than a son.

She couldn't go back in time and change what had happened. If she could, she would have, but the only thing to do now was to accept that her son was healthy. He was back home, where he belonged, and she prayed every night that the old Nick would return to her.

Veronica recalled when Nick had been the sweetest, most caring son in the world, but now she didn't know what to say or do about the situation. She didn't want to bring up his odd behavior to him, because she had a feeling that there was no changing what Nick had become.

Most days he would sit up in his room and come out only to eat and shower. She thought he was just sleeping and playing games on his computer. What she didn't know was that he was planning a murder.

5

ON THE OUTSIDE

On the first of July, Veronica passed away. The funeral took place three days later, and Nick hadn't left his house since then. He was tormented with guilt and sorrow that she had died so young. Cancer had finally collected her body, as it had so many others.

Nick was so furious that his mother died that when he first came home from the funeral he threw all the pictures of him and his mother together off the walls. After he'd violently flung them and cracked all the glass in the picture frames, he'd collapsed in the middle of the living room, weeping into the carpet and screaming, "Why, why, why?"

More days passed, there was no food in the house, and he had no job. To buy food, he had to find a job. Before he went into the coma, he'd had two jobs, but when he awoke from his coma, he was informed that his position had been filled. His mom had gotten money that had been raised to help cancer patients who can't afford to pay for treatment. The money had also helped with the house expenses a lot, although it hadn't been enough to cure her.

Nick found the courage to eventually get out of the house. He rode his bike around the city and came across a fish-bait shop that had a Help Wanted sign in the window. He parked his bike down an alley and decided to walk in. When he did, he saw a lot of different fishing equipment and everything you could possibly need for a camping trip. Nick eyed a man who seemed to be in charge, so he walked up to him and asked for a job application.

After Nick filled out the form, the man asked Nick to come into his office so he could ask him some questions. Nick turned into his kind, witty self again to charm the manager into hiring him. He knew that eventually he would be able to buy some of the equipment that he would need for his plan.

As he was walking out of the store, he felt relieved that he could start his new job the very next Monday. When he was walking along the sidewalk toward the alley where he'd parked his bike, he saw a familiar face—and it made his blood boil.

Sean was just getting out of his car in front of a nursery across the street. Nick crouched down behind a car that was parked on the opposite side of the street. He quietly watched Sean go into the nursery. Sean was wearing a button-up flannel shirt with black jeans and sneakers. What also caught Nick's eye was the very expensive-looking watch that he wore on his left wrist.

Nick looked behind him to where his bike was parked down the alley. He thought that he should follow Sean when he came out. He wondered whether Sean was still with Amy and whether she was still living in Boston. He still had a Massachusetts license plate, but that could mean he'd moved to a different area in Massachusetts.

Sean was only in the nursery for five minutes; Nick timed him by looking at his wristwatch. He emerged from the store with a bouquet of daisies and daffodils. He looked right and left at the curb as cars passed by him; then he walked out into the street to get into his car on the other side.

He put the flowers in the back seat, and then he got into the driver's seat. Nick would've given anything to beat him up right then and there, but there were way too many witnesses around. *He took everything from me*, Nick kept thinking.

As Sean started the car, Nick stayed crouched over his bike. He saw Sean drive away, and he got on his bike to follow him. Nick tried hard to stay far enough away from Sean's flashy black Mercedes so he wouldn't notice him but close enough so that he wouldn't lose him.

Nick was hoping that Sean wouldn't go on the highway, because then he would definitely lose sight of him. Pedaling was also going to be a struggle, and he was praying Sean wasn't driving too far from there.

Keeping his eye on Sean, Nick pedaled all the way to what seemed to be Sean's house. It was only a fifteen-minute bike ride for Nick. As he took a turn on Elm Street, he saw a brand-new house just around the corner.

Nick felt that he might be seen, so he rode his bike into the woods just past Sean's house. He got off his bike and peeked around a massive tree, keeping a close watch on Sean.

When he wrapped his hands around the trunk of the tree, he couldn't help but feel the scar tissue that was on his palms. He remembered how he'd fallen on that cold winter night, and he remembered how his mom had tended his wounds. His heart ached to think that she wasn't on this earth anymore. He took a deep breath, trying to put her out of his mind, and returned to focusing on Sean.

Sean got out of his car and grabbed the flowers from the back seat. As he was walking around his car to get to the front porch, a woman greeted him, emerging from the house.

It was a very cozy house, with a dark-blue paint on the wood and a big porch in the front. Nick thought that Sean was taking very good care of himself. He guessed that the flowers were for someone very special.

It was Amy, and she was glowing. Nick thought that she hadn't changed at all, but there was a huge difference when she turned to the side. Amy was with child, and Nick glanced at the diamond ring on her finger as the sun shined down on the porch. Amy appeared to have stuffed a basketball underneath her tank top.

Amy smiled at the sight of her husband bringing her flowers. "I got us a housewarming gift," he heard Sean say. As he said it, Nick felt sick to his stomach to think that Amy was still with Sean after all this time.

Nick caught a glance of packing boxes on the floor inside the house when Amy left the door open to greet Sean. They must have just moved in, and they were starting a family together.

Nick was repulsed when Sean kissed her on the forehead and she wrapped her arms around him. Sean whispered something to Amy and they shared laughter, talking about how much weight Amy had gained during her pregnancy and how she didn't have much longer to go. They were ready to welcome their daughter into the world.

As Sean shut the door behind him, Nick looked at the nearby street sign. It said Elm Street, and that was something he'd never forget. If Sean hadn't moved here, odds were that Amy would be having Nick's child, not Sean's.

Deranged at the sight, Nick had never felt so sure of his plan. He wanted to put it into action immediately. With them having a baby on the way, he could feel a little guilt for taking the baby's father away, but it soon faded when he recalled that Sean had taken Amy away from him—the girl he never stopped loving. Even though she was pregnant Nick thought that Amy was beautiful, as he watched from behind a tree near their house.

Months went by, and the season changed to fall. The leaves were starting to change from green to a light orange, and the cold air was starting to move in. Soon enough the leaves would begin falling from the branches as winter moved in. Nick had been contemplating every single night since he'd seen Sean at the flower shop. He wanted to walk down to Elm Street and give Sean what he deserved, what he'd had been coming to him ever since Nick had woken up from his coma.

Nick held down his job at the fish-bait shop, and he knew he was well equipped to get the job done. With his employee discount he bought the items that he needed to execute his plan. He was charming as could be when he was out in public, and no one would ever have suspected that this average man was planning a murder. People would have described him as kind, fun, and a hard worker at his job.

Nick bought a 15-inch fillet knife, along with black gloves and a ski mask. Those three objects were going to be used to complete his plan. After he'd purchased them, he left the store, shoved the items into his backpack, and then pedaled his way home. Night after night he contemplated flaking on his plan and returning all the items so he wouldn't be tempted ever again.

Nick would toss and turn most nights before eventually falling asleep. The voices were telling him to go through with his plan, but he didn't want to harm Amy in any way for his own selfish reasons. Every night he would find an excuse not to go to Elm Street.

One crisp fall night, Nick was sitting in his mother's rocking chair, enjoying a cold beer while watching TV. As he kept rocking the chair back and forth, his eye settled on the backpack that had been sitting over by the door. That backpack had the future murder weapon along with the gloves and the mask to conceal his face. He had been home from work for a few hours, and he changed out of his work clothes, into a black sweatshirt and baggy black jeans.

Empathy crept in as he thought about how Amy would feel. It would be like doing the same thing she'd done to him. Heartache was the worst feeling in the world. Also, thinking of the child growing up without a father made Nick get choked up, because Nick knew what it was like to be raised by a single mom.

What if the police catch me? I could end up going to jail. Sean could fight back and end up killing me. He took another sip of his beer and turned back to the TV. Behind him were still the shattered pictures of his late mother. He couldn't force himself to throw them out, so he'd left all the shattered glass in the carpet. Every step he took he would hear a crunch as the glass shattered into more tiny little pieces.

Suddenly, an urge of energy made Nick stand up from the chair and walk to the door, more glass cracking into smaller pieces along the way. It was just starting to get dark as he looked out his window. He bent down, unzipped his backpack, and took out the black leather gloves. He slipped them on and then grabbed the ski mask out of the backpack.

The first time he put it on, he put it on backward, so he couldn't see anything. He flipped it around on his face so he could see. Sticking out of the bag was the long, sharp knife. He'd almost forgotten one more important thing.

Nick walked into the kitchen and grabbed a towel from the drawer closest to the fridge. Then he walked back to the front door. He stuffed the towel into the backpack to go with the knife. Zipping it the backpack, out the door he went.

With no hesitation, Nick rode his bike briskly down the sidewalk toward Sean's house. Many cars passed him as he made his way to Elm Street with his backpack on his back. But they didn't know that Nick was going to commit a murder. And in his mind he wasn't really committing a crime, he was really only repaying a favor.

6

FULL MOON

As Nick made his final turn around the block, where he could see Elm Street, he recognized one major problem. Nick was concerned that if he wasn't careful, there is a slight chance that someone could see him acting suspicious. He hopped off his bike, as his legs were very tired from pedaling. Across from the street sign there were five other houses. In each house several of the lights inside were still on. He pushed up his sleeve to see his watch. It was well past eleven.

Nick then decided to cut through the woods and eventually get sight of the back of the house. While he was navigating his way to the back of the house, he noticed that in the top floor on the right side of the house a light was on in one room. In the first level of the home there were no lights on; it was completely dark.

When he got to the middle at the back of the house, surrounded by trees, he decided to stop and put his backpack behind a tree. He crouched, still looking up and seeing the light on in the upstairs bedroom. He could tell that it was a bedroom, because he saw a shadow of a man walk into the center of the room and then tumble onto a surface. Odds were that the shadow was getting into bed, Nick thought. As he continued looking up at the window, he leaned his bike up against the same tree that he'd put his backpack behind.

He bent down again to unzip his backpack. Pulling out the sharp knife, he grasped it tightly in his hand. Then he stood up as a gust of wind blew in his direction. He stepped around the tree and looked at the back door of the house.

His heart racing, he started to feel sweat flowing down his back. He was starting to get hot under the cotton ski mask he was wearing. A gust of cool fall air blew near and around Nick, only cooling him off temporarily. But then the sweat trickled down his back again as he started to make his way to the back door. He looked up at the dusky sky, seeing the moon full and bright. He took a deep breath and kept moving forward, toward the house.

He felt very clever, as he had a secret weapon to help him get inside. It was an enchanted key that could open any door, and it had taken Nick forever to get his hands on it. When he did find it eventually, in his home, he'd known this would be the perfect object to help him with his scheme.

Nick held onto his knife tightly as he slowly walked toward the door. It was pitch black, but he knew that he was at the back door to the house. Patting the door, he finally put his hand on the doorknob. As he took the key out of his pocket and started to insert it, miraculously it began to glow. The shape changed into a different key that would unlock the door. As he unlocked the door, the darkness around him suddenly became brighter for a short moment; the shimmer then faded away when he pulled the key out of the hole and entered the house. Quietly, he shut the door behind him and put the enchanted key back in his pocket.

Crouching at mid height, he still could barely see anything other than the darkness. Nick willfully grasped his knife tighter. He scanned the room that he was in but continued to only see the light that was shining down the stairs from the bedroom. The light came down from the staircase and stopped at the front portion of the house near the double doors.

Standing up regularly now, Nick stood in the middle of what he thought was the kitchen. Many times he had ridden his bike past their street and spotted Amy cooking dinner inside. The light had been on in the kitchen, and Nick had been able to see her clearly through the window.

He still grasped his knife strongly and had it ready for Sean. His elbow was pointed outward, and it bumped into a frying pan that was dangling from a ceiling rack. The frying pan came off the hook and crashed down onto the kitchen floor.

Nick cringed as he heard the sound. He didn't know what to do. They must have heard the clang from upstairs. Now all he had to do was hide and wait for the right moment to strike.

Upstairs, Amy was rocking Ariel to sleep in her arms. As she looked down at her daughter, Amy noticed that Ariel was almost asleep. Her eyes were just starting to close when she was awakened again by the loud clang that came from downstairs. This was followed by quick footsteps, and Amy looked up from Ariel into the hallway. Still holding Ariel in her arms, she looked at Sean and said worriedly, "Sean, what was that?"

Sean looked up from his book and answered, "I don't know." He closed his book, stood up from the bed, and put the book on his nightstand next to the bed.

Concerned, as the bang was followed by quietness, Sean needed to find out what had made that sound. His first instinct was that it was an intruder, but a part of him wanted to stay upstairs and away from harm. He had to have courage. He wanted to protect his family if there was an intruder downstairs. "Stay up here. I'll go check it out." Sean willingly passed by his wife to go downstairs.

Amy felt uncertain about Sean going downstairs; she was sure that she had heard footsteps. She couldn't help but think that someone had broken into the house, although she knew that she'd locked the back door before coming upstairs.

As Sean made his way down the stairs, hand skimming the railing, he couldn't see anything in front of him. He turned around to the upstairs lighting from the bedroom and that was his only guidance. When he turned his head it was pitch black, but he knew that there was a light switch at the bottom of the stairs.

The light switch was in the dining room, where the doorway had an opening to the kitchen. As he reached the bottom of the stairs, he felt the wall as a guide while he looked up the stairs to see the bedroom light still on.

When he walked closer to the dining room, he started to feel around for the light switch. He was at the right wall where the switch would be, but he couldn't get his hand on it. Sean felt all around until he finally felt the switch and flipped it. The room lit up from the chandelier above. He took two steps toward the center of the room, not seeing anything peculiar. The dining room was finally all put together; finally all the boxes had been unpacked. He was glad that he was officially moved in. Sean also admired the dining room table set his parents had given to him and Amy as a wedding gift. It completed the room perfectly. He turned to look out the window and saw some car headlights passing by on the road outside his house. It was then that he noticed a shadowy figure in the reflection of the window.

It was a man with a sharp blade in his hand and dressed in all black. Before Sean could turn around, it was too late. Nick had waited for the opportune moment to pounce, when Sean had his back to him. He drove his knife into Sean's side, causing him to fall backward, cringing at the pain in his side and letting out a loud wheeze. As Nick removed the knife, Sean started to fall back toward him, his blood covering the blade entirely. Sean tried to turn around as he fell and landed on his side.

Sean had not been able to see the intruder; Nick was unrecognizable in his ski mask. As Sean suffered, trying to put pressure on his wound while lying on the floor, he looked at the massive amount of blood that was gushing out of his body. There was nothing he could do. He watched his side leak out blood onto his hands. Sean started to feel cold, and his vision became blurry.

Meanwhile, Nick stood watching over him and saw him dying slowly but surely. Sean was in so much pain that he couldn't call out to Amy; he laid there helpless. Nick then bent down to the suffering Sean as he was almost going into the light.

Sean had no idea why someone would do this to him. He was frightened to think what this person was going to do to him next. Through his pain, he heard the masked man say to him, "You stole everything from me. You had it coming!"

Those were the last words Sean ever heard someone say. Nick stayed until Sean's eyes eventually became lifeless and his body became very still after he took his last breath. Nick checked for a pulse and couldn't find one. His thirst for revenge was finally satisfied after so many days of planning. He had finally executed what he had been wanting for so long.

To see Sean's deceased face was almost rewarding to Nick. He had at last given in to what the voices inside his head told him to do.

When Nick stood up again, he admired Sean's spiritless corpse. But he soon had to hide again, because he heard Amy yelling for Sean. "Sean, are you okay?"

He hid back in the kitchen where there was no light. Since he was wearing all black, he was completely invisible. As long as the lights weren't switched on in the kitchen, he would remain hidden. He wanted to see how Amy would react; he didn't know what to do in the moment. He just couldn't make an escape yet.

Upstairs, Amy was concerned when her husband had not returned after a few minutes. She looked down the stairs one last time, still rocking Ariel to sleep in her arms. She saw that Sean had switched the downstairs light on, but he did not answer her when she called out. It was unlike Sean to not answer. She also didn't hear any footsteps.

She didn't want to put Ariel down, because she didn't want her to start crying again. Ariel was almost asleep, but Amy had to check on Sean. Amy walked back into her bedroom and looked at Ariel. She held her up away from her body as she saw her yawn and her eyes just start to close. Amy couldn't ignore her gut feeling as she looked back into the hallway; she knew that something had gone wrong. She walked over to her closet, opened the door, and placed Ariel inside.

She did not put her in her crib, because the crib wasn't fully assembled for Ariel to sleep in. Sean had not made the crib stable just quite yet. Yes, it was standing, but the legs were still wobbly when she attempted to place her down inside. When it had started to shake, she had taken her out just in time before it had collapsed. Sean wasn't the most handy man around, and besides, Amy had Ariel sleep with her at night.

She laid her down, all swaddled up, and said to her daughter, "I'll be right back, sweetie." Amy felt that if something was wrong, no one would find her in the closet. She gulped as she closed the closet door quietly and stood up from the carpet.

Making her way down the stairs, she looked to her left to the opening where she could see into the dining room. "Honey, it's late," she said. She paused, and then she saw her lifeless husband lying on the floor with a puddle of blood around him.

Amy shrieked, flew down the rest of the stairs, and rushed to his side. "Oh my God!" she shouted over and over again. She knelt down next to his lifeless body. Her hands were shaking as she tried to find a pulse, and she recognized that he wasn't breathing at all. There was so much blood around him, and she saw the stab wound in his side that was still fresh. She cupped his head in her hands and started weeping. Not knowing what to do, she combed her fingers through his hair, whispering, "Sean!"

Amy tried to control her sobbing but could not. She screamed as she ran her hands through his hair again. She thought she was having a nightmare, but this was for real; there was no waking up from this one. She wanted to hug Sean and never let go, but she knew that she had to report this.

She got up from the floor, wiping her tears, and walked over to the phone in the corner of the room to call for help. She didn't want to believe this was actually happening. An operator came on the other line, saying, "This is 911. What is your emergency?"

"Please help me—please help me! There was an intruder in my house, and my husband was stabbed. He's not breathing! Please send somebody—anybody! He's not moving!"

Amy was so frantic on the phone that the operator could hardly understand her, but she heard enough to send help to the scene. Amy couldn't help but cry uncontrollably. The operator asked what her address was, and Amy replied, "One Elm Street, Dorchester."

As she was talking to the operator, Nick was just about to leave through the back door. He'd accomplished his job, done what he'd set out to do. Once he heard Amy make the 911 call, he turned back around.

He thought, *Amy can't call the cops; I can't let her.* So he walked back into the dining room where Amy was. She was on the phone, wiping tears from her cheek, and her back was turned to Nick. Nick was not in his right mind; he had gone completely unhinged. He had to stop her from saying anything further.

Nick raised his knife once again; she didn't see him coming. She only saw a reflection of a shadow in the window and didn't turn around in time. He had already plunged the knife into her side, and then he stabbed her once more in the back. The phone was on a table right in front of the window, so Amy had no idea who her killer was; he just looked like a dark shadow coming from behind. As she squealed, she looked down to her side and saw blood surfacing through her clothes.

Nick pulled out the knife, and he whispered very quietly behind her, "I'm so sorry." Amy felt the stab wound with her hand as she fell backward, pulling the phone and overturning the table. Eventually the phone fell out of her hand as she hit the floor. She cringed, weeping and knowing that this was the end for her.

Nick didn't understand why he'd done what he had in that moment, but he knew it couldn't be undone. He had only come here to kill Sean, but he'd had to keep Amy from calling the police. As Nick watched Amy die on the floor, he couldn't help but realize that her child was upstairs somewhere. He made his way around Amy and looked up the stairs.

In her final moments before she died, Amy saw dark-colored shoes walking across the carpet and heading to the stairs. She thought he was now going to go find her daughter, Ariel. She wanted to put up a fight with whoever this person was, but she had already turned cold, and a final tear dripped off her face as her heart ached for the loss of her husband.

If it wasn't for Sean, Amy and I would've had children of our own together someday. That child upstairs somewhere is rightfully mine, Nick thought. As he was about to go up the stairs to go and find the child, a familiar sound came from outside.

It was a police siren, and the sound was getting louder and louder by the second. He looked down at the phone, and he could hear the operator say, "Hold on, ma'am. Help is on the way. Ma'am, are you still there? Ma'am?" Amy remained motionless on the floor with her eyes open.

Nick panicked on hearing those sirens. He had to leave immediately. He felt so angry at himself for killing Amy, but it had had to be done. He accidentally tripped over the table that was turned over on its side. As he did that, he landed on his stomach, face to face with Sean. He quickly got up as he heard the sirens coming louder; he had no time to think about what happened. Nick then grasped his knife even tighter as he ran out of the living room.

He sprinted out of the house and found his bike by the tree

where he'd left it earlier. He shoved the knife that still had Amy's blood on it into his backpack after wiping the blood off with the towel. The sirens continued to get louder as Nick pedaled away from the house and into the woods in a dash.

As Nick was pedaling through the woods, the leaves on the ground started to get caught in the wheels of his bike. He didn't notice, as he was focused on getting far away from Elm Street. Dodging several tree trunks, he knew he had to dispose of the murder weapon as soon as possible. Everywhere he pedaled it was dark; he had no idea where he was going. All he knew was that he was going away from the police sirens, as he couldn't hear them as well as he had when he'd been running out into the backyard.

Intensely sweating through his ski mask, Nick started to fly faster and faster through the woods. He felt as if he were going down a hill, almost falling forward.

He still had no idea where he was going, and he tumbled forward as a leaf got caught in his bike chain, so that made him fall down the rest of the hill. Suffering hard blows to the head by rocks and rough surfaces, Nick finally landed at the bottom of the hill on his back. His bike landed right next to him, and that was when he realized he didn't have his backpack with him.

It had been on his back the entire time he was riding his bike, but it must have fallen off when he came down the hill, he thought. Nick went into search mode; he knew that he couldn't leave the backpack behind. Police would find the knife and match it up to be the murder weapon. It was still pitch black, and all Nick was feeling was leaves and tree trunks.

Still unable to see anything, Nick heard a skid coming down from the hill. He reached his hands out toward the sound, hoping it would be his backpack. He looked behind him quickly to see car lights and a road that was directly behind him. He had no idea where he'd pedaled to, but it was away from Elm Street.

Nick let out a sigh of relief as he finally put his hand on his backpack. He stood his bike up and got back on. Holding onto his pack tighter than last time, he made his way toward the street. He looked over his shoulder, and he could no longer hear the sirens. He must be in the next town over, which was Roxbury. Nick recognized the sign for the Franklin Park Zoo.

Nick knew what he had to do, and that was dispose of his backpack. He had to put it someplace where no one would ever find it.

He had to make a decision quickly but didn't want anyone to ever find it. Also, he had to dodge every passing car so that he wouldn't be seen. He squatted behind a tree that was just off the street; from there he could see the buildings across from him.

Then, instantly, he thought of one place that he could put his backpack. Definitely no one would ever find it there. He waited until no cars were driving by him, and then he hopped on his bike once again and started pedaling toward the Charles River. It was going to be a long bike ride, but he knew it would be worth it. He could hide his backpack in the river.

As he was riding toward the Charles, he reminded himself to stay calm. He took in some deep breaths, as he rode his bike frantically. His inner devil told him that he would be accused or at least suspected if passersby saw a man with a ski mask riding down the street. They could put two and two together, and someone could contact the police. It was a huge risk, but he chose to take his ski mask off.

As cars passed him, the headlights blinded him for a short amount of time while they passed. To drivers Nick looked to be just a normal person riding his bike. Hundreds of cars passed him that night. No one could've guessed what Nick had just done. He was a cold-hearted murderer, but to the public he was just a normal guy, living his average life, going to work every day.

As the cool fall night turned into morning, Nick was still eagerly attempting to get to his destination. The fog from the dusk was slowly becoming dawn, as Nick could see the sun almost peeking up to start a new day.

He huffed and puffed as he turned around the corner from where he could see the Charles. He couldn't believe how long it had taken him to ride his bike there. On his way down the street, he looked down at his feet, and something ahead of him caught his eye. He put both feet on the ground to stop his bike completely, and he picked up a brick that had fallen out of a building. Then he picked up two more bricks that were right beside the first one.

These would be perfect for sinking my bag to the bottom, Nick thought. He picked up that brick and then two more to make it heavier. He pulled his backpack off his shoulder, and unzipped it. The bricks were dusty, and he slipped them inside the bag one by one. He took off his gloves and put them in the bag too, along with his ski mask and the knife.

Now he pulled the heavy bag up over his shoulder again and headed over to the Charles. His legs were no longer legs in his mind; they felt like Jell-O, and he almost fell trying to get back on his bike again.

It had been a long journey to get there, but in his mind there was no better place to hide the murder weapon. He just hoped that no early runners would spot him while he was trying to dispose of his bag.

As Nick reached the bridge of the Charles River, he parked his bike next to the beginning of the bridge. Getting off his bike and leaning it up against the wall of the bridge, he carried his backpack in both hands, looking around to see if anyone was watching him. It was still very early in the morning, and runners weren't quite up yet, even though the sun was appearing over the horizon.

Nick was tipsy as he walked along the bridge, and he felt as if his legs might give out at any second. He looked right and then left, seeing water on both sides. He wondered for a moment whether this was a smart idea. He chose his original instinct and held the backpack over the ledge once he got to the center of the bridge.

Reaching out holding his backpack, he then let go, and it

splashed into the Charles River. Nick stayed there for a few moments to make sure the bag sank to the bottom. The backpack disappeared from view, and the ripples quickly went away.

Nick sighed, looking up at the sky while resting his forearms on the wall of the bridge. A strong gust of wind brushed his skin, and a new thought entered his head. "I've gotta get out of here," he mumbled to himself.

A new burst of energy rushed through his body as he raced down the bridge and got back on his bike. He headed home, turning his back to the bridge. Nick had lost control of himself. He wasn't the same person anymore; he was possessed by his inner demon. He was no longer Nick but a cold-hearted killer.

7

SECOND THOUGHTS

Now, at six a.m., Nick had finally made his way home. It had taken him much longer to get back home than it had to go to the Charles from Elm Street. His legs were cramping up and his eyes were starting to close as he walked up the porch stairs. Exhausted and mad at what he'd done, he just collapsed on the couch when he went inside, landing with his head on the pillow. Silence surfaced, but then he screamed into his pillow. He was confused as to why he had made himself go through with his evil plan.

He felt disgusted with himself, because he felt that his skin had brushed up against death. He had to wash it off, or he would be death's next victim.

He sat up on the couch, resting his face in his palms. Guilt over killing Amy started to enter Nick's conscience. He rocked back and forth, hugging himself, while repeatedly saying, "I'm sorry, I'm so sorry."

Nick's mental state was so far off into his own world that he couldn't go to sleep. He was thinking about whether the police would find him and arrest him for what he had done. He grabbed the remote and turned on the TV to see if the news had done a story about the murder.

Nick hated having the temptation of turning the TV on. He felt that it would make him more paranoid if he saw a news report about Elm Street. To get rid of the temptation he would have to get rid of his TV, but he couldn't do that, because then he couldn't watch any more episodes of Will & Grace. So he decided to keep the TV, but now he changed his mind and gave in to seeing the breaking news.

He turned the TV on and immediately changed the channel from Comedy Central to the CBS news. He saw what he most desperately didn't want to see. A newscaster was already on the scene of the crime; Nick recognized the background instantly. The newscaster was in front of the house on Elm Street. Behind her there was yellow police tape saying Caution.

It was a woman newscaster, wearing a navy-blue sweater and having dark-brown hair down to her shoulders and blowing back in the wind. Nick noticed that she was Chinese, as her eyes were very slim, and she had beautiful fair skin. She held the microphone in her hand with the CBS news logo.

"Yes, well, Boston Police Department responded to a frantic 911 call. A woman called about an intruder in her home. By the time police arrived, the two adults were found dead in their home. Now, the victims were Amy and Sean Howard. Whoever the intruder was fled the scene without a trace, but investigators will be taking this case head-on to find whoever did this."

In the newsroom, a man wearing a suit then asked the reporter, "Now, it says here that a toddler was found in the home but appeared to not be harmed at all. Can you tell us more about that, Shianne?"

Shianne answered, "Yes, absolutely. Detective Smith found the toddler in the upper level of the home, in a closet. The toddler, we know now, is Ariel Howard, and she was handed over to child protective services temporarily until a guardian of some sort legally adopts the young girl. With Detective Smith knowing the young couple, this case becomes extremely difficult, as the detective has no idea who would have done this to just a fun-loving couple. They had no enemies, so he told reporters, and Smith and his wife are now aiming to get custody of the child, as they were named Ariel Howard's godparents, which will be taken to court to make official. As of right now the case remains open, and investigators are questioning neighbors across and down from Elm Street to ask if anyone saw a suspicious character fleeing the scene or anything out of the ordinary. If you have any information regarding Elm Street, please contact Boston Police Department. Reporting live, I'm Shianne Wang, CBS morning news."

"Okay. Thank you, Shianne." Nick then turned off the TV. That was all that he needed to hear; they had no current suspects. He got a chill down his spine as he thought about how he'd left their daughter in the house. Now she would grow up not knowing her parents. He should've just taken her last night and raised her as his own, he thought.

Jealously is a deadly disease, and wherever you go in life, someone you meet always seems to have it. It's very easy to catch.

Somehow Nick felt that it was a good thing that Ariel would grow up not knowing her father. He thought Sean was nothing but a selfish, manipulative egomaniac of a man. Nick hadn't known the real Sean, though. When they had gone to high school together, Nick had been intimidated by Sean's New York swagger and the fact that he came from money. He also had had no idea that Amy was seeing Sean behind his back.

When Nick was in his coma, Sean had grown fonder of Amy every day. He'd wanted to spend the rest of his life with her and start a family. That was the kind of love that grows more and more each and every day. Nick was sure that Sean was the most selfish person on earth, but in reality, Nick himself was selfish. He had taken two lives for his own revenge, not thinking about how it would affect other people.

"Don't panic—don't panic," Nick whispered to himself as he stood up from the couch. He took some deep breaths and looked down at his feet. He was wearing blue socks, and he watched them wiggle and slide back and forth on the carpet.

Then Nick remembered something. He'd heard a familiar name on the news. The name was Smith, and the only Smith he knew was David Smith, whom he'd gone to high school with. He'd dated Allison, Amy's best friend. Nick thought, *It's probably another Smith; it couldn't be the David that was with Allison in high school. Could it? Maybe they aren't that close anymore. Who knows?* he thought. One thing he had to check, though, was whether David Smith had been the detective at the crime scene. Nick raced upstairs to his computer to look up David Smith and find out whether he was a detective for the Boston Police Department.

Nick sat down at his desk and turned his computer on. He had a hellish look in his eyes. He had to find out about Smith. Back in high school, David had been adamant about becoming a cop. As he went onto public records of police officers in the area, he came across David Smith. He found his date of birth, where he'd gone to school, and that yes, he had become a detective. He was the detective who'd found the little girl in the house on Elm Street. It was the first real crime scene he'd gone to as a detective. It was listed on the website that he had just been named a detective. Before that, he had been a Boston Police officer.

Nick leaned back in his chair, interlocking his hands and putting them behind his neck with his elbows facing outward. Nick went back into his mind; he couldn't believe how much time he had missed while in a coma. He looked at the picture the website had of David in his uniform.

David still had the same brown eyes and same hairstyle that Nick recalled, but the wrinkles on his forehead became more defined over the years. Nick decided to scroll down to the bottom of the page where it said spouse, and there he read Allison Garnier in dark-fonted letters.

Allison had also been part of Nick's graduating class. She and

David had gone to college out of state, while Sean and Amy had stayed in-state for college. Nick tilted his head in a neurotic way as he processed everything that had happened in the last seven hours. As he looked over to the window, the sun had just started coming through that window. Then he caught a glimpse of the alarm clock on his bedside table.

It read 7:39, and Nick had to get ready in a rush. He had to be at work for 8:00, and he was twenty minutes away from the fish-bait shop. He stood up from his chair, pulled open his drawers, and dug around to find the work shirt that had his name on it. Once he found a clean shirt, then he found clean pants. He changed and bolted out the front door. There was no time to eat. He had to get back on his bike again and pedal to work now, even though he basically had biked over fifty miles already that day. But there was no chance he was going to start up and drive his mother's car.

Nick couldn't let himself sell his mother's car, because it was the last thing of hers that he didn't destroy accidentally, and he didn't want to ever be behind the wheel again. It was the last part of his mom, and he felt comforted by the car still being in the driveway when he thought about her. Nick would try to make himself sit in the car and turn on the ignition, but he had a panic attack every time he tried and ended up tumbling out of the car.

His car accident had messed his mind up so much that he couldn't even drive a car. He was petrified of getting into another accident. With his mind being disturbed, the best thing for him was to ride his bike everywhere he needed to go. It was almost like therapy for him every morning to ride his bike to work.

He biked everywhere he needed to go. When he went to the grocery store, he would then have to carry the bags back home. He came up with a clever way to do this. He would put the plastic grocery bags on his handlebars and pedal away. Nick would ride his bike to work and to hit the gym on rare occasions. He saved up a lot of money by not paying for gas. To be honest, Nick loved not being stuck in traffic. Some mornings on his way to work he would ride on by people who were stuck in their cars while traffic was backed up for miles.

Nick still had to keep this in mind: he had to act completely normal and not act out of character on his bike ride to work. *Draw no attention to yourself,* he thought as he smiled with the right side of his mouth. He looked demented and twisted, but as he turned the corner he kept smiling, showing his teeth as he passed people and asked how they were that day. He was just being a nice, kind Bostonian, hiding the inside Nick who was criminally insane.

His happy-go-lucky mood instantly turned into a stressful one. On his way he had to dodge multiple cops on the street. They were questioning pedestrians just walking along the sidewalk. Nick had to avoid any contact with the cops. He could feel his face starting to become flushed as he raced by the cluster of cop cars. *Just stay calm; you don't know the cops are questioning people about what you did last night. Don't worry. Just get to work. You'll be fine; just get to work.*

Two cops turned and walked right away from Nick. They had their backs toward him, and he let out a sigh as they walked further away. *That was close,* he thought. *Jesus, man. Cops are like ants in the summertime; they're everywhere!* Nick had always been kind of afraid of police officers in the first place, ever since he was a kid. Cops were always walking around with guns on their hips, and they were very well built. He was almost jealous, as he himself was more on the slim side.

He clipped the lock on his bike chain and walked to the shop. He pulled open the door and saw his boss at the front counter. The bell attached to the top of the door rang when Nick swung it open.

Dozens of fishing rods, tool kits, and fishing knifes hung on the walls of the store. In the aisles were all types of fish hooks and fishing attire. The camping equipment was in the back half of the store.

Nick walked over to his boss through aisle 1. "Hey boss, what were those cops doing here?" Mark looked up from the desk, where he was polishing some of his expensive inventory and then putting the items back into the case below the desk for viewing.

"Oh, they were just here to ask a few questions about if I saw anything or anyone last night. Did you see the news last night? Some bastard killed a couple and then fled the scene. I can't imagine someone so heartless that could do something like that. Whoever did it, they have to live with that harsh memory forever. They deserve to rot in jail for the rest of their pathetic life."

Nick stayed neutral with Mark; he felt that he had to play along. "Yeah, that's just terrible." Nick could feel his face becoming red again. He hoped that Mark wouldn't look up at him and see him racked with guilt. He might then assume that something was up.

Nick took some deep breaths before he heard Mark speak again and looked up as he closed the viewing case under the desk. In the front of the desk it was all clear glass with shelves where the special fish hooks and very expensive fishing knives rested.

"So, you ready to help me move in some new inventory?" Mark clapped his hands together and started to make his way to the back room.

Nick followed him, saying, "Oh yeah." Nick tried to be sane on the outside, even though on the inside he was screaming.

As he was working, the whole day he was thinking about the chest back at his house. He remembered that before he'd had his accident and was still with Amy, he'd stored all of their pictures in a chest. That chest had led him to find the enchanted key, which had helped him out tremendously the night before. It had taken him a long time to find the key and open the chest.

Nick was thinking back to before he'd committed his crime. For days he had passed the chest in his room and tried to remember what on earth he'd put in there so long ago. When his mother was alive, she hadn't been able to remember what he could have put in there either. Nick also thought back to the day when he was at work and remembered exactly what was in that chest.

Now he knew, but there was one problem. He had no idea where the key was. The chest held memories of when things hadn't yet gone wrong. He chuckled to himself when he thought about how long it had taken him to find the key to the chest. Now he had the key in his pocket. He never went anywhere without it.

Distracted the whole day, Nick had a hard time concentrating on doing simple tasks. A customer asked for his assistance in looking for a particular item, and Nick went completely blank, not knowing what aisle it was in. Eventually he gave up and asked Mark what aisle to tell the customer to go to. He also dropped some boxes when he was moving them from the back room to be put on display.

Mark was a very forgiving boss, unlike some bosses. Back when Nick's mother had passed away, he'd told him that he could take all the time he needed until he was ready to come back to work. Mark noticed that Nick was a little off.

At the end of the day, Mark was closing up. Nick had just finished unpacking his last box and put the very last fishing rod together and up on the wall. Mark looked over to Nick and saw him just staring out the window. "You all right over there, Nick?"

Nick turned his head quickly back at Mark and came up with a lie. What he really was doing was thinking about getting home and opening up that chest again. "Oh, I just was admiring the moon. The moons in October are my favorite part of fall." He smiled, trying to cover up his thoughts.

Mark said, "Okay, I'll see you tomorrow then?"

Nick hadn't realized that it was closing time; his mind was really somewhere else. He became excited that it was time to go home. "Yes, absolutely! You have a good night, Mark."

Mark went to the back room to grab the broom and start sweeping up the floor. When he returned to the front, he said, "You too, Nick."

But Nick had already left the store. The bell over the entrance was still slightly ringing. *How odd of him, leaving in a rush like that,*

Mark thought. He began sweeping the floor as he made his way to the front door to switch the sign from Open to Closed.

Looking out the street, he saw Nick pedaling away on his bike at a very swift pace. Wherever he was going, he was going somewhere very important, Mark thought.

Nick went back to when he'd known what was inside the chest in the first place, and the chest had been right next to his nightstand. He wanted to race home and admire the lovely pictures inside the chest, and he laughed thinking about the day when he hadn't been able to remember for the life of him where the key was. He'd racked his brain for years, wondering what on earth could be inside.

8

THE KEY

A couple weeks earlier, when Nick hadn't yet committed the crime, he came home from work one day and decided he wasn't going to sleep until he found the key. He made it his priority to find it. Nick turned onto his front lawn and grabbed the brakes on the handlebars to come to a stop. He put his feet down, swung his leg over the bike, and ran up to the porch, leaving his bike in the middle of the lawn on its side.

He entered his home and immediately ran upstairs. He went up the stairs so quickly that the whole house shook. Standing in the middle of his bedroom, he gawked at the ancient chest next to his nightstand. He remembered his mother telling him about where she'd gotten the chest when he was a little boy.

Veronica's mother, Nick's grandmother, had come to America with all her belongings in that exact same chest, which made the chest over a hundred years old. Nick got closer to the chest and recognized the very familiar keyhole that he had been trying to crack for years. Nothing would open this chest except the key. He'd tried to pick the lock with everything he could find—a bobby pin, a paper clip, and even a knife to try and slice through the keyhole.

The chest had black leather around the sides and intricate chiseling in the wood of the entire chest. In the center of it was a small keyhole with black marble surrounding it.

Nick bent down and blew the dust off the chest. He closed one eye, while the other peeked into the chest. He was trying to see if there was anything valuable inside the chest, but it was completely dark.

He placed both his hands on the top of the chest, still thinking about where to start looking for the key. He didn't care that the pictures inside would cause him to feel more pain over not being with Amy or provide some closure. All he wanted was to see the pictures of when his life had seemed to be sparkling with happiness. Nothing could ever ruin the life Nick had planned for himself and Amy at the time. That had been before prom night, when things had been changed forever and his dreams for Amy and himself shattered.

Certain problems or issues can't be restored or repaired—just like the old Nick. He would never be back and never be repaired. Now all he thought about was finding the needle in a haystack.

Standing back up, Nick marched into the hallway. He passed the bathroom and then put his hand on the doorknob of his mother's room. He hesitated to open the door at first. A voice inside of him said, *You need to find the key to open the chest.*

Nick hadn't gone into his mother's room since she'd passed away. He couldn't bring himself to go through all her clothes and belongings, but this day he had a whole new purpose. Odds are that the key was in her room somewhere.

He purposefully opened the door and instantly started looking around her room. If the key was anywhere in the house, it would be there. Even though she'd claimed she couldn't remember where she'd put the key several years ago, he wasn't going anywhere until he found it.

Nick started with the top of her dresser. Maybe the key was in one of her jewelry boxes. Those boxes were the perfect size to fit a key in. He found pearls and seashell-patterned bracelets, the majority of what Veronica used to wear. Looking through all her jewelry boxes one by one without finding the key, he decided to move on to another spot.

Also on her dresser Nick found a variety of perfumes and nail polishes. The polishes were all arranged by color. He smiled at how perfect she had been at organizing. Then he looked through all the drawers, tossing all the clothing items out to see whether the key was at the bottom. Nick even pulled the dresser away from the wall to see if anything was behind it, but there wasn't.

The bedroom floor soon became covered by jeans, shorts, and tank tops. The key was not in the dresser, so he moved on to the closet. He opened the closet door and saw all his mother's blouses, shirts, and dresses organized by color. It was like an assortment of clothes combining into a rainbow. Red started on the left, and at the right were purple and black.

He looked down and saw several shoe boxes. Maybe the key was in one of those, he thought. Nick opened shoe box after shoe box. *How could a woman own this many shoes?* he wondered. When he reached the back of the closet, he found even more boxes filled with clothes and shoes.

Nick started to feel overwhelmed by all the places this key could be. It might not even be in this room! What if she'd lost it and it wasn't even in the house anymore? He was getting frustrated at not finding the key, but he wasn't going to give up. He searched every nook and cranny of her bedroom.

He knew that if his mother were still alive she would not let him go through her bedroom like this—no way! But he couldn't stop now. Not when he'd finally remembered what was in the chest in the first place. *Who knows? Maybe there's more in that chest that I don't even know about or I just haven't remembered*, he thought.

An hour passed, and still no key. Nick was almost sinking in the piles of clothes that he'd taken out of the closet. He had to laugh when he remembered the times Veronica had said that she had nothing to wear to go out to a party. She had plenty of clothes, but every woman always said, "Oh, I have nothing to wear!" Nick chuckled and then said, "Oh, you have plenty to wear."

Three hours had passed, and still no key. Nick started to think that he was never going to find it. So he climbed out of the volcano of clothes and walked back to his room. He scratched his head while walking, still trying to figure out where the stupid key would be.

Nick then raced back down next to the chest, saying, "Where would you be, key? Here, key!" As he peeked through the keyhole again, he still could see nothing inside. It was like a dark hole where you could see nothing in front of you.

He sat back on his heels, thinking about what to do. He then decided to stand up and pick up the chest. He cupped his hands around the sides of the chest—and felt something underneath the back right corner of the chest.

As he stuck his hand underneath that side of the chest, it felt as if something was taped to it, something metal underneath the tape. He desperately wanted to see what it was, so he lifted the chest up again with all his might. He grunted as he picked it up off the floor.

Closing his eyes, he swung the chest onto his bed. The chest was so heavy that it made the bed almost collapse. When it creaked, Nick was worried that the bedframe was going to give out. He looked under the bed and saw that the bedframe was, luckily, still intact. When he looked up again, he saw the chest lying on the bed with its bottom facing him and its front facing the ceiling. In the right corner of the bottom of the chest was an ancient key that was held there by tape.

Smiling, Nick couldn't believe that the key had been right under his nose the whole time! *Mom probably stuck it there because she knew it would be a good laugh for her watching me struggle to find it.*

The key looked ancient, made of silver and bronze, but most of the bronze had tarnished over the years. Nick pried the key away from the bottom of the chest and finally grasped it in his hand.

Excitedly, Nick then stood the chest up so that he could unlock it at last. His eyes narrowed in at the keyhole, and his hand guided the key into the slot. It was almost like two puzzle pieces that fit together perfectly. As he turned the key, he saw the top part of the chest pop open. There was a small crack to see what was inside. Nick decided to take the chest off of the bed and onto the floor for a better view. He knelt in front of the chest, placing his hand on top of it. Finally, he was going to get his hands on what was inside!

The chest flung open, and another cloud of dust puffed into the room. Nick coughed again before starting to rummage through the belongings inside. As the dust cleared, he saw a picture of his grandmother in a very old frame. The picture was in black and white and she was getting off a boat. Nick thought it must be the day that she came to America. He felt the back of the frame as he lifted it up. He took the picture out of its frame and turned it over. There was a date written on the back, May 25, 1948.

Nick noticed the lovely cursive handwriting under the date. It said, "The beginning of my life starts now, here in Massachusetts." Nick thought about how different his life would have been if his grandmother had not come to America from France. She never would've met Paul, his grandfather.

Lynette had met Paul shortly after she'd docked in Boston, and she'd fallen for him. He and his family were very well off, and Lynette had felt that she had no business being a part of that wealthy life. Soon after Paul and Lynette went their separate ways, Lynette had discovered that she was with child. This was Veronica, Nick's mother. Lynette had been adamant about providing a life for herself and her child in America.

Nick looked down at what was underneath; it was an old satchel. This satchel was the same one as in the picture. Lynette had traveled to America with nothing but the clothes on her back and a few belongings in her satchel and in the chest.

The satchel now, however, was completely empty as Nick peeked inside. But as he lifted the satchel out, he saw glittering diamonds at the very bottom of the chest. There were earrings, a necklace, and a sapphire broach. Pearls were in the mix, along with some emerald-green necklaces and earrings.

Nick was taken aback. How on earth was it that this kind of jewelry had been in this chest for all this time? Not even his mother had mentioned to him about this jewelry. He had no idea how much the jewelry was worth, but as he remembered his mom telling him about his grandmother's past, he then put together how she must have gotten the massively expensive jewelry in the first place.

9

THE FOUNTAIN

The year was 1948, and it was a warm summer night in Boston. Young Lynette was getting ready for a very important dinner date with Paul and his parents. She was a fiery French woman from Paris, and she was someone you didn't tell what to do. She'd turn it around, and you would end up following her orders.

Dark-brown, curly hair and brown eyes shining, Lynette laid out one of her best dresses across the hotel bed. Her hands were clammy, and she could feel the sweat from her neck dripping down her back. Then she heard a knock at her hotel door.

For the past few previous mornings, Lynette had been getting morning sickness. She did not want to tell Paul, because the pregnancy was too early, and she did not want him to be angry with her.

Lynette had had no place to stay, but when she'd met Paul, he had gladly paid for her to stay in a hotel. It was not just any hotel, it was the most elegant hotel in all of Boston. Only republicans and upper-class folks could afford to stay there. Paul had fallen in love with her the moment they'd met, and he wasn't going to let a beautiful woman like Lynette just slip by.

Lynette loved how sweet Paul was to her in helping her out, but everything was moving all too fast for her. She had only met Paul back in May, and now it was July. She was taken by surprise at how much he spent on her; she couldn't believe how extravagant his life was. He wouldn't flinch about buying her jewelry or renting out a yacht to go out on the Boston Harbor.

He even took the liberty of teaching her English. When she'd come to America, she'd only known a few words, but now her vocabulary had blossomed. She still had trouble pronouncing some words, but above all Lynette found it hard to grasp the Bostonian accent. She would pronounce her words fully; it was hard to understand why some locals would leave out letters in certain words.

Lynette opened the door and welcomed Paul in. He laid a kiss on her forehead as he entered the hotel room. Classy yet elegant, the hotel to Lynette was like a mansion. It was a five-star hotel, and it was more spacious than she could ever ask for. Having grown up in a one-room house, Lynette was very grateful to Paul. She still had no source of income, so Paul was her life preserver.

In the corner of the room stood a very fancy chest. The key to the chest was on the dresser. Lynette had used that chest to lug everything she owned over to America. Excited to start fresh, she'd had no idea that she would meet Paul on her first day.

"Hello, darling. Almost ready to go?" Paul had gold buttons on his jacket, and his black vest rested on his strong shoulders. A chain was visible coming out of his pocket, attached to which was a golden pocket watch. As he was eyeing the dress spread out on the bed, he was thinking to himself, *Oh no! She's not wearing that old thing, is she? Mother and Father will know that she is just some girl off the streets.*

Paul could read the tension and the stress on her face. He saw that she was very nervous about the evening that he had planned for her. "Yes, Paulie, I just have to put on my dress." That was one thing Paul loved about Lynette, her thick French accent. He hadn't met many girls that spoke with so much texture; some girls he had met in Boston talked like truck drivers.

As she bent down to put on her shoes, Paul said, "Darling, you not going to wear that old thing, are you?"

Lynette stood up in shock. She'd thought the dress beautiful. It was her only dress, for that matter. Although the lace on the sleeves was a bit ratty, all around it was still a charming dress for a night out in the city. Lynette only felt more uneasy when she imagined what kind of people Paul's parents really were.

"I was going to, yes."

"Don't worry, Lynette. There is a luxury evening gown shop right down the street from here. We'll find you a gown there." Paul knew very well that Lynette did not come from much, but with eyes and a smile like that, he didn't want to let go of her.

Lynette was puzzled, thinking, *How come my old dress isn't good enough?* She was worried about what she was getting herself into. Why on earth was Paul being so incredibly nice to her? Not just nice, he was spoiling her. *If this is how all Americans are, I think I'm going to like it here*, she thought.

She did not know that not all Americans were as well off as Paul and his family. They came from money and were country-club personalities. They were a very well-known family all around Boston. Lynette didn't like all the attention they'd get when she and Paul went out. They wouldn't just be able to walk by themselves; they would be followed by greetings and having conversations during which Lynette had no idea what they were talking about. The vocabulary they used especially threw her off.

Together, Lynette and Paul left the hotel and walked across the street to the shop. Lynette saw that the dresses she'd brought with her in her chest were mainly flowy and comfortable. The dress shop that she was about to go to sold incredibly tight and flashy gowns. They certainly weren't her style, and she wished that she could be herself. But she went along with Paul's suggestion.

When she got to the shop, she wasn't really sure how to tell the worker what she was looking for, because she had no idea what would've been considered presentable in Paul's eyes. So Paul simply told the woman what she needed. He didn't flinch at opening up his check book, no matter the cost. He told the worker that there was absolutely no budget.

Along with jewelry that Paul had already bought her, she wore a maroon gown that was tight around her waist and, as the skirt went down, proceeded outward. Shimmering sparkles covered the whole dress. At the bottom you could see her silver shoes when she walked, and the dress flowed from side to side. She emerged from the dressing room feeling uncomfortable in her own skin, but she saw Paul smile at her when she came out from behind the curtains. She was confused about why she had to wear such an uncomfortable get-up just to eat dinner, but again she decided to please Paul by going along with his decisions.

She wore a diamond necklace, diamonds earrings, and a sapphire broach pinned to her jacket. No one would ever have guessed that only two months prior to that she had been an immigrant with no money in her pocket. She'd barely wrestled enough money together for the boat ride over to Massachusetts. Now she was swanky and gorgeous as she walked back to Paul's car. "You look absolutely gorgeous, Lynette," Paul whispered in her ear.

Several people were gathered outside of the store, trying to catch a glimpse of Paul and Lynette. She swerved and managed her way through the wave of people and then waited for Paul to open the door of the car for her. Paul, of course, had a driver.

Lynette felt very uncomfortable going to meet Paul's parents. Having met him only two months ago, she felt that the relationship had progressed too quickly. She didn't know how to slow down. He was being so kind in buying her everything she needed or wanted, and Lynette returned the favors by giving him affection.

Lynette felt like telling him that she didn't want to meet his parents and she hated wearing those ridiculous clothes. She felt like the corset she was wearing was breaking her ribcage. It did make her more ravishing, she thought. She didn't know the English words to tell him off, so she just went through with his plan. After all, he has taken good care of her over the last couple months, and she was afraid to lose him, because she would probably end up living on the streets. Thus she chose to hold her tongue when it came to meeting his parents; she wanted no friction to enter their relationship.

Paul always made sure that she ordered room service, and he bought her new clothes almost every time they went out together. If they didn't see each other during the day, Paul would take Lynette out at night to go dancing. Paul was a man of excellent taste, and Lynette was afraid to lose him. Where would she go? She certainly wouldn't be able to live in a five-star hotel anymore.

As the car started to move away from the curb, Lynette felt extremely nervous. Paul sensed that Lynette wasn't herself. She was very quiet and just continued to gaze out the window. She was usually bubbly and would talk about her day.

"What's wrong, Lynette? You seem tense." Sitting next to her, he slid over closer to her and put his hand on her thigh. She turned her head away from the window and looked back at Paul.

"It's just that from what you told me, your parents seem very ..." she paused, trying to come up with the words without hurting Paul's feelings.

"They seem like what?"

She looked into his eyes and said, "They seem to be very opulent and domineering. I know you might not think that, but your parents are very well known in the state, and I don't belong in their world." Her eyes then turned away from Paul and to the complimentary champagne that was sitting in the cup holders.

"Lynette, don't worry about a thing. You're going to be in my world, not theirs." He kissed her on her forehead once more, and it wasn't too long until they were pulling up in front of his residence.

Paul lived in a beautiful community just outside Boston. Lynette's eyes turned to the massive black gate that was over twenty feet tall. As the gates opened wide, the car continued down a wide driveway with pine trees on both sides. The driveway went on for miles, and eventually Lynette saw the most marvelous mansion she would see in her lifetime.

With its all-brick walls and crystal-clear windows, this wasn't just a house; it looked like a mansion out of a movie. As the car got closer, Lynette became more and more amazed as each detail became more prominent. A white fountain stood right in front of the garden in the middle of the front yard. Wildflowers and a pond surrounded the fountain. On top of the roof were four chimneys, and she could see chandeliers shining from inside the mansion as they drove by the windows. The car came to a stop before a grand staircase that led up to a giant door with a silver knob.

Her jaw dropped immediately; she was taken aback by everything she was seeing. As Paul got out of the car first and came around to open her door, she was still mesmerized by the amazing architecture. She looked up at how tall the mansion was, and then she said, "You live here?"

"Yes." As he led her up to the giant staircase, she looked down at her feet. Then she looked at the railing at the sides of the staircase. The railings were made out of bronze, and they had a certain glow and shine to them. Then she looked up again, admiring the amazing mansion.

"Oh, darling, I'm sure there are even more beautiful buildings in Paris."

Lynette thought back to where she'd grown up, with barely enough money to buy bread. The Eiffel Tower was beautiful and miraculous, but in the part of Paris where she'd lived, it wasn't always exactly pretty.

As Paul opened the door for her, she had that bad feeling in her stomach again. She was afraid this wasn't going to work out. Meeting parents of a millionaire was not her style, and she felt that she wouldn't be able to be herself around them. The night was headed for disaster. She felt she was walking on eggshells just by entering the front door. She was afraid to sit down or drag in a speck of dirt on the rug of this immaculate mansion.

When she entered, Lynette was only more impressed. A long red carpet lay on top of the white marble floors of a long hallway with many windows and doors in front of her. At the end of the hallway was an elevator.

Only an hour into the dinner, Lynette fled the mansion, running out the front door, with Paul chasing after her. "Lynette, please wait up!" She ran to the bottom of the luxurious staircase and lifted her dress up off the pavement. She grabbed the railing to balance, and she took her shoes off so she could walk better.

When Paul caught up with her and grabbed her arm, she quickly swung away. "There's no way I'm marrying into that family. I don't care how much money you have! There's just no way." She then spoke a sentence to Paul in French that he didn't understand. She was cussing in French, and then she finally yelled, "Paul, your family is too overbearing, and I would rather go back to France than become a part of your family." Then she continued to cuss—thankfully Paul had no idea what she was saying.

She spoke so fast in her own language. Paul could only hear the difference in the tone she was speaking in, and he knew she was not happy. He hated seeing her in distress, and he couldn't believe that this was happening.

When she started walking away, Paul followed her. "Lynette, my parents can be a little overbearing; I get that. Just give them a chance."

Lynette rolled her eyes, turned back to Paul, and stopped walking. "Give them a chance? No way! They don't even speak to me like I deserve their breath! We're just from two completely different worlds. I can't handle the wrath of your parents. They only know I'm not like you." Lynette didn't want to change who she was, and she never wanted to be with someone who was going to change her.

Paul knew deep down inside that his parents were lethal to all the girls that he brought home to meet them. They always found something that they didn't like about Paul's newest girlfriend, and eventually he and the girl would break up because Paul knew his parents didn't approve. They just wanted nothing less than someone perfect for their son.

Even if Paul's family had been welcoming, as she'd thought they would be, she'd still had a bad feeling since they'd pulled up in front of the mansion. She thought about her future, and how she would end up being a reserved personality. Lynette hated the idea that she would always be critiqued and gawked at. During the short amount of time she had been there, she'd felt that they swallowed her up like quicksand.

As she started walking away, Paul caught up with her again. "Listen, Lynette, you can't leave me—I won't let you! I can give you a better life! Better than the one you already have." He grabbed her by the shoulder this time.

Lynette looked to her right and saw that they were close to the fountain. "Let me go!" She kept trying to scramble away from him. Her feet hurt from walking around in the ridiculous shoes. Lynette wasn't going to be forced into something just because Paul has given her a roof over her head. Happiness was more important to her than living a life of wealth if it meant being surrounded by phonies. Life was way too short to be unhappy. As she swung around, she placed her hands on Paul's shoulders. With all her might she pushed Paul backward.

"Lynette, stop!" Before he could finish his sentence, she had pushed him into the fountain, wearing his valuable suit. Lynette watched over him as he fell awkwardly, making a big splash—so big that her gown got a little damp.

"I don't need you or your money!" Holding her head high with pride, Lynette didn't look back; she left Paul soaking in the fountain.

Paul spit out the water that was in his mouth. He had seen the mean side of Lynette; he couldn't believe she'd gotten ticked off like that. Paul was furious as well as confused about why Lynette wanted to leave him. "Fine then—go! I don't need you!"

Lynette felt as if she could finally breathe as she walked away from Paul. No amount of money could be worth not truly being yourself, and Lynette felt that she couldn't do that if she married Paul. It would be a long and tedious life of being someone she was not. She didn't return the items of jewelry he had bought her; they had been gifts to her.

Soon after she'd broken up with Paul, she knew that she had to start creating a life for herself. Paul came back to the hotel to sort things out, but he was too late. She had already completely cleared all of her belongings out of the hotel. He walked into the center of the room and put his hands on his hips, looking around the room. He knew that another terrific girl had slipped through his hands. The city was way too big for him to try and track her down, so with a heavy heart Paul let her go. This wasn't the first girl his parents had chased away with their rude comments and intellectual remarks.

Lynette got a job, because she knew that she would have to provide for her unborn child. She regretted ever being with Paul in the first place, but in a way she was grateful, because out of that relationship he'd given her a child. She never crossed paths with him again, and when she gave birth to a daughter, she named her Veronica.

That was the story of Nick's grandmother. Nick took her jewelry out of the chest and placed it on his dresser. He knew that there was a lot of history behind the jewelry, and he felt the right thing to do was keep it.

Nick still hadn't found what he'd thought was in the chest. It appeared to be empty. But then he saw a small drawer inside the chest. He just noticed it because there was a small white Polaroid picture sticking out of the corner of it.

He pulled the drawer to find that there was a secret compartment.

Only little items could fit in there. As he pulled it open, Nick felt a sigh of relief. He had finally found what he was looking for, some pictures that he had put in the chest several years earlier.

Nick stared at the dusty and discolored photos that had been taken of Amy and him long before they were dating. That was the best part, before you started a relationship, when two people started out as friends.

In his hand Nick held the history between Amy and him, four pocket-sized pictures. He noticed that they had aged over the years from being in the chest.

The picture on the very top showed Nick on the left and Amy on the right. They were both in sixth grade. Amy was wearing a blue dress and black flats on her first day of middle school, and Nick wore jeans and a green shirt, with sneakers.

They were smiling wide in the picture, and Nick couldn't believe how fast time had flown by. They had been excited because they'd both gotten bigger backpacks that year, and Nick remembered how much Amy had loved the pink backpack that was in the Polaroid. He felt as if the picture had been taken only a day ago.

He pulled the next picture forward, moving the first picture to the back of the pile. This one had been taken in the summer; Amy and Nick were around the same age as in the first picture. They were sitting on a bench together, and Amy had just smooshed her ice cream into Nick's face. She was laughing intensely, and Nick's mom had been there to capture the shot. In that picture Nick had been mad, with ice cream dripping down his nose.

Nick liked that picture very much, because of how wide Amy's smile was in the picture. He could still hear how she'd chuckled that day when the picture was taken. He then had a sudden craving for ice cream. He thought about that day and how warm it had been on the first day of summer. Amy had gotten vanilla ice cream, and Nick had gotten chocolate.

The third picture was a rather great achievement photo. It

showed Nick and Amy now in eighth grade, and Nick remembered how he'd had a lot of acne in eighth grade. Just like in this picture, his face had been covered with it. Amy looked perfect, as always. She had her hair braided on the side and wore a pink top with blue jeans. It was their eighth-grade graduation, and it was also the year before they'd started dating.

Nick put his palm to his face as he looked at himself in the picture. He was so embarrassed looking back at this picture so many years later. He'd forgotten how he'd really looked before he'd entered high school. Standing next to the most beautiful girl in school, he had on an odd smile and baggy jeans and a blue shirt. He also was wearing the same exact sneakers he'd worn in the last picture. Nick hadn't hit his growth spurt yet, and Amy at the time was a couple inches taller as they stood in front of the school.

Then Nick looked at the last photo. This one was different from the others. This one brought tears to his eyes. A ton of emotions ran through Nick's body. He couldn't believe how artistic his mom had been with the camera. She'd shot so many irreplaceable memories. He missed her so much.

Nick knew that eventually he would be going to hell for what he was going to do now that he had the enchanted key. His hands then began to tremble when he thought about after the job was done and finished. *What if the cops do arrest me? I would have no hope and be found guilty.*

The last photo showed Nick and Amy going on their very first date. Nick recognized the picture immediately, because he remembered how nervous he had been that day. The two of them were walking side by side away from his house. Amy had her arm around his waist, and Nick had his arm draped around her shoulder. Her hair still went to the bottom of her back, and he'd gotten a nice short, spiffy haircut that afternoon. He'd wanted to look his best for Amy, because he'd wanted to impress her.

Nick glanced at each photo for what it seemed to be only a few minutes. But when he looked at his wristwatch for a second, he realized it had been a couple of hours. He was so confused at how things had ended up this way. Why he couldn't he have had his happy ending?

The pictures did give Nick some closure. He put them in his wallet to admire every day. He put his grandmother's jewelry back into the chest and locked it with the key. Then he pushed the chest back into its spot against the wall next to his nightstand.

As he locked the chest, he stared at the key and remembered how much of a hassle it had been to find it. He tried to think of a place to put it so he would always remember where it was and not have to go through that ever again.

Knowing that his grandmother's jewelry was probably worth a fortune, he knew that he didn't want to have the key in plain sight. "Where could I possibly put you so I'll never forget where you are?" Nick said out loud. Should he just put it back taped to the bottom of the chest? But he had already moved the chest back into place, and he didn't want to hurt his back by lifting it again. It had taken a lot of strength to move it once, and he wasn't going to do that again.

As his eyes caught a glimpse of his nightstand, he thought that maybe it wouldn't be such a bad idea to leave it in plain sight. After all, the odds of someone breaking into his home were pretty slim. So Nick placed the key right on top of the chest. After that, he slipped off his shoes and crawled into bed for the night.

He reached over to his nightstand and shut the light off. Nick was still having a hard time trying to get Amy off his mind. He was glad that he'd finally found the key that was so important to his scheme. Eventually, Nick would find out that this wasn't just any ordinary key. It was a key that could open any door.

10

UNLOCKING

It was fifteen days before the murder. Most workdays Nick would have to be the one to open up the store in the morning; his boss, Mark, had given him the earlier shift. Nick had to make sure that everything was in order and ready for the costumers. The only downfall was that Nick had to get up extra early, but he wanted to show Mark that he was a responsible person for the task.

Like every other American, Nick made coffee to wake his body up. As he looked at his watch, he would say to himself, "Why am I up so damn early?" Eventually those thoughts would subside when he took his first sip of coffee.

On the kitchen countertop lay Nick's keychain. On it there was one key to the house, one to the fish-bait shop, and one more key. This key was the key to the chest upstairs.

Nick had almost lost the key a few times, so he'd decided to put it on his keychain with the other keys. At this time Nick didn't know that the key to the chest wasn't just a random key but an enchanted key. The key's power was waiting to be unveiled at the right time and in the right person's hands.

Nick was getting ready for a normal day at the job. As he was brushing his teeth, he noticed that a few gray hairs had appeared in his scalp. With the lines on his forehead looking more prominent, he saw that he was getting older every year. Even his hands had aged; they had gained more freckles. He looked at his hands as he washed his face and then rinsed with cool water at the sink.

He looked at his wristwatch again and saw that he was running a tad late. He'd hit the snooze button on his alarm numerous times that morning. He grabbed his phone from the counter of the bathroom sink and went downstairs, shoving the phone into his back pocket when he got to the bottom.

He looked out the window and decided it might be a little chilly out there, so he grabbed his thick coat from the closet. Nick slipped it on over his shoulders and zipped it up. He looked around for his keys, thinking, *I put them here yesterday. Where are they?* Then he remembered and walked over to the kitchen counter to grab them. The metal scratched the surface for a moment as he grabbed his keychain quickly.

"Oh yeah, shoes!" Nick muttered. He placed his keys onto the table that was next to the door. When they were on the table, the keys were at the same level as the keyhole of the front door.

The key to the chest started to shimmer and glow. Since the key was close to the lock of the front door, the key morphed into the key that would open that door. Whereas the key had been the shape and size of the keyhole of the ancient chest, its body then changed to fit the front door. The key started gleaming with a purpose—this key changed when it was near another door.

Nick put on some shoes, and when he went to grab his keys, he noticed something was different. As the glow started to fade, Nick picked up the keys to see what was making the one key glow.

At first he thought it was a reflection of something, or the sun was shining on the keys through the window, but when he held the key away from the door, it changed back to its original form, the ancient-looking key. Nick saw it change before his very eyes. The glow dimmed and then died as he held the set of keys away from the door. Nick was startled. This was something that he'd never seen before!

That's weird! he thought. He wanted to see if the glow would come back if he held the key closer to the door, and it did. Nick thought he was hallucinating, but then he knew that this was real. He'd had no idea that the key was magic! He was shocked to see the power of this key revealed. When he'd found it, the key hadn't looked very promising. It had been very rusty and only looked as if it could work on the chest upstairs.

As the key now resembled the house key that was dangling at the bottom of his keychain, he was curious to see if it would work on the front door. When he slipped the key into the hole, he expected it to not work, but somehow it did. It unlocked the front door. As he stepped out onto the porch, he took that same key and locked his house with it. *How can this be possible?* he thought. *All this time I thought it was just an old washed-up key from France. I guess it wasn't, after all. But there's only one way I can test it.* Nick got on his bike and headed to work.

Nick had still not set foot in a vehicle since the accident. His mom's car was in the driveway even now, but it had turned rusty. Weeds and vines had intertwined in and around the wheels, and the windshield had a small crack running through it.

Nick was eager to find out whether the key could really open all doors. Nick had heard this legend but never thought he would have such a key in his possession. When he was a kid, he'd loved hearing the ancient stories and incredible legends that were said to be true.

Now that he had the enchanted key, he knew exactly what he was going to do with it. This was going to be very helpful in his plan to pay Sean a visit! He just had to see whether this key really did open any door.

Several hundreds of years ago, according to a legend, there had been five enchanted keys made for five chests. A powerful sorcerer had passed down the chests to his five daughters. As he'd married a mortal woman, his magical gifts had not passed down to the next generation. Even though they had not inherited his magical blood, he wanted each of the daughters to have something enchanted.

The youngest daughter had been given the very chest and key that Nick now had. She had been Lynette's great-great-great-grandmother. The message did not get passed on fluently, and when Lynette had come to America, she'd had no idea at all what kind of magic that key possessed; it had just looked like a regular key and chest to her. But now Nick was going to test the limits of the key and see if it was really the legendary enchanted key from France.

Biking through Boston, Nick navigated his way around people on the sidewalk. It was early in the morning, but the city was very awake. He heard cars honking behind him and also heard the train clacking along the tracks. Nick was proud to be a Bostonian; he would never want to live in any other city.

Once he got to work, he parked his bike on the bike rack down the alley next to the building. The building was all brick, and Nick walked by the brick wall until he got to the entrance. He pulled out his keychain and saw that the enchanted key appeared like any other ordinary key. Then he raised the hand holding the key up near the keyhole. It wasn't long until the key started to glow again. Soon it had morphed into the shape of the key that would fit that door exactly! It turned the lock perfectly, and Nick was amazed as he opened the door.

Once he was inside, Nick flipped the switch to light up the entire store. With the lights on, he looked back down at the key. What he'd believed was true—he did have the enchanted key! The key began to lose its glow and started to change back to its original form. He turned back around to switch the Closed sign to Open.

Nick had a hard time processing this. He wanted to go some-where after work to relax and think. During his whole shift he de-bating on whether it was a good idea to go to that place. He thought that in the future it would be a good place to dispose of a murder weapon.

After all the generations that the key had been passed down, Nick was now the prime holder. He remembered that his mom had had no knowledge of the key's magic, and he was still shocked at how his plan had just become so much easier.

It was a beautiful and soothing place just to clear his head. The view would take his mind off anything. There was a sense of safety in the feel of the gentle breeze coming off the water. That place was the Charles River.

Fifteen years had passed since Nick found out that he had the en-chanted key. Yes, it had been fifteen years since Nick has committed his villainous crime. He'd avoided the police department and con-tinued to hold down his job at fish-bait shop.

Every night after work he would go down to the Charles to clear his mind and then go straight home and order pizza. Every day was pretty much the same for Nick nowadays. He was starting to get even older, but he kept his secret to himself. He had not told a single soul about what he had done.

Tonight he was at his regular spot at the same time as most Wednesday nights. He sat on the same bench next to the same tree every evening after work, enjoying the view and taking it all in. He closed his eyes and speculated on just how idiotic and clueless the Boston Police Department really was. In fifteen years not even a single suspect had been taken into custody for questioning. That was long enough for the crime to be labeled as an unsolved case.

In hindsight, Nick wanted to make Amy's mother pay for bring-ing her up to be the person she had become. Her family had not appreciated the gem Amy had been when she was alive. He re-membered all the times when he and Amy had been together. Her mother had been bringing Amy up to be just like her, valuing only the wealthy, having common etiquette, and being particular about who she was dating. She'd even told Amy right in front of Nick one time that she thought Nick was a low life who wouldn't be able to take care of her. Amy would just tell Nick to ignore her mother's comments. She didn't care who the person was on the outside or whether he had a luxurious future ahead of him. She cared about what was inside, and that was something Nick had loved about Amy. She'd loved him for who he was—that is, before Sean had moved to Boston and before he'd moved in on Amy.

As a gentle breeze blew, Nick was sitting comfortably on a bench looking out at the Charles River. He had one leg resting on top of the other while he spread his arms along the back of the bench and felt the wind blow through his hair.

While looking out onto the water, he noticed the brightly colored sailboats that kept floating by his view. One after the next, each sailboat had different colored sails. Also, several strong canoers were paddling hard against the water and then continuing under the bridge.

That was the bridge where Nick had thrown the murder weapon off into the water many years ago. Even though Nick spent most of his nights sleepless and racked with guilt, he had a certain peace of mind in knowing that he had the enchanted key right at his side, in his pocket, disguised among the other keys on his chain.

He was still amazed that he could have had the key within a few feet of him for decades and not know it. He was the one who had unlocked its power. He thought about who the other four lucky key holders might be. It was possible that they, too, didn't know the true capability of their keys and, like Nick, had assumed they could just unlock the chests.

Nick gazed out into the revolving water while joggers ran past him. Since there were only five keys in existence, this key must be worth a great deal of money, certainly enough money so he would never have to work again. A key that could open any door, well, it would be worth millions. If he announced that he had such an object, top buyers would all gather at an auction. But that would be revealing to the world that a sorcerer had existed hundreds of years ago. It was possible that some still did exist, and Nick felt that the world was not ready for that kind of news.

Suddenly Nick heard a burst of laughter, and he turned to his right. As far as he could make out, three young people were walking toward him, two boys and a girl. He blinked repeatedly, trying to make out who these three people were walking toward him, but turning to look back at the river, to make it seem as if he wasn't watching them.

The young girl resembled a person he'd loved very deeply a long time ago. As they walked closer, Nick's heart began to beat faster, and he could feel the sweat dripping off his forehead. His sanity then crept in, and he remembered that he had to look natural and normal. In fact, he was feeling just the opposite.

After school, the three young teenagers were walking along the Charles River. The young lady had long blonde hair and a tiny physique, while the young boys were tall and lean. One was wearing a Celtics sweatshirt and jeans, and the other was wearing a Bruins sweatshirt and jeans. With every step they got closer, and Nick listened in on their conversation. Soon they came close enough for Nick to realize that the boys were, in fact, twins. Then his eyes immediately returned to the girl. She was smiling brightly and laughing as she looked down, blushing, at her shoes while she continued to walk.

Nick realized in that instant that she looked exactly like Amy— but no, it couldn't be true! It had been fifteen years already since he'd committed his crime. He took a guess at how old this girl was. She might be Amy's daughter, but he wasn't sure. He thought back to that night on Elm Street and how he'd regretted not taking the infant when he had the chance. It had been a rather big gamble, to risk getting caught by police, so he'd decided to flee the scene instead.

There was a flaw in this girl's appearance, some features that Nick hated. In some ways she resembled her father. The group reached the bench Nick was sitting on, and without hesitation, they kept on walking by. Nick kept a serious look on his face, trying to act like a normal guy just taking in the scenery.

"Oh my God, you guys are insane!"

The boys chuckled on hearing Ariel's remark. "No, you have to trust me, Ariel," one of them said. Then they passed right by Nick, and he could no longer hear their conversation. He was looking at Ariel's back, how her golden-blonde hair flowed in the wind down to the bottom of her back.

Then a car pulled up to the side of the road while Nick was still watching the young group walking further away from him. He noticed a man driving the car, and he saw the window being rolled down. He instantly recognized who that man was.

"Ariel, Aaron, Eric, come on! Mom's making suppah!" *It's David*, Nick thought. He hadn't changed a bit, with only a few gray hairs and a few more pounds in muscle. Nick watched the three teenagers walk faster over to the car. *Those must be David's kids, and that's got to be Ariel.* While other cars sped past David's car, he had his blinker on as he waited for the kids to get in the car.

"She's making meatballs tonight. Let's get home!" The three kids got into his car, and he pulled away from the curb onto the main road. Ariel sat in the passenger seat, while the boys sat in the back.

Nick returned to looking out at the water. David must have adopted Ariel when she was a toddler, and she was apparently all grown up now. She must be living with those two boys, David's sons.

Nick following David on Facebook, using a fake name. He knew that David and Allison had gotten married, but he'd never thought that he would see his two boys. Certainly he never would've guessed that he had been taking care of Ariel all this time. Nick thought it would be nice of him to pay them a visit.

Nick got up and walked toward the route the car had gone. He was hoping he would get lucky and find out where David's family lived. He pulled his bike from where it was resting up against a tree, hopped on, and quickly started pedaling in the direction the car had gone. He needed to catch up to them before they got too far ahead of him.

It wasn't long until he spotted David's car. He was stopped in a traffic jam, and Nick was actually riding so fast that he thought he might pass them by accident, so he slammed on his brakes, coming to a rough stop.

The traffic was barely moving, and he noticed that David had put his signal on to go right. He couldn't turn right yet, though, because the cars in front of him were blocking his way down that street. All during the traffic jam Nick had a hard time trying to focus on keeping an eye on David's car. Being around all these cars so close together and hearing horns repeatedly honking gave him major anxiety.

Nick waited patiently and very still, just waiting for David to squeeze by the cars in front of his, but he was driving a very expensive black Infiniti. If he tried to pass those cars, he could easily scratch the meters or the cars that were parked on Beacon Street.

David was just in the right position, looking at the side mirror on the Infiniti, that Nick could see Ariel in the front passenger seat, laughing and singing along to the song on the radio. The boys had the windows rolled down in the back seat of the car.

Finally, David turned right and continued down that street, and Nick followed them very carefully all the way back to their home. David pulled into a big parking lot just to the side of a very grand apartment building. *To live here certainly would cost a pretty penny,* Nick thought. The building had just been completed a year ago, and it hadn't taken long for people to start renting. David and his family lived in that building.

This place was way out of Nick's price range. He could barely afford to keep his own house. To buy an apartment in Boston, with a view, would be almost impossible for him. He watched carefully as David pulled into a parking spot near the building, while he rode by them.

Nick then looked around to find a safe spot where they couldn't see him. He decided to go behind a power pole that was far enough away from David that Nick wouldn't be seen yet close enough to hear their conversation. When David shut the car off, Nick could hear the loud, boisterous laughter that was coming from inside the car.

David and his kids got out of the car and walked toward the entrance of the building, while Nick hid behind the pole. Nick's mind then instantly went to the enchanted key—with it, there would be no problem entering the building. David was in front of the kids, and Nick could see David punching in a code of some sort on a keypad next to the door. The digits were the key to entering the building. Sadly, Nick couldn't see what the numbers were.

Four easy numbers, and the door unlocked and they went inside. There was no keyhole to the front entrance, so the enchanted key would not be useful to him. Nick looked all the way up at the top of the building; it was very high. Then he saw another person heading toward the door to enter the building. It was a lady, and she had her back turned to him, so he crept closer to try and catch a glance of what the code was. He had no luck in doing so, because the lady entered the code too quickly, before Nick could even glance at the keypad.

He wanted to try and figure out the code himself, but when he glanced at the building, he spotted security cameras on the sides of the building, angling downward at the front entrance. If he got on camera, he would look suspicious while trying to crack the code. It would get him in trouble, and he would be questioned by authorities. He would hate to blow his cover now, after flying under the radar for so many years and not leaving a trace at the crime scene. It would be idiotic to take a risk like that.

As hours went on, he continued to watch people enter codes

and then go into the building. The street lights came on, and the sky turned black; as stars poked out of the grim clouds, they shone across the city.

Nick was too focused on what he was doing to notice how gorgeous the night was. He noticed something was off: every single time someone entered a four-digit code, they punched different digits into the keypad. The same code was not entered twice.

Nick could then see the inside of the building, because the outside was all glass, and inside lots of people had their lights on. He looked up at the very top, and he saw two boys hanging out on the patio. It was the two boys he'd seen earlier. They were on the top floor, sitting in patio chairs as music played from their stereo.

So David and his family lived on the top floor. But what number could that be, he wondered. Still glancing upward at the top deck, he found it hard to make out, but he saw a woman also on the deck. It was probably their mom. The lightbulb went on in Nick's head. *That must be Allison. She really has stayed with David all this time.* Allison had been Amy's best friend back in high school, and now Nick's motivation to get into that apartment building was a lot stronger than it had been before.

For the next several days, Nick watched dozens of people go in and out after he got off of work, to try and see a code that someone punched in. That was the only thing he needed to get into the building. Then he can think about acting on his next diabolical plan.

Nick figured out the system just by watching people enter their codes to be let in. When a person entered a code and got in, it wouldn't be long until lights came on at a certain level of the apartment building. Nick was able to match the code with the number of levels when a light came on in that section of the building. Every person punched in either a four-digit or three-digit code to gain access—it was his or her apartment number.

Since waking from the coma, Nick had returned to one of his most favorite hobbies, computers. For the plan to work, he would have to hack into the apartment emergency system to turn off the smoke alarms and the sprinkler system. Also, he would have to hack into the security cameras so that we he wouldn't be seen exiting the building at the wrong time; it would show him leaving an hour earlier, before he started the fire. He needed to lay low, and the only way he was going to keep his record clean was to hack into the camera system so he would not be pointed to by police investigators.

Nick thought it would be a good idea to have the fire start two floors below where the Smith residence was. That way the fire would grow and not alert the Smiths up above. The sprinkler system would be turned off before he even started the fire. Nick was very excited when he started to imagine his idea in his head, but he knew it was going to be very difficult to execute.

Back before Nick's accident, he wouldn't have hurt a fly, let alone take the lives of innocent people. Now, mentally crooked and very vile, Nick felt pure when he committed his crimes. The guilt would set in shortly afterward, but he knew deep down in his mind that what he was doing was right.

Almost like I'm returning people a favor for what they've done to me over the years, he thought. *They deserve everything that's coming to them, and tomorrow will be the finale.*

11

PLATFORM

After thinking about different ways to execute his plan, Nick had decided to go with his first idea, which he thought was the easiest. Today he was going to start a fire inside the apartment building where David and Alison lived along with their three children, and where dozens of other families lived.

After seeing David and his kids over by the Charles that day, he couldn't resist putting his plan into action. If he didn't do it today, then he wasn't going to do it at all, he told himself. Having had the pleasure of seeing Ariel all grown up, he felt that she, unfortunately, must be erased as well. It wasn't her fault. Nick was just repaying her parents for what they'd done to him all those years ago before Ariel was even born. Nick was one person you didn't want to have a grudge with, because he could hold a grudge longer than you would imagine.

Even though she looked like her gorgeous mother, the part of Ariel that reminded Nick of Sean made him even more motivated to execute his plan. He loved the way his mad mind worked, and he easily came up with a solution to get inside—after, of course, finishing the hard part, which was hacking into the apartment's emergency system to shut off the sprinklers and smoke alarms.

Nick was simply going to disguise himself as a UPS delivery man. He got a big box from the attic; he would put all the materials needed to accomplish his plan inside the box. A cigarette lighter went in, to light objects inside one of the apartments two floors down from the Smith residence. Along with the lighter he needed a container full of flammable gas of some kind, so he thought of different places where he could get some.

First he pedaled down to the nearest gas station to fill up a gas container. As he was putting gas in the container, he tried to appear like just a normal guy who might have run out of gas and used his bike to get to the gas station. But that wasn't the case. The gas was intended to burn the apartment building down to ash.

Then, once the container was full, he pedaled back home on his bike, holding the container with one hand. When he got back inside his house, he then placed the container gently inside the box.

Once he'd placed the lighter inside the box, he sealed the box with sealing tape. No one would ever suspect that it was going to be used to start a fire, because on the outside the box looked completely normal. He even printed out a delivery seal to make it look more believable.

There was one problem that he had to face. The box was way too hard to carry and balance while pedaling on his bike. There was absolutely no chance he was going to drive his mother's car. That was the one detail that he had trouble figuring out, a way to do it and not look suspicious.

He couldn't steal and drive off with a UPS truck. That would be a complete and utter failure. He had all day to figure this out, thankfully, as he had the day off from work. Some days he had a hard time concentrating at work when he knew that he had to go home and recheck everything that he needed to fully complete his scheme.

Regular-delivery-guy work uniform, check. Delivery box, check. Enchanted key in breast pocket, check. Lighter, check, and container of flammable liquid, check. Nick went through the checklist in his head and then thought maybe this could work if he took the train. After all, the station was only a few miles from his house. He could just walk to the station with the box and then get on the train.

Before he left his house, he looked at the T schedule online, finding the stop that was the closest to the apartment building in the heart of the city. That would be his best shot. He felt the enchanted key in his pocket before lifting the box from the floor. Then he had to set it down again to open the door.

Nick's stomach grumbled, as he hadn't eaten in hours. He was too anxious to get his plan underway, and food slipped his mind. There wasn't much food in the house anyway. He thought he would probably order pizza again.

He opened the door and proceeded outside, carrying the box down the street. Wearing his delivery uniform to fool people into thinking that he was a delivery guy, he swiftly headed toward the train station. Wearing all brown, Nick was identifying himself as a UPS delivery man just finishing up some last-minute deliveries. He felt that to execute his plan he had to stay distant from people as much as he could.

His arms were starting to get tired, but he could see signs for the T just up ahead. The box was small enough that Nick could just see over the top. He could feel the movement from inside and could hear the lighter moving around inside the box, so he decided to move more slowly to avoid making a sound. Nick was praying that he would see the least amount of people possible today. *The less people the better; hopefully not too many people will be on the train today*, he thought.

Once he reached the train station, he set down his box on a bench and then bought his Charlie card for both ways so that he could get out of there and back home as soon as possible. He headed through the card swiper with his box and then waited for the train, standing on the platform above the tracks. He was the only person on the platform for a few minutes, simply waiting for the train, while the station was quiet. He could hear a leaky pipe dripping from above onto the tracks.

It wasn't long until several other people arrived to wait for the same train. Nick started thinking to himself, *Just stay calm. Don't attract anyone's attention. You'll be fine. Don't sweat it.* To people who rode the train every day, Nick looked like a normal man just carrying an abnormally large delivery box.

The people assumed he was just going to deliver his package, because he was wearing a well-put-together uniform. More and more people started to enter the platform, waiting for the train to arrive. All the time that everyone was walking onto the platform and standing next to, behind, and around Nick, he simply stared at the tracks.

He breathed in and out slowly, trying to stay composed and not blow his cover. Nick, in that moment, feared that someone would recognize him. He'd heard some of his co-workers say that they hopped the train to go to work every day. He felt an intense breeze flow through the station and onto the tracks. In the back of his mind he wondered whether what he was about to do was really necessary. Nick knew he couldn't tell the truth if he accidently ran into one of his co-workers. He pulled down his hat slightly to cover more of his face.

Gulping about every thirty seconds, he thought to himself, *Where the hell is this train?* The more people that ended up on this platform, the more possible witnesses if they did give a police report, he thought. But why would they point their fingers at a regular UPS guy just delivering a package? He then calmed himself down. No one was going to do that.

But Nick continued staring at the tracks, not looking at anybody, just hearing conversations behind him. Some were in Spanish, and he couldn't understand them. Nick glanced back slightly and saw two Hispanic women wearing colorful dresses talking to each other. One was wearing an orange dress, and the other woman was wearing a blue dress. Nick then went back to staring at the tracks.

He wanted to avoid running into anyone or giving anyone a chance of seeing his face. Everyone around could only see the side of his face, and his hair color was hidden by his brown hat.

He'd gotten his UPS delivery uniform from a party store. As he thought that his clever plan was working, Nick kept replaying the digit code number in his head. His whole plan would be ruined if he suddenly forgot the code, which was extremely difficult to memorize while trying to keep calm with everything going on around him. But eventually, the code came back to him.

Nick had extreme social anxiety; he hated big crowds. You would think he would have wanted to live somewhere completely different than a big city like Boston, but Nick had learned to cope with his struggles. He loved Boston too much to move away.

Before he left the house, he used his computer skills to hack into the security system in the building. He shut off the sprinklers and smoke alarms. Lastly, he made the cameras on the outside of the building near the entrance show a different time on them. When he rushed out of the building after setting the fire, the camera would record that he was leaving an hour before the fire even took place.

If Nick's plan succeeded, the cameras would be completely destroyed in the fire. He had the whole plan mapped out in his head. Once he punched in the code on the keypad, he'd make his way to an apartment a couple floors below the Smith's. Then he'd use the enchanted key to get inside. A few weeks ago, he'd seen a woman punch in her code while talking on the phone with someone. He'd heard her telling that person how she was going on vacation in a few weeks, and the apartment was going to be completely empty. So that was the apartment he was going to hit. The code he had to memorize was 806; that was the key to entering the building. But first he wanted to check on the Smiths before he put his plan into action—almost like saying a farewell to them once and for all. Nick knew how evil and twisted this was, wanting to see the family before setting the building on fire. But it was something he'd been wanting to do for a while, and now he could, because he'd finally got hold of the right code.

He was very anxious to just get to his destination and punch in the 806 code. With the sprinkler system turned off, the flames would have no trouble reaching the top floor, he thought. The Smith family lived in apartment number 1004. Nick was curious to see what the Smiths were up to, and he also wanted to see them that one last time before starting the fire in the building.

Nick was constantly worried at night, thinking, *What if this isn't such a good idea?* When he'd woken up that morning, though, he'd felt that he had no choice but to go through with it. Now he started to hear the train clacking down the tracks. He looked to his left and saw the train's lights coming up the tunnel toward him.

The screeching noise came in increasingly louder until eventually the train emerged from the tunnel. He heard the conductor slam on the brakes. The train brought a breeze toward the platform, and it slowed to a halt in front of the platform.

Seeing the reflection of himself holding his box in the clear windows of the train as several train cars passed him, Nick thought about his mother and what she would think of what he had done to Amy and Sean so long ago. Now he was spreading more tragedy to the Smiths just to sooth his own demon-invaded soul. He hated himself for what he was about to do, but he knew it had to be done.

The train's doors opened wide, and Nick entered, along with the rest of people just going about their everyday business. In a way, he felt good about himself when he saw so many people riding the train. He wasn't the only one who didn't drive a car to get to places. Some of his co-workers had mentioned to him that he was too cheap to buy a car, but even if Nick had the money to buy a new car, his fear wouldn't have allowed him to.

He sat down in the corner of the train car and placed the box gently down on the cold, hard floor. With people sitting directly across from him, he then decided to pick the box up again and rest it on his lap; that way no one would see his face during the ride. It was probably a better idea to hold the box anyway, because the contents might slide around. He hadn't been on a train in years; the last time had been with his mom, when they went to the aquarium when he was nine. The train ride then had been pretty rocky, so he braced himself now as the train started moving. The continuous clacking sound and the fast movement gave Nick a feeling of motion sickness. He swallowed and closed his eyes, knowing that the ride wasn't going to be that long.

Although it seemed like forever, the train ride was only a few short minutes. After making five stops, they were at Nick's stop. He got off the train with his delivery box in his arms. Stepping onto the platform, he proceeded out of the train station, along with the other people who had gotten off.

Nick still held the box high in his arms in front of his face, concealing his identity to possible witnesses, while he walked to the apartment building. He had to be extra careful of people seeing his identity. The less people crossing paths with Nick the better. He didn't want to speak with anyone while he was on his way to the apartment building. Nick didn't want to have a sudden change of heart or empathy. When he bumped into people as he tried to get by them on the sidewalk, some would turn to him with rude remarks, like "Watch where ya goin'," as the pointy corner of the box would poke into someone's backside or hip. Nick wouldn't return a sorry or excuse me. He just kept on walking, and the people he ran into thought that Nick had very bad manners.

Continuing to the apartment building, he could feel his heart starting to race. He orientated himself as he looked up at the tall buildings around him, and he knew exactly where he was. He promised to himself and to his late mother that this would be the last crime he would ever commit.

Nick had contemplated taking his own life because of the horrible things he had done already. He was scared of what he would think of himself after this awful tragedy, for which he would be responsible.

But Nick had a very crafty idea on how he wouldn't get caught, just as he had deluded Boston Police Department all those years ago on Elm Street. He would be careful to cover up his tracks and not leave a single clue behind. If he were to accidently leave a clue behind, it wouldn't matter. In the end, all the evidence would be destroyed in the fire, while Nick walked away a free man, heading back home on the subway.

He had to concentrate on the task at hand, which was going to be very difficult to execute. The walk from the subway to the apartment building was only about a thirty-minute walk, which wasn't too bad. But carrying the box was a struggle, and Nick felt relieved by the time he could see the tall apartment building in his view.

The sun was just starting to go down behind the tall buildings of Boston. It was around supper time, and Nick figured that the whole Smith family would be at home. Family time and being there for one another was so tedious in Nick's mind.

If Nick hadn't been so clever and hacked into the surveillance cameras, he would have looked awful suspicious at the wrong time. He'd been proud when he took down that final firewall online and was able to proceed.

When he made his way up to the front entrance of the building, he put his box down gently as he looked at the keypad in the doorway. He remembered the key code was 1004, which was the apartment that the Smith's lived in. He wanted to first see the Smiths inside their apartment before he started the fire.

Nick had an evil look in his eye, and he looked at the keypad. He swallowed hard and thought, What if he hadn't overheard that lady talking on the phone that day about going on vacation? Then he wouldn't have been able to use her apartment to complete his mission. Then he would have had to come up with a backup plan.

Nick punched 1004 into the keypad, and soon after that he

heard, "Access granted," followed by a loud noise and vibration coming from the doorway. Nick pushed on the door and it opened. He quickly picked up his box again. He used his hip to balance the box and keep the door open as he slipped into the building.

12

ASH

Nick looked down at his feet, at the rug he was standing on. It had beautiful spirals of all colors incorporated into it, with the spirals all coming together as one. He looked at the rug continuously as he walked across the floor, eventually coming to an elevator. When he looked up, he saw a crystal chandelier hanging from the white high ceiling. Nick was taken aback at how exquisite the building was. It was a shame that this beautiful building had to be turned to ash, he thought.

As he looked forward, he saw the gorgeous black marble surrounding the elevators. When he walked toward them, he felt a sudden urge to turn back. It was as if Nick had a devil on one shoulder and an angel on the other.

At this point he didn't know who to listen to anymore. He'd listened to the devil the night he went to Elm Street, but this time he actually listened to the angel, who was talking in a soft tone. "Nick, why would you want to kill all these innocent people? They have done nothing to you. If you get caught, you'll pay a life sentence." That soft tone was then overpowered by an arrogant loud voice, that of the devil on his other shoulder. "What do you mean, they've done nothing to you? David and Allison deserve what's coming to them! Besides, no one caught you the last time. What makes you think cops are going to get a brain and catch you this time?"

The devil and the angel were figments of Nick's imagination, or at least that's what he thought. Not long after his accident Nick had started hearing the voices. The angel was really his mother's spirit trying to guide him on the right path again. Now, the devil, that was the devil himself, or an evil spirit controlling him to do harm to others.

Nick pressed the elevator button to go up, and it was only a few seconds until it arrived. The Up arrow next to the elevator lit up as the doors opened wide. Several people came out of the elevator, probably people who also lived in the building. Nick waited for all of them to exit the elevator entirely before he got on.

Once he was in the elevator, he pressed floor 10. As the elevator doors were closing, he was musing that the people who'd left the building just now shouldn't come back if they knew what was good for them. If they did, they would be in for a rude awakening. Best for them to stay away if they wanted to keep their lives.

Nick took some deep breaths as the elevator went up to the tenth floor. Containing his thoughts, Nick tried to block out the voices in his head. He closed his eyes, because he knew they weren't real. Sinful thoughts passed through his mind, thoughts that he must stay on the mission. The voices started to grow louder and clearer. Luckily, they all went away with the slight ding as the elevator doors opened again. Nick saw that he was on the tenth floor and he stepped out of the elevator. Adjusting the box to his right hip, he looked at the numbers on the apartment doors.

He walked to where the lower numbers were, and then he stood in front of the Smiths' door. He couldn't believe that he was standing in front of their home. After all this time, on the other side of that door was Amy and Sean's daughter. She was living with two people who had helped Amy deceive Nick and keep the truth from him decades ago. Now he was unleashing his revenge one last time.

He put the box down onto the floor next to the door and crouched down. As he did, he looked through the keyhole to see inside of the apartment. It was very dark, but he could soon make out what was going on inside, even though he had no side vision while looking through the keyhole.

He saw Allison cooking in the kitchen, while the two boys were playing video games on the big TV in the living room. A man was coming out of the hallway, and he recognized David. He had just shut off the hallway light. In the corner of the room was Ariel, who was taking her shoes off as if she had just come home. Laughter filled the room, and he could hear the loud TV all the way out in the hallway.

It's a wonder I didn't run into her on the elevator; she must've just come home from somewhere, Nick thought. Nick hadn't been there long, but he told himself to get up off the floor and get focused back on his plan. If he admired them much longer, he might have a change of heart at the very last minute. So he slowly walked down the hallway with his box and pressed the elevator button to go down. He waited patiently until the elevator doors opened up, and he went inside. He pressed the button for floor 8.

Nick stood in the middle as the doors shut. Then he was moved two floors down. In a few moments the doors opened wide again, and he stepped out holding his box.

The elevator was in the middle of the floor, so Nick again followed the doors going down in number. The first door he looked at was 814. Across the hall the door read 813. So he continued down the hallway, grasping his box tightly as he held it on his hip.

Finally Nick found apartment 806. His arms were getting tired from holding the box. He hadn't thought that his arms would be this tired, since he constantly carried boxes around at work, but not for this length of time, he supposed. He exhaled as he finally got to the door that said 806. He shifted the box onto his left hip as he fished around in his pocket to get hold of the enchanted key. He felt it in his breast pocket and pulled it out. It still looking like an old, ordinary key, so he moved it closer to the keyhole of the apartment. It didn't take long for the key to glow and change into one that would fit the slot as exactly as the apartment key would. Still balancing the box on his hip, he slipped the enchanted key into the keyhole, and the door opened.

Entering a very luxurious apartment, Nick took the key out of the keyhole and held it in his hand while he closed the door behind him. He put the box down on the kitchen floor, admiring the key as it morphed back. The glow faded and the teeth of the key went back to looking rusty and scratched; it had returned to its original shape and color.

When he looked at the empty apartment, he was taken aback by how spotless it was. Every kitchen appliance was in its place; meanwhile, the living room didn't have a speck of dust anywhere. This lady was certainly a clean freak, he thought. Nick waited a few moments and then recognized that what he'd heard was true. The apartment was completely empty; you could hear a pin drop.

Black leather couches and a gigantic-screen TV dominated the massive living room. He put his box on top of the kitchen counter. Nick pried off the tape from the box and revealed what was inside.

Nick felt a sudden urge of adrenalin upon opening the box. Inside was the single lighter and the container of highly flammable gasoline. He took the container and lighter out of the box and thought about where he was going to put the empty box.

He knew that he couldn't very well exit the building holding the same box. He would instantly be targeted by police, because it would seem odd if a delivery man entered and exited with the same box. He turned and saw the patio outside the slider doors. He walked over to the doors and admired the beautiful lights that ranged across the city. He couldn't imagine how beautiful Boston must look from the top floor of the building.

When he opened the door, he could hear several honking horns from cars below him. He looked down from the patio and saw that there was a dumpster at the bottom. He thought that it would be a good idea to let go of the box and have it land in the dumpster. That way he would not be seen with a package on the cameras, just in case the cameras didn't completely disintegrate.

Nick went back inside to grab the empty box, walked back out to the patio, and held the box over the railing. Then he let it go and watched it fall into the dumpster with a quiet thump—he hoped it was as quiet down below as it was from up where he was. He could see from where he stood that there was a large amount of garbage in the dumpster, so the box was camouflaged neatly. Then he went back inside.

Nick closed the patio door behind him, and he thought, *Now it's time to get to work.* He twisted the cap off the container of flammable gas and started pouring the toxic liquid all over the apartment. He poured it on the floor, around the kitchen tiles, and even on the drapes that were hanging above the patio slider. He had to move quickly and spread the flammable gas as far as possible before the jug became empty. His trail led near the doorway, where he poured the last drop. He then went out to the patio and dropped the empty container into the dumpster below.

When he went back inside, he grabbed his lighter off the counter and tried to get it to light using his thumb. Soon a small flame was peeking out of the lighter. It was so small, but it was going to become very big, very soon.

He held the lighter down toward the floor near the beginning of the trail of gasoline. It didn't take long for the gasoline to catch fire, and once it did, Nick was out of that apartment in a flash, shutting the door as soon as he could hear the fire starting to catch.

He ran to the stairs, knowing that the elevator was going to be too slow. While he was running, all he had on his mind was that he had to get out of there before anyone noticed. Flying down the stairs, he eventually got to the bottom level, and he reminded himself that he had to act natural.

He opened the door and casually walked by people in the lobby. Walking fast and not making eye contact, he thought that this was going to work. He was anxious to leave and not turn back.

Once outside, he felt relief at knowing that what he'd done had needed to be done. Now he just had to go home. Once he got out of the camera's sight, he checked his phone to see if the time on the camera was still an hour behind. He did that while he was sitting on a bench waiting for the train. He still had to conceal his face from the public; he'd had his hat turned downward while he navigated through the crowds.

Meanwhile, in the apartment, the fire was starting to wreak havoc. It was burning everything in sight, and it had reached the drapes that were hanging over the slider door leading out to the patio.

Just a few doors down was a young girl named Chelsea. She was Ariel's friend, who lived in apartment 802. She was sitting on her couch and smelled an odd smell. She got up from the couch and looked in the kitchen to make sure that the oven wasn't on by accident.

She walked around the kitchen, still smelling a smoke-like aroma, and she followed the trail of scent over near the door. Just before she opened the door, she looked down to see black smoke coming from the crack underneath the door and traveling into her apartment. Startled, she immediately opened the door, which was followed by more black smoke entering the apartment.

Chelsea coughed as she breathed in the black smoke. She looked down the hall and saw that the smoke was coming from one of the apartments. She was petrified by seeing flames, and then she heard a neighbor across the hall scream her name, "Chelsea!"

She answered, "Mr. Sanchez!" She saw Mr. Sanchez come toward her, and he led her away from the smoke. He gave her a towel to put around her face to avoid inhaling any more smoke. As he was leading her to the stairs, she said, "Wait! What about everyone else?"

Mr. Sanchez had already ordered everyone on the eighth floor to get out of the building. He was a father of four kids, and his wife and children were already safely out of the building. He'd come back to make sure that no one else was on floor eight where the fire was blazing. His wife anxiously waited at the bottom for his safe return.

He answered, "Don't worry about everyone else. Let's get you out of here." Then they made their way down the stairs and out of the building. Chelsea heard police sirens on their way to the scene as she removed the towel from her face to breathe some clean air.

Heat and smoke started to fill the apartment. There was a propane gas tank attached to a grill on the patio. It wasn't long until the fire reached the patio, and a massive explosion resulted from the propane tank colliding with the flames.

Nick started walking faster as he made his way toward the train station. There was a cluster of pedestrians just like him making their way to the station. He was surprised how busy the train was later at night. The sun had finally disappeared from the sky, and Nick made his way to the underground station to go home.

Nick didn't turn back for one second to think it was terrible what he had just done. Now, he felt powerful, and nothing was going to ruin it. He didn't have to wait for a train this time; it was waiting for him when he got there.

He felt the lighter in his breast pocket, along with the enchanted key. He ran down the steps of the station and into the train car. When he sat down in the train, he realized he didn't have the box to keep his face unknown to the public. His eyes widened in surprise; he was uneasy to think that someone would look at him.

Luckily, the three women sitting directly across from him were occupied by their phones and weren't tempted to look up from their screens. He took slow, deep breaths during the whole ride to his stop.

When he'd gotten on the train, there had been people shoulder to shoulder because there were no more seats. Nick had managed to grab the very last empty one, and everyone who came on after that had to hold onto a railing while standing. Nick had starting to feel claustrophobic, but then he was relieved as more and more people got off at their stops. He was counting the stops until he could get off.

Nick's prayers were finally answered when his stop came. Snaking his way through people again, he got onto the platform and started walking to the exit. Nick could hear the sound of feet stepping on the concrete platform. To Nick it sounded as if people were trying to catch up to him for some reason, which only made him more paranoid. He decided to walk a little faster, in front of the crowd.

Outside of the train station, he noticed that the street lights were on, because it was now nighttime. He continued to walk back to his house, but he was getting frustrated at how people would innocently get in his way every time he came to a stop or took a moment to look around. His patience had worn out, and he wasn't going to wait any longer. Avoiding cop cars passing him by on the street, he would walk slowly for a few minutes until he thought they were out of his range, and then he would pick up the pace of his walking again. He looked behind him, because he knew that they were going in the direction of the apartment building.

It wasn't long until he saw the street he lived on. He immediately started running down his street to get inside. At this point he didn't care if he drew attention to himself; he just ran as fast as he could to his house. There were no cars, so he just ran up the middle. When he reached the steps of his porch, he bolted up them while he felt around for the enchanted key in his pocket. Now that he had the enchanted key in his possession, there was no need for all his other keys, so he had thrown them out.

When Nick felt around in his back pocket and didn't feel the enchanted key, he went into full panic mode. *What if I left it in the apartment by mistake? What if I left it on the train? Oh my God, this isn't happening to me right now! If I left the key in the apartment building, then it will be blown to bits!* he thought.

Feeling around in his breast pocket, Nick gave a sigh of relief when he felt the metal under his fingers. He pulled the key out of his pocket, along with the lighter, and then he exhaled again as he unlocked the door and went inside the house. *If not for the enchanted key, it would've been almost impossible to pull this off,* he thought. If he'd accidently left the key in the building, that would have been a huge mistake on his part.

Once he was inside, he kicked off his shoes and face-planted into the couch. Aching all over, Nick felt as if he had just walked a marathon, though it had hardly been that.

After a few minutes of catching his breath, he pulled out his phone to insert a scene of footage that he'd recorded. It had been taken an hour prior on the security cameras. He inserted that footage after he'd left the building, so when he'd finished the job, it appeared that Nick had left the building an hour before the fire had started, and dozens of other people had entered and exited the building in that time. Once he'd completed that, he switched the time back to what it had originally been. What he didn't know was that he didn't need to change the camera's time to cover his tracks, because the fire was going to do all the work for him.

The fiery debris that fell from the building would completely cover the dumpster that he'd put the box and the empty bottle in. The remains would be almost unrecognizable. The investigators on the scene would not know what part of the apartment they'd come from, if they could even identify disintegrated rubble. Nick felt that his tracks were going to be completely covered, and he tried to put his mind at ease.

Nick put his phone back in his pocket, got up from the couch, and sat in his recliner. He grabbed the remote that was sitting on the windowsill and turned on the TV. Nick was obsessed to see how the public would react to this tragedy.

Nick especially wanted to know how much of a mark his one bottle of flammable liquid would leave on the building. He expected that there wouldn't be a luxurious apartment building any longer by the time the fire department got there.

Patiently waiting for breaking news, Nick had kept a close eye on the time shown on his phone screen. He had never felt so empowered and reckless. He kept thinking about the innocent faces he'd passed while getting out of the building. He'd known that with each minute passing by the flames were growing inside the building.

He prayed for the people whose faces he'd seen before he set the fire and thought that he didn't want them to get injured. But Nick's deed was destined to bring hurt to a lot of people in that building. It would bring destruction and hatred to people and their families who'd had nothing to do with Nick's problems. He had finally listened to the devil on his shoulder, but he felt a strong feeling in his stomach. It was guilt. The angel on his other shoulder was very disappointed in him.

He kept checking his phone every minute, waiting for it to reach the top of the hour. If there was a breaking news story, it was usually shown at the top of the hour, which was just minutes away.

In the distance, Nick heard police sirens. His paranoia made him get up and look out his window. He imagined the police were pulling up in front of his house, because they somehow knew that he was responsible for setting the fire.

When he looked outside, he didn't see cop cars in his driveway, but at the end of his street he saw fire trucks driving quickly in the direction of the fire. Red and white flashing lights passed his street momentarily, followed by flashing blue lights, which meant police cars following the fire trucks.

He let out a huge sigh after seeing the last cop car pass his street. He told himself, *Don't get worked up like that. You're just paranoid.*

It would be impossible for them to think that you did this. He kept whispering this to himself. He looked away from the window and walked into the center of living room to sit back down.

Nick looked back at the TV. There was still no breaking news or even subtitles running across to tell the public what had happened. His eyes stayed glued to the screen. It was almost eight o'clock.

His mind then turned to David and Allison. They'd deserve this. They'd known about Amy cheating behind his back. Neither Allison nor David had told him about Amy's betrayal. There was no right way for this to end, but he must end it.

Nick's eyes turned bloodshot from thinking about the situation all over again, about how he'd felt the day he'd woken up from his coma in the hospital. He was furious that this had happened to him, and he made a promise to himself that he would make the people suffer who had made him suffer.

13

VOICES

Nick had committed another unspeakable crime. He was all comfortable in his recliner, watching the news and simply waiting for a report to come to the newscaster. Meanwhile, helpless, innocent people were struggling for their lives. Nick stared at the screen, waiting, and then it seemed that the people in the studio all of a sudden took liberty and looked down at the paper that had reached across their desk. A few moments went by, and then finally breaking news came up on his screen.

"Sorry for interrupting the evening weather, but this is breaking news coming from the heart of Boston, where a fire is wreaking havoc on the eighth floor of an apartment building, and the flames have started to travel to the top of the building. This is a very dangerous situation for people who live in this building. While several people have fled out of the building, we are unsure about the people situated on the higher floors. It appears that the building is currently on fire and fire officers are getting into their ready positions. We currently do not know what has caused this horrible fire, but we will soon find out. It says here that a Boston detective lives in that building, but we cannot confirm whether he is inside. Here's Monica Grant, reporting from the scene."

The studio then transferred the broadcast to the on-site camera crew with Monica Grant at the scene. Fiery debris could be seen falling from the building, while the two top floors had smoke coming from the windows, and flames were visible at the very top.

Frantic people were pouring from the front entrance as if there was no tomorrow, and Nick tried to spot any familiar faces. Holding their family members and crying, these people were soon out of camera range. He heard the sobs from people coming from the building. Some people were coughing from the smoke intake. They were soon passed by firefighters who were running toward the fiery building.

In the background, some more people were escaping down the fire escape. They were looking back up at the top of building but would soon be escorted by firefighters back far away from the building. The camera angled to the top of the building, where the smoke was rising into the sky more and more thickly by the minute. Meanwhile, the fire on the top floors was starting to travel down to the floors below.

The news reporter then said, "Yes, I have just had it confirmed that detective David Smith from Boston Police Department and his family live in this apartment building. His children have made their way out of the building, but Smith and his wife have not been accounted for. Several other people have not been accounted for that live on the three highest floors, while every single tenant below the eighth floor, where the fire began, has made their way out of the building safely. We will keep giving you updates every half hour. Reporting live, this is Monica Grant for CBS Evening News."

Instantly grabbing the remote to shut the TV off, Nick started panicking. He got out of his recliner and headed to look out the window. The stars were shining brightly, and the moon was full. Nick started trembling as he covered his mouth, now realizing what kind of harm he had done to David and Allison's family.

He wished he could do this day all over again, but he couldn't. No amount of magic could turn back time. *My luck will run out,* he thought. *But why on earth would the police department come and question me? Why would they, after I left the building in plenty of time for them to question many other people?*

"There's no need to panic. There's no need to panic," Nick whispered to himself, trying to calm himself down. Meanwhile, voices inside his mind were telling him otherwise. In the moment, Nick knew that he had gone mad by what the voices were telling him. He tried to cover his ears so that he wouldn't hear them.

In a snake-like tone he heard, "You're gonna go to hell for what you've done." Nick whirled around to look behind him but saw no one there. "You're gonna live in a cell for the rest of your pathetic life!" a raspy voice said to Nick. "You killed them a-l-l-l-l-l-l."

Nick then looked up as the ceiling started spinning. Saying the same verses over and over again, the voices started to grow louder and louder, followed by a thumping noise. He couldn't control his thoughts, and the entire room was spinning.

He looked out the window again, and he could almost see the stars turning around each other rapidly. The reoccurring thumping in his head wasn't stopping, and it was becoming louder. Almost like the sounds of drums, it was really his heartbeat. His ears started ringing, but he could still hear the voices in the background of the thumping.

This was followed by a soft voice saying, "Your mother would be very disappointed in you." Nick let out a scream. He folded his hands and put them behind his head, as tears dripped off his cheeks. He'd listened to the voices in his head that had made him bring destruction, but now they were turning it around on him, making him out to be the bad guy.

The room was still spinning, and Nick tripped on the carpet and fell backward. He landed on the hardwood floor next to the stairs. Sealing his eyes shut, he kept breathing heavily, pulling his knees to his chest.

Still trying to block out the voices, Nick covered his ears once again. That wasn't going to help him, though. The voices he was hearing weren't coming from the room, they were coming from inside his mind. They were all around him, he felt. The loud voices sounded like ghosts just revolving in and out of his home. He even thought that the drumming noise was coming through the walls. Then the drumming sounds turned to vibration, and Nick thought that the floor was moving as he lay there covering his ears on the floor.

He screamed, "Leave me alone!" But they didn't; the voices just grew louder and louder. That only made Nick more and more agitated. He just couldn't take it anymore, so he grabbed the closest object he could to silence the evil voices in his mind. This was a vase on a small table next to the door. For the longest time he'd meant to fill it with flowers, but he'd never had the chance to. He grasped the vase quickly and smashed it into his skull, rendering him unconscious.

As the vase broke into dozens of little pieces, Nick fell asleep and the voices disappeared, because his mind was now asleep. Nick had been driven to hurt himself in order to silence the voices in his mind.

What Nick didn't know was that while he was passed out, David and Allison had been trapped in the apartment building as it started to collapse, resulting in their tragic deaths. The Boston community would be devastated by this traumatic event.

Boston Police Department was adamant to find who was responsible for this. Since the cameras has disintegrated, as Nick had predicted, the investigators turned to what was a pretty obvious clue. After the fire started, it had caught onto a patio on the eighth floor. On that patio there had been a propane tank. The resulting explosion had caused anyone from the eighth floor up to have little chance of survival. The owner of that apartment was outraged when she heard the news that police knew the fire had started in her apartment before spreading to other parts of the apartment building.

Yes, she was in for a rude awakening when she came back from vacation. She had lost her home and everything inside, but she was thankful that she had left when she did, because she was still alive today. Unlike the Smith family, which had not been so lucky.

They had lost both their parents in one day, and nothing could prepare them for what they had to go through. They were emotionally wrecked. The children of David and Allison Smith not only had to mourn their parents' deaths but had to go through with a funeral and services six days later.

Since David was a police detective, his wake was broadcasted on live TV for the whole city to see. Still sitting free and pretty, Nick watched David's ceremony, while the public still asked for answers. Even though the investigation was ongoing, there were still no leads after the building had turned to ash, but the public was very suspicious. The Boston Police Department told the public that David and Allison's death had not been an accident; someone had planned for this to happen. The community was disgusted by how the police department stood by their original statement, while they didn't bring justice to David and Allison's family. The woman on the eighth floor must have left her propane tank on by accident, some thought, but the woman swore that she had turned it completely off before she left for vacation.

With heavy hearts and love and support from the city of Boston, Ariel, Aaron, and Eric had to go on with their lives. At the time they still had to finish high school, so they moved in with their grandmother Regina.

As their parents would've wanted them to, they stayed strong in going where the wind had blown them. Their parents had always encouraged them to just be themselves, to be whoever they wanted to be, because life was too short to be anyone else but yourself.

Nick awoke the morning after the fire with an ungodly headache—along with a small cut on the back of his head from smashing the vase against it. The sun was shining through the glass window in the front door. Nick squinted at the broken glass that surrounded him. As he slowly sat up from the floor, he looked at the stairs and wondered why he was sleeping on the floor. He blinked as the sun crept through the front windows of the house.

He felt the back of his head, and it hurt to touch. When he pulled his hand away and looked at his fingers, he saw dried blood on the tips. Sitting up and looking behind him, he saw a puddle of blood where his head had rested for the night. He pulled himself up using the railing of the stairs; he was still seeing stars. He couldn't remember what had made him sleep next to the stairs last night or how he had cut his head.

He yawned and looked over at the rocking chair by the window. It was rocking all by itself. He didn't know whether what he was seeing was real or not, but he felt a weird presence in the room. Then, all of sudden, the chair stopped rocking and stayed still. He thought it must be just his imagination as he rubbed his eyes, trying to wake up. That was his mother's rocking chair, and ever since her passing Nick had not sat in that chair, because it was hers. When he saw it rocking all by itself that morning, all he could think of was that maybe her spirit was present in the room with him.

Stepping and crunching on the broken glass, Nick stumbled his way toward the kitchen. A little dizzy as he walked, he eventually found his way to the kitchen cabinets underneath the sink. He knelt down, looking for the bottle of hydrogen peroxide. Grabbing the brown jug out from under the sink, he placed it on the countertop closest to the sink. He then turned around to grab a towel from a drawer to clean his wound with.

Nick was a little hesitant to treat the wound by himself, but he sure as hell wasn't going to the hospital just over a little cut. But it wasn't just a little cut, it was a giant gouge in the back of his head. As he felt the back of his head, he quickly pulled his hand away from the fresh wound. After spending four years in a hospital room, Nick never wanted to go back to a hospital again.

When he was younger and his mother had been going through

treatments, he'd hated seeing her go through so much pain and agony. All those memories of hospital rooms and appointments made Nick's stomach turn. Nick knew that he would rather die in his own house, on his own terms, than to die in a hospital. Before he died he would have to be taken care of 24/7 by nurses whom he didn't even know. It sent a chill down his spine just thinking about it. Then Nick snapped out of the dark thought and tended to his wound.

He untwisted the hydrogen peroxide cap and poured a good amount onto the towel in his other hand. Nick took in a deep breath as he raised the towel close to the back of his head. He didn't want to do this, but he had no choice. He was not going to step foot into another hospital. Besides, it wasn't that major, he thought. He could take care of it himself.

Blowing that deep breath out, Nick then placed the hydrogen peroxide-soaked towel on the back of his head. The stinging pain brought tears to his eyes. He stomped his feet on the floor and bit his lip, followed by some quick breaths as he held the towel on his wound.

He kept repeating that sequence until the wound had completely stopped bleeding and he didn't see any more blood after pulling the towel away from his head. His headache soon started to subside. He remembered all of what had happened yesterday, his starting the fire in the apartment building. Mysterious and evil voices had taken over his thoughts, and the only way to silence them had been to make himself unconscious, which was how he'd gotten the cut on the back of his head. Nick turned around for a quick moment to see the broken vase on the floor over by the stairs.

Nick then looked at the clock on his stove. It read 8:32 a.m., and he needed to be at work by 9:00. He had to hustle to get his work clothes on, and he put on a large Band-Aid and then a Red Sox hat to cover the gouge on the back of his head. The hat covered the large Band-Aid perfectly. He grabbed his key and went out the door to go to work, acting as if nothing had happened the night before.

By acting completely normal and keeping out of the police officers' eyes, he would easily be able to avoid arrest yet again. Nick was a little uncertain about going to work that morning, but if he didn't, it would just make him look suspicious to his co-workers and boss, he thought.

No amount of preparation can help control how you feel after you know that you have done something really horrible that you shouldn't have. Yet, you can feel amazing while doing it and even feel that it's the right thing to do. But soon the guilt starts to creep in, slowly, as the hours go on. As hours turn into night, you end up staring at the ceiling, regretting that you did such a horrible thing in the first place. Nick had often missed sleep over what he'd done on Elm Street. Now he had another awful event to keep him up at night.

When Nick arrived at work, he immediately hopped off his bike and parked it where he always did, in the alley just a few feet from his work. He checked his phone, and the time was 9:07. Nick was worried that his boss would fire him if he was ever late. He then thought about Mark's personality. He was a pretty reasonable guy, and he'd probably let it slide. But Nick had seen Mark get mad at some of his co-workers before over the smallest things. He wasn't sure which side of Mark he was going to get today.

He walked into work and he saw his boss at the front counter. He was cleaning the glass countertop with Windex. Nick saw him look up, and he called, "I'm sorry I'm late, boss. I didn't set my alarm when I went to sleep last night."

His boss stopped what he was doing and looked at him again. Nick was expecting him to say something loud or harsh. The room was silent for a moment, as Nick waited to hear his response. But Mark just smiled at Nick, saying, "Nah, don't worry about it, Nick. You've been punctual all the time you've been here. Don't sweat it, kid."

With a sigh of relief, Nick said, "Yeah, I guess I worry sometimes about the little things. Is there a shipment today?"

"Yes, Nick, there is. The truck came by this morning, so let's get to unloading," Then he clapped his hands as he made his way to the back room, and Nick followed right behind him. Nick scratched himself; he was silly to think his boss would ever get mad at him. He was the most down-to-earth guy he'd ever met, he thought. Of all people, why would he be mad at Nick for being a few minutes late? Unlike some bosses, who would rip the head off an intern who'd put two percent milk instead of almond milk in their coffee.

Nick felt like an actor playing a role. Out in public, when he was working, he was perceived as a happy-go-lucky, nice guy. He was like a character so unrealistic to his true self. By himself, Nick was insane, very unpredictable, and very afraid of what the voices in his head would tell him to do next.

The voices had only been inside his head since he'd woken from his coma. They'd changed his personality, and they'd changed his life by making him take the life of the girl he loved. Nick feared what the voices would make him do next. Honestly, sometimes he wished he would not wake up at all in the morning.

Oddly, when he was out talking with people at his job or just out and about, it would be as if his mind was on a vacation. He felt that he could control his own thoughts again, but his mind always changed when he got home. Then his inner self started to take over.

The previous night the voices had kept growing louder until he'd had to go to extreme lengths to stop them. The voices had never been that bad before. Most of the time he was able to ignore them, but he'd just snapped last night, unable to stand their taunting anymore.

Now Nick was pretending it was like any other day at his job, telling customers what aisles things were in and sweeping the floor by the front entrance. Nick's mind wasn't clouded by demonic thoughts when he was working; it was almost as if the voices in his mind were nonexistent then.

When he was stocking shelves, a plastic package of fish hooks fell off the rack onto the floor. As Nick went to pick up the package, his hat fell off his head, revealing the large Band-Aid across the back of his head. He picked the hat up quickly and slipped it back on, hoping that no one had noticed. But his boss was close enough that he caught a glimpse of the Band-Aid just as Nick was covering it with his hat again. "Hey, Nick, what happened to your head there? That's a pretty big cut."

Nick, still facing away from him, had to think up something that didn't too suspicious. Nick knew that if he told him the truth, his boss would think that something was up with him mentally. So he thought up a lie, hoping it would stick.

The angel on his shoulder kept saying to Nick to tell the truth, but like every other time, he listened to the devil on the other shoulder. He turned around slowly to face his boss, still standing at the end of the aisle. He said, "Oh, I slipped and fell on my bathroom tiles."

Trying to sound convincing, he continued with his lie. "Yeah, when I fell, my head smacked right on my razor that I'd dropped, and it cut my head. It's only a scratch." He swallowed after finishing his sentence.

Then his boss said, "Oh man, that sucks. Be more careful next time." Then Mark returned to scanning the inventory on the shelves behind the counter.

Nick exhaled, relieved that Mark had believed his fib. "Yeah, I will." Then Nick turned back to organizing and placing new items on racks and shelves. Feeling quite clever, Nick had forgotten for a while about all the horrible things he had done over the years. For now he felt normal—but it would all go away when he returned home and the voices inside his head returned as well.

14

PATH

A few years had passed, and Nick was still walking the streets of Boston a free man. Nick still worked at the fish-bait shop part time, but he had decided to start a new chapter in his life, by getting an education. It was something that he wanted to accomplish, getting a degree.

Due to his accident, he hadn't quite attained his high school diploma or even thought about attending a college. He now finished high school, earning his diploma by doing schoolwork online. It was much more convenient for Nick to do this online, because he could maneuver his school time around his work schedule. Now all he needed was the money to go to the next step in finishing his education, enrolling at a college.

He had no car payment each month, because he still only took the train or rode his bike everywhere. His mother had given him the house in her will; he had no mortgage payments, as the house was completely paid off. He lived by himself, so he only needed groceries, electricity, and water for one person. Over the years, he eventually saved up enough money to enroll at a college.

Even though he was a little older than most freshman, Nick felt extremely motivated to get an education in business. Business was a major he had been considering when in high school, so now that he had the time and money, why not make it a reality? Nick thought there was no better place to get an education in business than Simmons University, a small college located in the heart of Boston.

Since Nick lived in Massachusetts, that helped him save money. His tuition was a lot lower than it would have been if he'd lived out of state. Also, since he didn't live on campus, he saved money by not having to live in a dorm. Just thinking about living in a small dorm gave Nick major anxiety and made him feel claustrophobic. He didn't want to have to put himself through that kind of terror. As well, the main campus was only fifteen minutes from his house, within biking distance, and Nick appreciated riding his bike through campus every day

Boston in the fall was absolutely gorgeous. Colored leaves were falling off branches, the fresh, brisk air was gusting through the buildings, and Nick had a clear mind when he went to his classes. He felt that the voices in his mind were going away more and more each day. He felt that the more he was out with people the more he was his old self. He felt happier and thought less about his past. That would all change when he returned home. It wouldn't take long for Nick to start hearing the pounding drums and slithering voices that lived deep in his mind.

On a regular Monday, Nick was on his way to one of his classes. He had a blazer on, with dress pants and hard shoes. His hair was almost all gray now, mainly on the sides. Nick knew he had every right to be there, just like all the other students. Education was one thing that someone couldn't steal from him; it was his right and better late than never.

Nick wanted to redeem his character to what it had been before he'd become a criminal. He felt that it was necessary to break out of the box that he had been living in. Going to work and coming home every day was kind of a drag. He felt that something was missing in his life, so he decided to go back to school and take up where he'd left off.

He parked his bike in one of the bike racks near the building of the business department that was a little past Fenway Park. Simmons campus was located on the same street as the stadium, and Nick would often hear the sounds of fans cheering from high above in the monster seats as he rode by. He was close enough to smell the hot dogs and popcorn.

Nick knew that at an exceptional university like Simmons there was going to be a very high intelligence rate among his classmates. At that time, the acceptance rate was pretty average; they accepted 60 percent of the applicants. Nick was shocked but happy when he received the acceptance letter in the mail. After finishing his senior year online with a 4.0 GPA and getting his diploma, he wanted to go somewhere he would be challenged but also close to home.

Entering the building, he found his way to his first class of the day. It was the start of a new era for Nick. He'd earned his education, paying it by himself with no support. He was clearly the oldest person taking the class, and as he passed people, Nick thought he might be mistaken for a professor.

Nick simply didn't wish to make any friends or acquaintances. He wanted to earn his degree and be done with school once and for all. He'd wanted to go back and finish school a few years prior, but he'd been occupied with other plans that had come first in his mind.

He eyed a seat in the back row in the middle. With his backpack, he walked around a few people to enter the aisle. Once he did, he made his way to the seat he'd seen free from across the room. He sat down and watched the rest of the class settling into their seats.

Two rows ahead of where he was sitting he saw a young girl with long blonde hair making her way down the aisle. She sat down right in the center, directly below Nick but with one row of seats between them. Nick was curious who this young girl was, because her hair reminded him of Amy's. He blinked, looking at how silky and soft her hair looked as it hung off the back of her seat.

Once everyone was seated, the professor entered the room from his office situated in the back. A rather under-average-height man, he wore a suit and a bow tie. Nick thought, *Oh boy, is this guy for real?* The man introduced himself and then ventured to do what he got paid to do, teach.

Nick was not paying any attention to the professor at all. He had his notebook out on his desk arm, but he took no notes. His eyes were locked down at the mystery girl two rows below him. She was taking notes with her purple pen when, all of a sudden, it seemed she was out of ink. She tried scribbling on the side of the page, but still no ink.

She bent down to look inside her backpack for another pen, but no luck. She then turned around, still sitting, to ask the man who was sitting in the row between her and Nick. Nick was close enough to listen in on the conversation, quietly leaning forward to hear what she had to say.

"Excuse me, do you have an extra pen I can borrow?" The student she'd asked was a well-put-together Bostonian. Nick could tell he was from Boston because he wore his Celtics sweatshirt and black joggers, along with his black beanie hat.

"Yeah, sure," he answered as he reached into his pocket and handed her a pen.

"Thank you," she whispered to him as he held out his hand again.

"I'm Damien."

She reached back over to shake his hand. She smiled again, looking at his strong upper body. She said, "Gia. Nice to meet you." Then she turned back around to focus on the professor's words.

Nick sat quietly, almost not believing that it was Ariel. He knew deep down in his gut that it wasn't her when he heard her say her name, but they looked very similar. He slouched back in his chair with a sigh of relief. Curious, he decided to look Ariel up on social media and to see where she had gone to college. Using a fake name, he followed her and her brothers on social media.

From Ariel's bio he learned that she was enrolled at Boston University, not too far from Simmons. Her brothers were enrolled there as well. They were going to be graduating the same year Nick was.

Out of all the colleges in the States, Ariel had to pick BU, Nick thought. There were over thirty thousand students enrolled at Boston University. Ariel had become a fine young lady, Nick saw; she had matured a lot since Nick had last seen her. In Boston, a lot of universities are very close together, and campus lines literally run into the next campus, interlocking like puzzle pieces. Nick feared that eventually one day he would run into her.

Nick then scrolled through her social media page, and he could see the happiness in her smiles in the pictures. Nick slumped more into his chair. He could not believe that Ariel was so happy after all she'd gone through. He would very rarely look at her social media page; he did not want to be tempted to do any more harm.

He remembered back in high school, when Amy had sat next to him in class and wanted so badly for the bell to ring so he could take her out on a date. That was before Sean had enrolled in high school, of course. So now Nick was in college and enrolled in the same year as Amy's daughter, and he felt mixed emotions. It was lucky they were not at the same university, he thought.

First off, he felt old. It had been so long since he'd seen Amy smile, and he still cherished the time they'd spent together as teenagers. His heart still ached with guilt, and when he saw pictures of Ariel on his phone, it was all he could do to just remain calm.

He kept trying to tell himself, *You're fine; you're going to be fine. Just stay calm; she has no idea who you are. You're just a slightly older college freshman. If you ever run into her, she probably won't know who you are.* Even though Ariel had no idea that her parents' murderer was following her on social media, she didn't get a weird vibe from him, because Nick just had pictures of food and Boston landmarks on his page, under a fake name, so she didn't choose to block him.

Once class was dismissed, Nick rushed to get out of the aisle before anyone else did. Exiting the building in a flash, he wanted to pedal out and away from his classmates. His next class was on the other side of campus, but it wasn't for another hour.

He decided to cool off for a bit and think about everything. He did have an hour, so he thought of a place where a lot of college students went when they needed a little pick-me-up. It would also help him blend in with the younger crowd, he thought. He got on his bike and started heading away from his fellow students. He wanted some quiet time; he didn't like being in such a large hall with so many students. But Simmons was a very popular school in Boston, and majoring in business was also very popular for new enrolling students.

Nick was sitting at Buick Street Market & Café. Nothing tasted better than a cup of hot chocolate in the morning. Nick thought about when his mother had made him hot chocolate on cold nights after a long day; it had been just the perfect thing to warm him up. His first day of being a freshman hadn't been too bad, he thought to himself. He had been intimidated at first after not being in regular school for so long, but it hadn't taken him long to adjust.

He was sitting by a window, and he saw another small blonde girl walking toward him. He put down his hot chocolate for a moment. The young girl was wearing a BU sweatshirt and leggings, with black boots. She had long blonde hair, and Nick felt in his stomach that he was tripping again, but this time he knew that it was Ariel.

A lot of college students from all different universities would come to the Buick Street Market & Café, not just students from Simmons. There were students from Northeastern, Emerson, Suffolk, and BU. A lot of them came to study in the café as well. It was calming, and they could enjoy coffee and other beverages.

Nick quickly checked on his phone, pulling up Ariel's social media page, and started to compare the facial features to those of the girl who'd just walked into the café. She was waiting in line to place her order at the counter, and Nick was going into full-on panic mode. When she got to the counter, she ordered to go.

Nick listened closely to their conversation, as his table was rather close to the ordering line. Then the worker asked, "And your name?" She responded with Ariel, and Nick's heart plummeted. He was utterly sweating through his jacket as he stared at her waiting there. Luckily, she didn't look up from her phone while she was waiting. He had never seen someone look so gorgeous in person. All of a sudden she looked up from her phone, and Nick looked away and back out the window. He just looked away just in time so that she didn't catch him staring at her.

Ariel received her order from the counter and started making her way out of the building. Nick simply glanced at her back as she went out the door. He watched as she walked the other way across the street, carrying a tray with three coffees. He was stunned to have seen Ariel, and couldn't believe after all the pain he had caused her, she resembled a happy-go-lucky, bubbly person. He looked out the window again to see that she had vanished.

A new thought entered his mind. What would happen if he ran into her again, but this time with words? He wouldn't know what to say or do. But he knew that Boston was a big city, and the chances of them running into each other again were very slim.

Nick gulped down his hot chocolate in that moment. He looked at the time; he had to get to his next class. Nick thought about transferring to another college outside of Boston. He wanted to be as far away from Ariel as possible. That was just the beginning of his paranoia. Nick thought that maybe, just maybe, he would get lucky and never cross paths with her again.

Nick got up, walked out of the café, and got on his bike to go to the other side of Simmons campus. He was concerned that Ariel was going to start clouding his judgement, and he was afraid that he might not be able to focus on his grades. With major emotion running through his mind, he didn't want his grades to slip out of his grasp. This was his second chance to finish his education. Nick knew that to transfer to another school would be a complicated situation for him. Simmons was a perfect distance from home, and he didn't want to give up that convenience.

Nick remained hopeful and decided to stay at Simmons, reminding himself why he'd chosen it in the first place. It was close to his house and work, but he hated that he was within walking distance of the BU campus, where Ariel attended college. When he'd seen in the café he'd barely been able look at her in the eyes. He thought to himself, *If I do, I know I will become weak and unleash my secret out of guilt.*

The first day of college had gone nothing like he had planned. He had been completely blindsided by seeing Ariel, and he felt extremely nauseous on the ride home. *Don't worry maybe this might be the only time you see her,* he kept saying to himself over and over again. It had been a very stressful day for Nick, and he'd had trouble focusing on his later classes.

Once Nick returned home, the voices started to take over his inner thoughts again. He decided that it might be a good idea to talk to somebody about these extreme hallucinations. Nick knew that what he was hearing was not normal, but he also knew that he would have to open up about his past, about the death of his mother and how it had affected him over the years. There were certain things that he didn't want to reveal to any soul, particular events he thought he would take to the grave.

Therapists are insanely expensive, and I'm better off talking to a bartender instead, Nick thought. *I don't have to pay him or her by the hour, and I can relax and watch the Celts' game while I have a beer or two.* While he was paying for his college tuition and also providing for himself, he snooped around for therapists in the area, but he decided at the last minute not to go through with making an appointment. He was terrified of completely stripping himself down to a vulnerable state and talking to a total stranger.

Letting someone into his deepest thoughts and trying to resolve them was too emotional an idea for Nick to even think about. He kept his emotions all bottled up during the day, but when he came home he let out his frustrations and grief.

Normally, when he came home from a good day from work, he would almost forget that his mother had passed, and he would open the front door and say, "Mom, I'm home." There would be no answer, and Nick would remember when he heard the quietness that filled the house.

Feeling unsettled, he knew firsthand that he wasn't going to get a wink of sleep that night. He lay down in his bed in a straight line in the center of the mattress. He was still wearing his shoes; they hung at the bottom of the bed as he stared at the ceiling all night. Nick desperately wanted to fall asleep, but his mind couldn't shut off.

He yawned and yawned, but he couldn't close his eyes for the life of him. When he did eventually close them for a few moments, it didn't take long for them to pop open again at any noise from outside. When it was a police siren, he'd think that they were coming to arrest him, while they just happened to be cruising by to get to the next neighborhood. As the house was very old, it creaked every time the wind blew at night. Before he knew it, the sun was up and shining in his bedroom window. Not having slept at all, Nick had no choice but to get up and go to class; it was day two of college courses.

Nick would often have a hard time interacting with other students because he was so much older than they were. His heart and mind were still in the 90s, but the other college students lived in the present year, which was 2017. It was hard for Nick to adapt to school life again after so long. College was a lot more difficult than high school. Even though there was not the drama and the grind of high school, the classes were harder and more time management was required.

He thought about the previous day and seeing Ariel at the café. He wanted absolutely nothing to do with that girl. If he had a chance to see her again, he would immediately walk or ride his bike the other way.

Yawning uncontrollably, Nick had to make his way to his eight o'clock class. He somehow stumbled his way outside onto the porch, where he was blinded by the sun. He found his bike and headed toward campus. On his way his stopped to get coffee at Dunkin' Donuts. After that, he decided to use the back roads to get to campus. Nick thought that he would have better chance of avoiding too many people if he went the less popular route. He was riding down a road where a lot of students lived in apartments or houses just off campus. These houses were specifically for students that attended Simmons, Northeastern, and BU.

Ahead Nick saw a woman with bright-blonde hair walking down the sidewalk with two young men, one on each side. They had just ventured out of their house and onto the sidewalk. He thought to himself, *Oh no. That better not be who I think it is!* As he pedaled closer, he could hear their conversation.

The boy closest to the street yelled, "Three freshman taking the world by storm!" This was followed by Ariel laughing and the other boy, to her left, shaking his head. Once Nick had pedaled past them, he turned around for a moment to see that it was Ariel, laughing in between what looked to be her two brothers.

Nick was extremely surprised that they'd stuck together all this time. It appeared they were all going to the same university and all living in the same off-campus house.

They didn't even notice Nick zooming by on his bike. He almost crashed into a fire hydrant after taking his eyes off the road to look over his shoulder at Ariel. They were all laughing and having a good time. Nick figured they, too, were on their way to start their day of classes. He could still hear the laughter from far away as he continued on his way to campus. He couldn't believe that he'd seen Ariel for the second day in a row.

When Nick was parking his bike at the campus, he thought about one of the twin boys carrying a sports bag. There was a possibility that he'd become part of an athletic team at Boston University. But which one, he wondered.

After Nick had finished all his classes for the day and made his way to work, he decided to go snoop through Boston University's athletic page, trying to find the last name Smith. Lo and behold, he found the name Aaron Smith under the men's basketball team. The profile picture right next to his name was the same face that Nick had seen this morning.

He was surprised that he did not find the other brother in any athletics. It might just be that sports weren't his thing. This made Nick more apt to go and watch some basketball games. If he just stood in the cheering section filled with students, no one would think anything of it or try to bother him.

Nick loved the game of basketball, but the game didn't always love him back. He'd stopped playing in the beginning of his freshman year in high school, when he got cut after trying out for the team. He'd felt so defeated and angry at not making the team that he lost his passion for the game. *What's the point of practicing if I'm not even on the team?* he thought to himself. The truth was that so many boys had tried out for the school team, and Nick was just cut short. Amy was right by his side when he found out he hadn't made that team, and she comforted him.

In spite of not playing, he could never turn down placing a bet during March Madness tournaments. The college games were certainly a treat to watch, especially when the team he'd bet on was up by twenty points with two seconds left and he knew he was going to win big bucks. Nick knew that he had a gambling problem, especially when he lost money. He just couldn't resist when his bookie called to ask whether he wanted to place a bet. He had to say yes, even though he knew sometimes he would just lose and waste money. But it was a great feeling when he won big!

The months seemed to be going by fast, and Nick felt that he was pretty much invisible and succeeding well in all his courses. Occasionally he would go to one of Aaron's home games and be full of team spirit. There was no doubt that Aaron could make a professional career out of basketball, as he was coming off the bench as a freshman. He was a phenomenal sixth man who averaged 18 points a game, ten rebounds, five assists, and three blocks.

Nick was studying all hours of night in the massive library with ceilings that looked to be as high as the Prudential Tower. The library was Nick's new home, and he took his studying very seriously. Some nights he wouldn't even go home; he would stay at the library all night and then have to go to class the next morning. It was a struggle to stay awake some days while reading about marketing strategies.

Running on Dunkin' Donuts coffee was one of the lovely parts about being a college student. It kept you going morning till night. Nick was a creature who wouldn't be able to function without his coffee in the morning. After drinking around four cups a day, he would dread the headache the next day if he didn't have it available.

Although he was still holding down his job at fish-bait shop, Nick felt as if he'd left his old life behind him and invented a brand-new one. He looked forward to all the years to come. He didn't really think of his past much; only when he tried to sleep did the voices in his mind return. But other than that, he very much enjoyed his time being a freshman.

The first year with anything new is always the best. Nick felt that he had reinvented himself. He didn't feel as suffocated staying in his house as when he'd just gone to work every day. He was out and interacting with people he never would have met if he hadn't enrolled at school. Things were just starting to look up for Nick.

15

GRADUATION

Four years had passed by, and it was a lovely spring day in Boston. The leaves on the trees were just starting to bud, and the city had finally received a break from the frigid temperatures in the previous months. Just as spring is a sign of new beginnings, Nick was also entering a new beginning—he was finally getting his college diploma.

Between those long study nights and the stressful projects that he'd turned in at the last minute, Nick had managed to earn enough credits to graduate. Nick couldn't believe that he'd maneuvered his way in and around the Smiths and avoided crossing paths since those first couple days of his freshman year. He realized that if one of them was to spot him, they wouldn't even know who he was, so his mind eventually relaxed. Looking back at how stressed he'd been about the whole situation, Nick felt that he could finally breath. Catching some sleep now did his body good and made his mind more functional during the day.

Throughout the years Nick had only caught small glimpses of Ariel and admired her from the distance. She would be walking downtown Boston or casually crossing the street, and Nick would calmly ride his bike in the other direction, away from her. He did some more snooping on social media and discovered that she was an artsy person behind the scenes. She had sketched several portraits and posted them online. Nick automatically guessed that she was majoring in something to help expand her artistic mind.

Most afternoons Nick would ride his bike down to the Charles and sit on the same bench he always did to just clear his mind. He would often bring homework when the library was too crowded for his liking. He would find himself staying there till dark, when the bright-blue lights lit up underneath the bridge over the Charles. Once he saw them flicker on he knew it was time to go home; it was too dark to see anymore.

Since there were a lot of colleges in Boston, they arrange for schools to graduate on different days or different weekends. With thousands of families coming to support their graduating sons and daughters, it would be impossible for all the colleges to hold graduation on the same day. The coming weekend the Simmons graduating class would be holding their ceremonies on the Saturday, and BU's graduating class would be holding them on the Sunday.

Nick was in the bathroom of the gymnasium, putting on his navy-blue cap and gown. The year now was 2021. He was so eager to finally get his diploma.

Thinking about his mother, he felt a little emotional because she had not had the chance to see him graduate, not even from high school, and now he was graduating from a top university. He missed her so much and wished that she hadn't left him so soon. Deep down in his soul he knew that he never would have turned into the monstrous person he was today if she'd been by his side. He hated himself for what he had done. Some mornings he didn't even recognize himself in the mirror. The old Nick had completely vanished, and he welcomed the voices in his mind to inhabit his persona.

Still he felt guilty of what he had done in his past. He knew his mother would have been so proud of him finishing his education. Still, the voices inside his mind haunted him at night; he couldn't deal with their taunting anymore. So he'd gone to a doctor and told him he had trouble falling asleep at night and that he would sometimes go days without sleep. What he'd told the doctor was half true; he just hadn't quite told him the whole reason why he couldn't fall asleep.

The doctor had prescribed medication for when Nick couldn't fall asleep on his own. Soon enough, the voices had grown softer as Nick entered REM sleep. The medication was giving great help to Nick, and every morning he woke up refreshed, like a new person almost.

Getting extra hours of sleep had made him realize that he didn't need coffee anymore to help him stay alert. He'd gone through withdrawal for a couple weeks, but he knew it would be good for him in the long run. Soon after the morning headaches stopped, he'd noticed how his hands were less jittery because he had less caffeine in his system. He'd stopped dropping product at work and felt less rushed doing day-to-day things. It had been hard to let go of the taste of coffee, but it was worth it. As well, he was saving a lot of money not having to buy coffee every morning. He'd used that extra money to treat himself to something nice every once in a while.

Just because Nick was thirty or so years older than all the other graduating students, that didn't mean that he had any less reason to be here. He looked at himself in the mirror as he fitted his cap over his receding hairline. Aging can take certain luxuries from your body, some that you take for granted.

Nick had had to get contacts, because he'd noticed that he couldn't see the price tags on the shelves at work. He'd had his eyes tested and had decided to go with contacts, because he hated the way glasses shaped his face. He'd tried on over a dozen pairs of glasses but just hadn't liked the way they fit his face. At first he'd wanted to go the less expensive route and pay for glasses and just wear them, but then he'd chosen to go with the contacts instead.

Wrinkles at the sides of his eyes were becoming more noticeable, and they didn't vanish after he smiled. The gray hairs in his beard were visible. Since he had not shaved in three weeks, his gray beard now connected with his sideburns and eventually to the hair on his head. But that was covered with the navy-blue cap.

As he looked at himself in the mirror, he couldn't believe that he was finally graduating. His first week of being a freshman he'd never thought he would get this far. The tassel on his right side swayed back and forth while he looked right and left before leaving the bathroom wearing his graduation gown.

Nick then made his way over to where a bunch of other Simmons graduates were standing. They were surrounded by their parents, siblings, and good friends, and Nick soon grew sad that he had no one coming to support him. It wasn't that he didn't feel his mother's presence from up in the clouds, but he wished that she could be here in person to see this historic event for her only son.

As the graduating class made their way down to the Blue Hills Bank Pavilion, Nick was surrounded by hundreds of students, some of whom he did not even recognize. He only knew a handful of students by name, but he realized just how many people went to Simmons when he saw the whole lineup of graduates. He then remembered that since Ariel and her brothers were graduating from BU, they would be graduating the next day.

It was a gorgeous day, and Nick was pleased that good weather had decided to arrive. During the rehearsal graduation the committee hadn't been sure whether they would have the roof of the stadium open or closed, but since the weather was perfect, it was open, and the sun shone down into the pavilion while a warm spring breeze flowed in and out of the building.

Nick looked up into the stands as he walked to his seat. He saw the stands filled with adoring family members cheering for their sons or daughters who were graduating. Nick then spotted an empty seat on the end, and he pictured his mother sitting there. He imagined that she was wearing a Simmons sweatshirt and dark jeans and clapping and smiling as Nick walked by the section of bleachers. Nick imagined her healthy and back to her normal self. Her long dark hair was beautiful and shiny. She was smiling widely and was so happy; he pictured her being happy toward the end of her days. That was the hardest part for Nick, because physically there had been nothing Nick could do to make her feel better or save her life. All he'd been able to do was make her comfortable, knowing that he was right by her side. Nick then blinked, and when he looked again at that same section, he saw that the seat was really empty.

Nick found his seat, sat down, and waited for the president of the college to begin his speech. From his seat almost at the back, he could look around and see a sea of navy blue and yellow. He listened to what the president and some of the professors had to say, and then it was time to stand and make his way to the podium to receive his diploma. There had been multiple days of rehearsal, during which getting everyone on the same page had been a struggle. When it was time for Nick's section to stand up, he had to follow the line alphabetically. Since his last name was Williams, he had waited patiently for a long time, but when the row he was in was finally able to stand up, Nick got butterflies in his stomach again. Sweat started to form on his forehead, making his cap very uncomfortable and itchy. But he stayed composed and slowly started taking steps out and away from the empty chairs in his row.

While walking down the aisle, he looked down at the scars on his palms. They were from the day he'd fallen on the icy sidewalk, and his mother had been there to help attend them. They weren't just scars to him, they were symbols of how far he had come as an individual. He looked down at his palms and then clenched them into fists and let them fall to his sides. Against the smooth texture of the robe, he felt another gentle breeze blow around him.

Step by step, getting closer and closer to the podium, Nick was only a few seconds from receiving his diploma. The orchestra was playing loudly, and along with cheering from the crowds, it made it hard for him to even hear the names that were being called before his.

A girl in front of the stairs had just been called. She went up and shook the president's hand, receiving her diploma. As the president spoke into the microphone again, he said, "Nick Williams." Nick stepped onto the steps and then to the stage, walking toward the president.

Still unable to hear very well over the orchestra, he went up to the president, shook his hand, and took the diploma from one of the head professors. He crossed to the other side of the stage to walk down the stairs and back around to his seat in an orderly fashion, following the girl he'd been behind before.

Once he was back in his seat, he admired the beauty of black cursive font on the covering slim binder. He opened the binder up, rested it on his lap, and admired the diploma with his name at the bottom.

Closing statements seemed to go on forever, but it wasn't long until the president said, "Students, you may move your tassels to the left side of your caps." Nick did exactly that, along with the rest of the students. He looked at the tassel on the left side of his cap and waited for the president to speak again.

"Congratulations, class of 2021! You have officially graduated. Your new journey is now beginning." At that moment, everyone threw their caps up in the air as a sign of being officially graduated and done with school—no more teachers, no more projects or exams. Now they were entering a new phase of life, and that included finding a job—except for Nick, that is, who felt that he already had a lifetime job at the fish-bait shop.

Amid loud cheers, the orchestra started playing yet again. All Nick wanted to do was get out of the crowd of people in blue and yellow and make his way back to his work.

Nick had talked to his boss about him getting his degree in business, and his boss had told him he would name Nick head supervisor and manager of his store in the Massachusetts district. He'd told him numerous times that he felt Nick was very qualified for the job, but he wasn't supposed to give such a high-ranking job to someone who didn't have a college degree.

Now that he had a diploma to show his boss, Nick would have to prove that he could handle that big responsibility. After working as a normal employee for so long, he was finally going to move up in the ranks of the business and get paid much more than his regular salary.

When Nick eventually made his way out of the massive flood of people, he had to try and find his bike. Holding his diploma rather tightly so he would not accidently drop it, Nick couldn't wait to get back to work and see the look on his boss's face when he showed him the diploma.

He found the familiar-looking tree that he'd leaned his bike up against; his bike was still there, right where he left it. Right next to his bike was his attached backpack; he'd woven his bike lock around it and the tree. Nick bolted out of the crowd to avoid the traffic that he knew was about to come. Every time the college held an event of some sort, it would take hours to get out of the parking area. Nick was lucky in that department; he didn't need a motor vehicle. He would just ride on by the raging people in their cars trying to bust out of the traffic jams.

He unlocked the chain and whipped his robe off. Now wearing dress pants and a button-up shirt, he put the robe in his bag along with his cap. He then gently rested the diploma in its protective folder on the handlebars of his bike. Even though it was a temporary diploma, it was still proof to Mark that he had officially graduated. He would receive the real diploma in four weeks. Then Nick hopped on his bike and started making his way out of campus. He was no longer a student. He was a man on a mission to go get a promotion at his work place.

Ahead of all the traffic coming out of ceremony, Nick then turned the corner toward the fish-bait shop. Extremely excited, he parked his bike down the alley as he always did. With his backpack still on, he eagerly walked inside with his diploma in hand.

Pushing the doors open wide, Nick called out, "Well, you didn't believe me, but I did it!" His boss was over by the counter as always and saw Nick make his grand entrance. A few costumers in the store gave Nick weird looks as he pranced around the front entrance; they eyed him up and down as if he were from a different planet.

"Well, let me see," Mark asked. Nick made his way down the aisle, skipping about. Then he finally placed the diploma on top of the counter. The folder said Simmons College, and he opened it up to reveal the diploma with its beautiful cursive writing.

"I told ya I'd do it! It really doesn't matter what age you are. You can always get your education!" Nick glowed for the first time in a long time. He had never been so proud of himself as he was in that moment. He just hoped that Mark would be true to his word and give him the position he'd promised him. Nick's fear was that he'd found somebody else for the position, that he hadn't been able to wait for Nick to finish up his senior year. Nick swallowed, waiting to hear Mark's reaction and feeling worried that Mark might go back on his word.

"Wow, Nick, that's really awesome!" He high-fived Nick to congratulate him on this tremendous accomplishment. He'd wondered why Nick hadn't gone to college after high school. Every time he asked Nick about his past, the facts seemed to change. He never gave Mark the same answer or the same story, so Mark had just stopped asking him about it. He could sense that Nick's past was dark, but he felt deep down that he was a good person. That's why he'd hired him in the first place.

Mark knew that Nick needed this job, that his mother had passed away and he needed a steady level of income. Nick had proven himself to be a loyal employee, so Mark had overlooked some odd things. Nick's personality came in different ranges every other day. Mark just ignored it, because Nick was one of his most hardworking employees. He was always very kind and helpful to customers and almost always on time. There was not much more you could ask from an employee, Mark thought.

As Mark grazed the side of the diploma, he looked back at Nick and said, "Why don't we talk about the promotion in my office?" Mark saw the happiness in Nick's eyes and felt good that he held out for Nick this long.

"Yes, I would absolutely love that, sir." Nick closed the diploma up and put it neatly inside his backpack on top of his cap and gown. The two of them then went into Mark's office to discuss the promotion and what exactly Nick was going to be doing.

Since Nick had shown him that he finally had his degree in business, Mark couldn't have anyone else more perfect for the job—especially since Nick was so loyal and had been working for the company for such a long time. Nick felt that he had this in the bag. When Mark offered him the position, Nick accepted gratefully. He promised Mark that he would not let him down; he would work very hard to keep his promise.

The very next day, Nick was on his way to another graduation. He was going to see the 2021 graduating class of Boston University; he knew that the Smiths would be graduating with this group. It was something that he'd thought about for a long time; he was curious to see if all three of the Smiths were going to graduate. He did not relish the idea of sitting through another graduation ceremony, but he wanted to see Ariel and the boys one last time—or what he thought would be the last time.

Although he was still getting the hang of his new position, Nick had Sundays off, luckily. He picked this day to just go to the graduation and enjoy his day off. He felt that his criminal years were completely behind him, and nothing would ever ruin the new life he'd set up for himself.

He found a seat in a corner of the stands that was pretty close to the stage. He could see all the graduates in their seats. They were all wearing the same red gowns, very different from the Simmons colors. There was no way he could spot Ariel out of a crowd like this. He had to wait until they started to line up at the stage to get their diplomas. There were hundreds more people graduating from BU than there had been from Simmons, Nick thought.

After the opening speeches were over, the graduates eventually started lining up to get onto the stage. The A's through R's all went, and Nick started paying close attention to the next set of people that were lining up, which would have been the names started with S.

As the first few graduates from the S section made their way up onto the stage and off the other end, it didn't take long for Nick to spot Ariel's beautiful long, blonde hair falling straight down her back. She was talking to Eric, who was behind her, but then she would look front again to hug Aaron. Nick could tell the twins apart, because he'd frequently watched Aaron on the basketball court during the season. His body was a little more athletic looking than Eric's; his upper body was also much wider. Nick could see his broad shoulders beneath the robe that fell all the way down to his dress shoes.

The Smiths were still all happy and together. This was a momentous occasion for them all, and Nick couldn't keep his eyes off Ariel. She had a stunning smile, and he could tell that she was laughing as she chatted back and forth to Aaron and Eric as they moved up closer to the stage.

This graduation was outside too, the ceremony taking place on the football field, and the sun was just peeking through the clouds onto the stands. Luckily, Nick was on the other side of the stadium. The sun was not in his eyes, so he could see very clearly.

Soon enough the Smiths got to the stairs leading to the stage, and the president was ready to call up the first Smith brother. The President said, "Aaron Smith." Aaron walked up to the stage as Ariel and Eric clapped while he shook the president's hand.

"Ariel Smith." She then stepped onto the stage. As she was walking back off the stage, a gust of wind blew out from beneath it, and Nick saw that she was wearing a full-length maroon dress underneath her gown. She pushed the robe down in a humorous manner before her dress blew above her knees. When she walked off stage, she met up with Aaron again, and he gave her a big hug as they waited for Eric to cross.

"And last, but not least, Eric Smith." It was certainly a first for BU to have three siblings in the same year, so they had to say something special for them. Eric got his diploma and then rushed off the stage to have a group hug with Ariel and Aaron.

The sun shone down at the right angle onto Ariel's hand, where a diamond ring appeared. Nick saw the glimmer from up in the stands. The night before, Aaron had proposed to Ariel. Nick had witnessed the amazing proposal taking place without them knowing he was there. He hated it that he had broken his promise to himself to leave the Smiths alone, but he couldn't bear to stay away now.

They all had stuck together over the years and became more and more close after everything they'd gone through together. That was the power of love, and it was unbreakable. Nothing was more powerful or meaningful than that. Nick started to feel that guilty feeling entering his stomach. He felt that he had tried everything to break them apart, but they'd stuck together like magnets. Wherever one went, the other two followed. If one fell, the other two were there to help catch him or her.

He tried to keep an eye on the three, but it wasn't too long until he lost them in the crowd. Nick gritted his teeth together and felt a chill go up his spine. He looked up into the sky to see puffy clouds and sun pouring through them. It was a sign that summer had arrived; it was almost 80 degrees on that Sunday.

Quietly he whispered to himself, "Forgive me, Mother." Then he looked back down onto the football field. He was thinking that this wasn't going to be the last time he would see the Smiths. Another plot was brewing inside his mind. After a long time, the voices were starting to speak out in public again.

Nick had felt that if he obeyed them they would just go away, and they had for a while, or so he'd thought. But they'd never truly gone away, only floated around waiting for the right moment, when he was weak and unable to resist them.

"Follow them. You must keep an eye on them. They ruined your life." Nick tried to block the voices out with the boisterous clapping and loud orchestra, but that didn't work. They took over his mind, driving him to do what the devil in his imagination wanted, and that was to watch Ariel's every move every day for the rest of her life. Nick made a promise to himself right then and there. He sat on the bleachers of the football field, collecting his thoughts, while the graduates threw their caps up in the air.

16

CLOSE EYE

After graduation, Nick wanted to take a step further and admire the last remaining Smiths from afar. He found it a bit odd that they still all lived in the same apartment on campus.

Weaving in and around his schedule at the fish-bait shop, he found it difficult to always find where Ariel was around the city. Then he put a small tracking device on one of her car tires, so he could always see where she was and where she was going. He soon knew what she was doing each day of the week. Ariel was a person who needed to be on a schedule, and Aaron was a man of habit.

Aaron would go to work every single day and leave the house at the same time on the dot. Nick knew this because every morning when Aaron left Nick would wrote it down in a journal, while hiding in the woods next to the house.

Since Nick was a big shot at work, he didn't have to show up in the office until nine or ten, so he would do his observation before he went to work. In his journal, Nick would write down everything he saw Aaron or Ariel do, what they were wearing, and what time they left the house. He would also write down how their facial expressions appeared in the morning. Ariel seemed to be more of a morning person, and Aaron was just the opposite.

On Mondays, Wednesdays, and Fridays, Ariel would get up and go for a run at seven sharp. After she ran around the city, she would return to the house around eight with an ice coffee in her hand. She would get this from the closest Dunkin' Donuts and walk back sipping it.

Eric, on the other hand, was quite hard to track. Most days he wouldn't even leave his home, and only occasionally would he go out with Ariel and Aaron. Nick thought maybe he worked at home, maybe working at building something crafty.

You would think they would want to buy a place of their own and get off campus, he thought. But what he didn't know was that Aaron and Ariel were saving up for a wedding and to eventually buy a house of their own. There were plenty of houses and apartments off campus for other college students, and Aaron didn't want to part with the apartment just yet.

Nick, thinking back, he was even there the night Ariel and Aaron had the fight that resulted in Ariel storming out with her boyfriend Jordan, at the time on that cold night in January. He was far enough away from the house, behind a car parked on the other side of the street, but Nick could hear Ariel bashing Aaron to her boyfriend at the time, Jordan, as they made their way to the bus stop. After they left, Nick heard Aaron screaming. Nick did not know what the fight was really about, but it had to be something major.

He also logged into his journal that while Ariel was standing her ground and living somewhere else, Aaron had left the country. It was probably to pursue his basketball career outside the country, he thought. He'd seen Aaron's passport sticking out of his pocket the morning he left to go to the airport.

Nick was the eyes in the bushes across from the apartment, viewing all the Smith family drama over the years. He was even there when the cops were called to the apartment, and he heard one of the cops say that Ariel had gone missing. He'd been riding home from work through that same street and decided to stop behind his usual hiding spot to watch for Ariel. He almost had a heart attack when cop cars started pulling up to the apartment. He knew he had to get out of sight before anyone saw him, so he dashed out the back way through the woods. The flashing blue lights were blinding as they reflected off the trees.

What he didn't know was that Ariel had run away to the house on Elm Street, with a blizzard brewing. Nick was glad he'd left when he did; if he had left later, he would've gotten caught in the storm. Days went by with him not knowing whether Ariel had been found. One morning he saw Aaron driving home with Ariel in the passenger seat and his brother in the back. It appeared that Ariel had suffered through the harsh conditions of the storm. She had tons of layers on to keep her warm, and Aaron helped by carrying her in his arms. Nick thought that maybe she was too weak to lift up her own body, and he was very concerned about what had happened to her. Nick didn't know this yet, but Aaron was in love with Ariel, and he wasn't going to let her go ever again.

Nick started to suspect that Ariel and Aaron had a connection, a connection that only a handful of couples have. As soon as Ariel was well recovered, Nick watched their relationship progress. He caught glimpses of them walking through downtown Boston holding hands and running together side by side along the Charles. Nick would see them as he sat on his usual bench in the morning before work. Ariel and Aaron would run on by him with not a care in the world.

One day Nick was surprised that Ariel had managed to get Aaron out of the house so early to go for a run with her, which only happened on rare occasions. They were wearing color-coordinated workout clothes, and they had no idea that they had just passed a person who was incapable of being normal. Nick turned his head to watch them run away, and then he returned to looking at the water when they were out of sight. Nick was even there the night Ariel got engaged to Aaron, the night before graduation. He had kept a close eye on them over the four years, but now it had become a bad habit.

Once his college classes were over, Nick only had to worry about work and then returning to the Smith residence either before or after work. Still on the bleachers of the football stadium, Nick kept pondering the previous night and how close a call it had been when he'd stayed in the window of the Smith's residence for a long time.

He replayed the night in his head. It had just been starting to get dark. Nick had felt more secure in his hiding spot, because the only way he could be spotted was if anyone shone a flashlight directly at him. He took an extra precaution and wore all black to further blend into the darkness.

The Smiths lived on the very last apartment house off campus, and it was the closest house to the woods. After living there for so long, they had made it their own; it appeared that they all actually could stand each other's living conditions. It didn't look like your typical college dormitory.

Once again Nick wrote down what time Aaron and Ariel came home. With all the lights on in the house, Nick could see inside certain parts of the house. He thought that they were celebrating a special occasion of some sort, because before he got to his spot in the trees, he saw Eric walking back to the house carrying large bags.

When Aaron arrived home, he was holding a very small jewelry box in his hand and was smiling ear to ear as he looked into the window and saw Ariel inside dancing in the kitchen. Nick wondered about the jewelry box. The only object small enough to fit in there was a ring.

Nick wanted to get closer to what was going to happen inside the house, but he didn't want to risk being caught. He took a gamble and crept closer to the window. He could hear a car approaching where he was on the street, so he quickly jumped behind Aaron's car so that the headlights wouldn't shine on him. Once the car passed, he decided to look up into the window.

Just as he did, he heard a crack of thunder in the sky behind him, and rain started to pour down. Nick thought to himself, *Oh, great!* He put his hood up over his head as the rain smacked onto the driveway, making puddles within seconds. Nick looked above him to see the lightning flashing in between the dark clouds. The loud thunder strikes made Nick jump as he crouched down under the windowsill.

He hated being out when it was raining, but he didn't want to miss out on what was going on inside. So he took a deep breath and looked into the window, putting his hands on the side of the house to keep him balanced while staying in a crouch position.

It appeared to Nick that a fancy dinner had been set up. Aaron didn't have that small jewelry box in his hand. Nick intrigued about what might happen. Ariel had no idea what was taking place. Very fancy lights had been strung up around the kitchen, and the lights had been dimmed slightly, while candles glowed brightly all around the table. Eric seemed to be preparing dinner for Ariel and Aaron, using a ridiculous French accent and a fake mustache. Nick could hear their laughter from outside the window, in between loud cracks of thunder.

He could tell that the night was set for something very special. Ariel was stunning, as always, and Aaron was a superior man, with a nervous energy. He kept fidgeting with his fingers underneath the table. From Nick's view, he could tell Aaron was nervous about something. A light bulb went off in Nick's head—he couldn't believe that he hadn't thought of it sooner. Aaron was going to propose to Ariel!

Nick was getting dumped on with rain; his clothes were soaked. He wanted to go home, but he wanted to see whether Ariel was going to say yes. So Nick stayed in the spot for hours while Ariel and Aaron had dinner. Nick was careful every time Aaron or Ariel turned toward the window to back away slightly to avoid being seen.

Watching the momentous evening take place, Nick only thought about how he hadn't been in the dating game ever since Amy. It was because his heart was still broken about what had happened back in high school. The guilt consumed him every day over ending her life, but he had to go about his life and continue to live.

As time went on, Nick found it harder every year to mourn the loss of his mother. His heart was empty as it searched for her motherly love. He knew deep down that she was watching over him as he continuously made horrible decision after horrible decision. The thought of what his mother would think of him after all he had done to innocent people haunted him at night. He knew that if she had been alive, he never would have committed those horrible crimes. Nick felt keenly the loss of love in his life.

After finishing dinner, Eric brought out a cheesecake from the fridge. Laughs were exchanged after Eric set the cake down on the table. When Ariel was about to cut a piece, she gasped and covered her mouth with her hands in shock.

Nick thought to himself, *Oh boy, this is it.* From that angle, Nick could not see what had surprised her so much, until Aaron grabbed what looked to be a diamond ring out of the cheesecake. He got out of his chair, walked over to Ariel's side of the table, and got down on one knee. He was proposing to Ariel, and Nick had a front-row seat. Nick could hear very little of the conversation through the window, as the rain started to come down harder, and thunder continued to go off in the distance.

He observed Ariel as she said yes. Aaron slipped the ring on her finger after sweeping her off her feet and kissing her passionately. He set her down, and she admired the gorgeous ring he had picked out for her. Nick was surprised. He'd thought that Aaron would be gone for a matter of months, but when Ariel had been reported missing, Aaron had returned on that horrible snowy night to help find her. Then the stars had all aligned when she was found, and it had turned out that Aaron was the one for Ariel after all. He'd decided to not pursue a career in basketball but come back to the States to win the heart of the girl he had loved since he was a teenager.

Nick never would've guessed after Aaron had left that they would become an item, but he'd been wrong. He felt mad at himself for not seeing this. He'd thought that the relationship would eventually just run its course, and they would break up. But Ariel was going to officially be a Smith, and there was nothing Nick could do about it.

After seeing enough joy and happiness, he had to walk back home. When he was on the sidewalk in front of their house, he looked back through the window to see Ariel and Aaron looking so happy. It tugged at his heart to see two people so in love, and he thought about how he'd lost the girl that he'd truly loved so many years ago. He had also been the one to make her spirit leave this earth.

He swallowed, thinking of his beloved Amy and how, long ago, they'd been happy together. Then Amy had chosen Sean over Nick, which had ruined his life. He could feel his chest starting to get tight, and his throat started to get scratchy as a tear rolled down his face. The rain continued to pour down on him, and he shivered. He had his hood up, but it didn't keep him dry; his clothes were completely soaked from the rain.

All of sudden, the voices returned to Nick, saying, "That should be you in there. He's stealing your precious Amy." Nick shook his head. He knew that the women inside waltzing around the kitchen was Ariel. He snapped his neck quickly to the left and right again and looked back into the window. His vison started to change; he didn't see Ariel and Aaron anymore. The two people he thought he saw in the window were Amy and Sean. He forgot what year he was in and thought he was his younger self again. Trying to stay true to himself, he wanted to believe that Amy was dead.

Nick blinked and rubbed his eyes with his sleeve; then he looked again. He thought his mind was playing tricks on him. He knew that this wasn't Amy and Sean's house, but he could've sworn he saw them in the window.

There was no way Amy and Sean could still be alive. It wasn't possible, he thought, but it was hard not to think that when he saw what was going on through the window. As he turned away and started walking down the street, he kept turning back and staring at the house, questioning what he had just seen.

It had finally happened. Nick had gone off the deep end. He was convinced that Amy and Sean lived in that house, and he had completely forgotten that he'd killed Amy and Sean over twenty years ago. The voices in his mind were starting to take over again. At that point, he couldn't tell whether something was real or not.

Nick wished that he had his bike to get back home, but when he'd looked at the forecast, he'd known that it was going to rain. He didn't want his bike to rust up any more than it already had. When he was younger, he'd been neglectful and left the bike out in the rain. The bike had rusted up over the years, and now that it was his main source of transportation, he had to take care of it. So he did what he should've done many years ago; he left his bike in the shed in the backyard when it rained.

When Nick got home, he was drenched. Every step he took left a puddle on the hardwood floors. He was cold and shivering; he needed to get out of his wet clothes. He grabbed the blanket off the couch and laid it out neatly. He took off his wet clothes and placed them near the fireplace to dry. After that, he rolled up in the warm, dry blanket and stayed there for the rest of the night. His body shivered uncontrollably. He had walked in the pouring rain for miles, and he could still feel the rain pouring down on his skin. He should've brought his raincoat. His head was at the end of the couch closest to the fireplace, and he could feel the warmth of the fire as he lay there.

He turned his head slightly and saw his drenched pants on the floor next to the fireplace. He noticed the bulge in his back pocket. It was the journal that he had been using to track the Smiths for the last couple of weeks. He worried that it might be ruined by the water, so he got off the couch, still wrapped in his blanket, and grabbed his damp pants. They dripped water onto the carpet as Nick rummaged through the back pocket. He pulled out his journal, feeling the cover limp from the water. Also in his pocket was the enchanted key. He shook the water off it and placed the dry key on the coffee table.

Laying the pants back down in front of the fireplace, he held the journal close to him as he sat back down on the couch. He pulled the blanket up around his shoulders again.

When he flipped the cover page, more water leaked out of the journal onto the floor. Nick looked at the pages, and each page looked the same. The ink had streaked the pages, and he could hardly read them. He could barely see any of the white in the pages, as the black ink was smeared all over.

The journal must have gotten wet when Nick had crouched down to get a better look in the window. Then he'd forgotten he even had it in his back pocket when he was walking home. He'd been thinking only that he had to get home and out of the rain.

All those weeks of tracking and following the Smiths had been a complete waste—watching them from afar and writing down their every move in that journal! Even their names were gone, which only made Nick believe his crazy vision more, that Ariel and Aaron were Amy and Sean. But he remembered that their graduation was coming up the next day, and that reminded Nick that it had been Ariel and Aaron who he'd seen in the window.

The demons were raging in Nick's mind. They wanted to take control of his life. They'd already gotten what they wanted in 1999, and they'd also made Nick bring terror to the apartment building when he'd murdered Allison and David. The question was, what were they going to make him do now?

Nick got up from the couch and walked over to the trash can, throwing his journal in. Then he scuffed his way back to the couch, where he fell asleep in the warmth of the fireplace. Strange thoughts crept into his mind, waking him up at all hours with night terrors.

These were about the cops coming to his house and arresting him and then him standing trial in court. As the dream continued, he saw himself in an orange jumpsuit and meeting his new fellow inmates. He woke up before the dream went any further.

Nick's prescribed medication wasn't working. He was petrified to go to sleep, but he didn't want to take any more pills than he'd been prescribed. So he just ended up staring at the ceiling until his mind gave out. The odd part was, when Nick would wake up and then go back to sleep, the dream would start all over from the beginning. Nick didn't want to endure the same dream over and over again.

He wanted to skip sleeping to avoid having night terrors, but he needed to be alert to perform at his job the next day. He was also afraid that if he went back to sleep a completely different dream would brew in his mind, something much harder to witness. This made him sick to think about and made his heart ache even more.

This other dream was that if he didn't get Amy and Sean first, they were going to come after him. His mind completely blanked out the fact that he'd already taken care of that situation over twenty years ago. Ariel and Aaron's identities were being mistaken for Amy and Sean's.

When he woke up, Nick immediately sat up on the couch, breathing quickly until he realized it was just another dream. The fire was still going strong, but Nick was still cold from being out in the rain. He got up from the couch to see if his clothes were still drenched. He felt his pants; they weren't as wet as they'd been earlier but were still a little damp.

He'd been meaning to get a new clothes dryer, but he hadn't got the chance. What with his new position at work and watching the Smiths, he'd been extremely busy. Thus he'd been washing his clothes and then having them dry near the fire. It wasn't ideal for drying time, but it was certainly cheaper than buying a new dryer, he thought. He sat back down on the couch and wrapped himself up in his blanket again. Nick was mainly concerned that he would get sick after being in the rain so long, that he would contract a cold. There was nothing he hated more than being sick.

In his mind Nick was viewing the graduation again. The flashbacks from the previous night tormented him. He was extremely overtired, having only gotten a couple hours of sleep and no REM sleep whatsoever. He saw himself surrounded by people who were clapping and happy for whoever they were supporting, someone who had finally graduated. Looking at the sea of red robes, he lost sight of Ariel. He tried to spot her blonde hair but wasn't able to pick her out of the crowd. He decided to give up looking for her from his seat and left for home.

That night, Nick knew he wasn't going to get any solid sleep again. When he woke up from the same reoccurring dream, a new plot had entered his mind, something that was very despicable and not to be spoken of. He had to be patient for the next seventeen years for it to begin.

17

FLASHLIGHT

In a stealthy stance, eyes firmly on his target, Nick found a spot behind a bush near the skate park. The year was now 2048, and Nick still had to take his pain out on the Smith family. His thirst for bringing hurt to the next generation of the Smiths was still very much alive. Nick wanted nothing more than to continue with yet another villainous plan.

A lot of things had changed throughout the city of Boston. Cars had a certain glow to them, as cars now had advanced engineering. But a lot of things about the city had stayed the same over the years. The same buildings with centuries of history still stood tall, and a mastermind lived who hadn't been caught for his crimes.

Shade Smith went to the skate park every day after school; it was only five minutes from where she lived. She lived at 1 Elm Street with her parents, Ariel and Aaron, and her three siblings. The landmarks, like the Prudential Tower, TD Garden, and the Charles certainly never lost their beauty. To this day, Nick would chuckle every time he rode on by the magnificent river, knowing that the murder weapon that he'd used on Amy and Sean was still lying at the bottom.

Nick had just retired from fish-bait shop, having turned seventy-one a few weeks earlier. He could barely recognize himself when he looked in the mirror every morning. He'd lost the muscle tone in his body due to not being as active as when he was younger—along with the drinking every night and not caring about what he was eating after he came home from work.

He'd never had much muscle tone to begin with but never felt the urge to go to the gym. Nick had felt that riding his bike every day was enough exercise for him, especially when he had to go out numerous times a day to do errands. The arthritis in his body was so bad some days that he couldn't even ride his bike to go do those errands. He would have to wait to go out the next day, or until his body felt better. He had lost his youthful complexion, wrinkles had taken over his forehead and temples, and the hair on his head was completely gray.

Now only the front of his head was visible, as he had his hood up, covering the top of his head. He had his eyes locked on Shade. She was sitting on top of a skate ramp next to Jonny, as he rolled his skateboard back and forth with his foot while holding her hand. Several other skateboarders were practicing and trying crazy tricks and skills all around them on the ramps and railings. Neither Shade nor Jonny had any idea that they were being watched. Nick was a very clever stalker; he hid in the darkness where no one could see him.

"I'm so glad we finally got a chance to do this," Jonny said while he brushed the back of her hand.

"Me too," she replied. While Shade had envisioned this might happen, she couldn't think of a single topic to talk about. Tons of times she had imagined how she would talk to Jonny if they ever got a chance to be alone together, but now her mind was just completely blank. For so long she'd dreamed about This night, but now she was afraid she would say something awkward or stutter as she spoke, which she had done in her past when nervous. Most of the time she was unable to speak clearly when she gave an orientation in front of the class. Eventually, her mumbling would stop at the halfway point, once she felt more comfortable with all the eyes on her.

As silence filled the air, she worried about him losing interest, so she said the first thing that came to her mind. She nudged Jonny with her shoulder playfully and saw him look down at her. "So, are you excited for the summer?" Shade was hoping that this would break the ice. The car ride there had been awkward enough, with them just listening to music.

"Oh yeah. My mom's friend has a place down in Cape, so I'll be going down there a lot."

"Do you have any aunts or uncles?"

Jonny replied, "Nope, I don't, just me and mom."

Shade looked at him and noticed the golden chain around his neck and his bright smile as she said, "What? What are you looking at?"

"You're just not like other girls at school. You're different."

Shade asked, "Am I a good kind of different?"

He chuckled, looking down at the concrete, and said, "Well, yeah. You have a beautiful heart." He turned back to her, fixated on her eyes. "You have a real heart, and I really like you for you. You don't try and be anybody else."

Shade blushed. She knew the type of girl he was talking about from school. She grinned, looking down at her shoes so Jonny wouldn't see her cheeks turn cherry red.

"Why do you always turn away when I look at you?"

Shade smiled, shaking her head. "I dunno." Jonny saw the kind of girl Shade was. She was comfortable in her own skin, and he was glad that he'd asked her out.

Shade then felt comfortable enough that she moved over closer to Jonny. She rested her head on his shoulder as he wrapped his arm around her. She smelt his strong cologne as a large gust of wind blew back in the direction of the skate park. The butterflies in her stomach started to subside as she felt more and more comfortable with Jonny. She felt confident about herself as she thought about what he'd said.

A few moments passed, and Jonny's phone rang in his pocket. Shade lifted her head up from his shoulder and saw Jonny checking to see who it was.

"Ugh, it's my mom. Do you mind if I answer it?"

She was surprised that he would ever think she would mind. Family came first and always had in her book. "No, it's fine. Take it."

Jonny pressed the answer button, and before Jonny could even say hello, Shade could hear his mother screaming on the other end.

Startled at the alarm in her voice, Shade sat up farther away from Jonny's shoulder and gave him some space. "Mom, wait—slow down! Can you just chill!"

Shade heard his mom say to him, "No, Jonny, I will not chill. I come up to your room to find out you're gone! Now, where the hell are you?"

Shade quickly became uncomfortable. Maybe Jonny had sneaked out of the house to be with her and taken the car without permission. She'd assumed that Jonny was completely free tonight and was surprised to see him as a rebel. Even through the phone it was obvious that his mother's rage was very intense. Jonny told her, "I'm at the skate park."

Shade looked out toward the woods. She couldn't see that far out from the park, because the park lights only lit up the area where the ramps and bars were. Next she heard his mother say, "Jonny, you better get your butt home right now. I don't care who you're out with!" Jonny tried explain himself, but she cut him off. "I don't wanna hear any excuses. I told you I don't want you driving my car out at night! You better be home in ten minutes!"

"All right, Ma! All right, fine, I'll come home." Then he hung up and put his phone back in his pocket.

"Shade, I'm really sorry, but my mom is fired up right now, and she wants me to get home. Come on, I'll drop you back to your house." He picked up his skateboard and held out his hand to help her off the ramp and onto the grass beyond the concrete.

She thought about his situation and felt awful for him. She was even a little touched that he had broken his mother's rules just so they could spend a little time together. There wasn't really any point for Jonny to drop her off when she was only five minutes away. She could just walk home. She looked down the street and saw multiple cars passing by. "Hey, that's all right. I can just walk home."

Jonny looked back at her after putting his skateboard in the trunk. "Really? Are ya sure?" he asked.

"Yeah, plus it sounded like you and your mom aren't doing too hot right now. I don't wanna get you in more trouble. I'll be fine. You just go on home."

Jonny wasn't thrilled with the idea of not giving Shade a ride, but his mind was consumed by what his mom was going to say to him when he got home. He knew that she didn't want him driving her car after dark, but he wanted to spend time with Shade. The anticipation started to make him sweat, and he wanted to run away with Shade.

Shade was adamant on walking home by herself. She didn't want to be the cause of more trouble between Jonny and his mom if he was out longer than he needed to be. One thing she hated about Jonny was that he was very stubborn. When he wanted to do something he'd try his best to do it his way, even though it might be the more difficult way.

"Are you sure you'll get home okay?"

"Jonny, don't worry about me." She reassured him, and he finally gave in.

"All right. Just text me when you get home, okay?"

"I will."

Before getting in his car, he wrapped his arms around Shade and pulled her close for a tight hug. He whispered, "I'm sorry our date was cut short." Shade stayed in his arms, and he said, "Don't worry about it, okay? We can try this again if she lets me out of the house this summer."

Shade laughed as Jonny got in his car and pulled away from her. As he did, she kicked up her skateboard with her foot and started walking back home. The date had been cut extremely short, which she hadn't expected at all. She was fearful that it would be the last time she went out with him this summer.

Shade was unaware of someone who was lurking in the shadows, calmly watching and waiting for the right moment. When she got further and further away from the skate park, she realized that her path became darker the farther down the street she ventured. Shade looked behind her; she could barely see the lights of the skate park. The space around her became darker every step she took.

The only light she would get briefly was from the headlights of passing cars. She felt uneasy and regretted not getting a ride back from Jonny. No cars passed her for a while. Shade just kept trying to continue straight, listening to branches crack as the wind blew.

Taking deeper breaths, she noticed how all alone she was in the dark, and she started to walk at a faster pace. She needed to get back home. She had a weird sense that someone was behind her. She looked over her right shoulder, but no one was there. She couldn't really see much of anything; she couldn't even be sure she was going in the right direction to get back home. All of a sudden she saw a radiant beam of light behind her. It wasn't a light as wide as a car's headlights; it appeared smaller. It must be a flashlight. She found it odd, so she turned around, thinking it might be Jonny.

Blinded by the bright light, she could not see who was holding the flashlight, but she could hear the man's voice. "Hello there. Are you Shade Smith?" She still could not see the person's face or anything—only that the person who'd spoken was wearing a sweatshirt, and his hood was up.

About twenty feet away from the person, Shade didn't recognize his voice. But she decided to answer him. "Yes, and who are you?" She held up her hand, trying to block the strong light from her eyes to get a better look at this person.

"Oh, I'm Jonny's uncle. He sent me to make sure you got home safe."

She squinted as the light continued to shine in her face. She thought, *Oh, how thoughtful of him.* But then her thoughts changed as the flashlight was turned off.

"Oh dear, the battery is dead in this thing." His voice came in clearer so Shade could tell that he was walking closer to her.

Shade was hoping that a car would drive by soon so that she could get a good view of this person. As they started walking, the man asked, "So you're Shade. Jonny has told me all about you." Shade didn't think anything of it, but she felt a weird vibe as she started walking back with the man who claimed to be Jonny's uncle.

She smiled at his remark, and a thought entered her mind. Something was just not quite right. She felt it in her gut. She needed to get home right away. She felt like sprinting away from the person who claimed to be Jonny's uncle. The two strangers had a quiet few seconds together, until Shade felt like she had to say something.

"Hang on. Jonny didn't tell his family about going out tonight." Shade's heart started to race—she knew that this person wasn't who he said he was. "Jonny doesn't even have an uncle!"

The man had no reply to that. It was as if he were completely numb and no words fazed him. But then Shade felt him grab her lower back, and not in a good way. The man's flashlight began to flicker on and off. While Shade tried to push him away, she saw a glimpse of what he looked like, a much older guy. He clearly was trying to attack her. She shoved him back and then started to run, but he caught up with her again. This time he was a lot more forceful as he grabbed her wrist, pulling her backward. She thought he must be a robber, as she tried to break the hold of his hands. "Let go of me! Let go!"

They got tangled with each other, falling backward into the woodsy area off the street. Shade tumbled backward onto her behind, while he was grabbing at her feet so she wouldn't get away.

When she fell, she let go of her skateboard, and she felt around for it on the ground.

As she was doing that, she felt the man start to grab at her legs, and she tried to kick away from his grasp. Luckily she found her skateboard. She grabbed it and swung it with power, hitting her attacker in the face. He grunted as he let go of her legs. Pushing back away from where she thought he was, she got up from the ground and started to run deeper into the woods.

She managed to kick and scramble away from her attacker. Once she got up onto her feet, she ran straight into the darker part of the woods. Squealing, she knew she couldn't go back up to the street, because was where her attacker was. She had no other option but to sprint faster and not look back.

Nick lied on the ground with a bloody forehead, but he didn't want to let her get away. Soon after she started running, he got back on his feet and blindly went after her. The only color he saw was black, and he could feel the blood dripping down his face. He heard the sounds of her rapid footsteps and snapping twigs, so he followed these noises.

Shade was in full-on panic mode. She had no idea where she was going, but she was running away from him, whoever he was. She had to find her way back home, but she couldn't see anything. She kept bumping into trees, as the only light that was guiding her was the light from the full moon and the flickering flashlight of the insane man chasing her. Branches smacked her in the face as she tried to feel around for a clear path. Looking behind her again, she could hear the man scream, "You'll pay for that! A-a-a-a-a-h!" This only made her run faster, as his shrieks became louder.

As she looked behind her again, she could see his flashlight flickering again. Soon enough he would be close enough to see her. She tripped a couple times but sprang back up, knowing that he was right behind her. Tears streamed down her face. She was terrified that he would catch her. She thought about using her phone light to help guide her, but it would only give up her location to him.

She had no idea where she was going, and there were absolutely no cars out on the street to help guide her back to her house. There was nothing but trees, roots that kept tripping her long strides, and a crazy man chasing her. She had no idea where she was or how to escape him if he caught up to her.

She looked behind her to see the flashlight was shining on her back, and she tripped once more. She saw the hooded man getting closer to her, and Shade pushed herself to get up again. But he grabbed onto her and pulled her down once more.

18

YELLOW DOOR

Back on Elm Street, Ariel had fallen asleep on the couch next to Aaron. Her eyes opened, as she looked at the TV and the start of the eleven o'clock news. She rubbed her eyes, thinking, *Is that the real time?* The blanket that was on top of her slowly slid down as she sat upward. She rubbed her eyes and yawned, realizing Shade had still not come home yet.

Her movement woke Aaron, who was sound asleep as well. Ariel stood up from the couch and walked over to the door. As she was looking out the glass, Aaron sat up from the couch and saw his worried wife standing near the front door with her arms crossed and her back toward him.

Ariel was gazing outside, only seeing light as far outward as the porch lights. Everywhere else it was dark, and the moon was bright in the grim sky. "She's still not back, Aaron."

"Wait—what? She's not back yet?

Ariel turned back away from the door, looking extremely worried. "I'm calling her right now." She quickly snatched her phone off the end table next to the couch and called Shade's phone. She anxiously waited for her to answer as she paced in front of the door.

Breathing quickly and with a fearful look in her eye, she was thinking that it wasn't like Shade to be out past curfew. There was no way she would just be out like this without an explanation. Shade's voice-mail message came on, and Ariel immediately hung up.

Aaron stood up from the couch and said, "Okay, let's not worry. They might've gotten a flat tire or something."

Ariel called her again and got the same voice-mail message. "No, Aaron, something happened. I know it! This isn't like Shade. I'm gonna go look for her."

Ariel tried calling Shade one more time as she put on her shoes near the door.

"Hold on a second, babe. Let me call Eric. Maybe she ended up there."

Ariel stopped what she was doing and waited.

He put the phone on speaker so they could both hear, but it rang several times before Eric picked up. Yawning, Eric said, "Hey, Aaron, what's up?"

"Hey, Eric. I know it's late, but is Shade with you? She went out with Jonny, and she still hasn't come home."

Eric cleared his throat and then answered, "Um, no, she's not here. I don't think you guys have to worry. I'm sure Shade is fine."

Ariel, however, had a motherly instinct that not everything was fine. It was very unlike Shade to not be home at curfew. Ariel remembered how excited she'd been about going out with Jonny and how she'd smiled before walking out the door.

It was possible that something had gone wrong, and Ariel still felt uneasy that she saw a shadowy figure in the backyard. Ariel thought that maybe it was a person after all.

"No, Eric, I'm going to go to the skate park."

"Look, Ariel, Shade isn't the kind of kid that'll just run off. I'm sure she's fine."

"Well, I'm still going to go look for her." She grabbed her keys and then headed for the front door.

"Do you want me to come with you?"

"No, you stay here in case she comes back, then call me if she does." Ariel frantically grabbed the handle of the door, and Aaron grabbed her other hand before she could leave. She was wearing the bracelet Aaron had made for her all those years ago. Its shape and color hadn't changed at all over the years, and neither had their love for each other. When he grabbed her wrist, the bracelet made a slight jingle, and Ariel looked back at him.

When she turned back, he said, "All right. Please call me when you find her."

"I will," she answered before he kissed her on the forehead. She opened the door and walked onto the porch and out to the driveway. *Maybe I should've been stricter with her*, Ariel thought. *I shouldn't have let her go out tonight.*

Before she got in her car she heard Aaron say, "Be careful."

"I will." Then she got in, backed out of the driveway, and drove onto the main street to the skate park.

Aaron then grabbed his phone again and decided to call Shade. It rang and rang as he kept trying. If she checked her phone to see all the missed calls, normally she would call back—but this time she was busy running for her life.

Ariel looked at the clock on the dashboard inside her car. It read 11:04. She was surprised that Shade had disobeyed her rules. She didn't think of herself as an overly strict mother. Shade just had to be home by a certain time and keep up with weekly chores. Ariel kept thinking, *Why did I let her walk out that door?*

Ariel remembered a conversation she'd had with Shade a week ago. Shade had mentioned to her mom that she thought of her more as her best friend then as a mom. Her words had warmed Ariel's heart. Now she knew in her gut that something just wasn't right. Shade wasn't the kind of kid that didn't respond to calls or texts.

As she was driving and getting closer to the skate park, thoughts in the back of her mind were clouding her judgment. But that soon changed as she pulled into the skate park. The skate park was completely empty. Her heart sunk into her stomach when she did not see Shade anywhere. Jonny's car was also nowhere in sight. *They must've gone somewhere*, she thought.

Ariel wanted to get to the bottom of this, so she decided to drive to Jonny's house to see if that's where they were. She was anxious at not knowing where her daughter was. She gritted her teeth and wondered where the hell she could be. She immediately backed out of the parking space and drove back onto the main road. While she held the wheel with her left hand, she called Shade again. It rang, but still no answer as her voice-mail message came on. Ariel decided to leave a message this time.

"Shade, it's your mom! Where are you? It's 11:15 at night. Please call me when you get this. I'm heading over to Jonny's right now. I went to the skate park and you weren't there, so call me back!" Then she hung up the phone and angrily slammed her other hand against the wheel.

Jonny lived in the opposite direction from Elm Street and closer in the city. Ariel was praying that she would find Shade there. Her phone rang, and she grabbed it off the passenger seat.

"Shade!"

"No, it's Aaron. You still haven't found her?"

"No, she wasn't at the skate park. Aaron I'm really starting to get worried. I'm heading over to Jonny's now. Oh my God, Aaron! Where the hell did she go?"

Ariel was becoming frantic. She was speeding to Jonny's as quickly as possible. "Ariel, honey, calm down. I'm sure that wherever she is, she's with Jonny. They're probably at his house. Do you want me to meet you there?"

"No, you stay at the house in case she comes back. I should be there in five minutes."

"Okay, babe, keep it under eighty, okay?"

Ariel looked down to check, and it turned out she was going way over the speed limit. When Ariel was nervous or angry in the car she would always speed. Aaron's words calmed her down, and she went a little slower so she wouldn't get pulled over or, worse, get in accident. "All right. I'll call you soon." Then she hung up and continued to drive at only forty miles an hour.

Ariel pulled into Jonny's driveway and recognized the differences compared to when she'd last seen it when, back in second grade, Shade had been invited to his birthday party. She didn't recognize it at first, probably because it was so dark out, and only the front porch light was on so she could see the yellow door. The exterior of the house had aged over the years, but the yellow door was the only part of the house that looked the same. She then recognized the car in the driveway. It was the same car that Shade had been picked up in.

Now she started to panic. *If Jonny drove home, why didn't he drop off Shade? Where is Shade?* Maybe she was inside the house, she thought, or maybe somewhere else.

She stepped onto the low porch and rang the doorbell. Looking up and seeing that there were absolutely no lights on inside the house only made Ariel more uneasy. She rang the doorbell multiple times; she could hear the ringing inside. She thought to herself, *I know they can hear me.*

Then she started knocking on the door and yelling, "Hello! Hello!" She knocked so hard that she broke the skin on her knuckles. Luckily it worked, because Ariel saw a light turn on inside the house. Pretty soon, standing on her tippy-toes and looking through the window at the top of the door, she saw a woman in a purple robe coming down the stairs. *This must be Jonny's mom,* she thought to herself.

Ariel backed away enough so she could open the door, and the woman said, "What is it? Do you know what time it is?" Ariel at first felt bad about waking her up, because this woman certainly needed some beauty sleep. She had a pale complexion and dark circles under her eyes, while her light brown hair was all knotted.

"Hi. I'm sorry to disturb you. I don't know if you remember me, but I'm Ariel Smith. Your son went out with my daughter, Shade, tonight."

Jonny's mom eyed her up and down as she realized who she was. "Oh, you're the lady with them four kids?"

"Yes, that's me," Ariel replied. "Now, is Jonny home?"

"Ya very rarely do you see big families anymore. One kid is enough to handle for me. He took the car without permission tonight to go out with your daughter." Ariel felt that they were getting slightly off topic; it seemed she was trying put the blame on Shade for him taking the car without asking.

Ariel shook her head, blowing off her last remark, and said, "Is your son here? I checked the skate park, and they weren't there, so I came here." Ariel was starting to get a little annoyed with this woman; all she wanted to know was whether Jonny and Shade were here!

Roxanne was still a little drowsy after waking up to hear someone yelling and knocking. She said to Ariel, "Yeah, Jonny's upstairs sleeping. Come on in. I'm Roxanne, by the way." She led Ariel into her house, closing the door behind her. She turned on another light as Ariel stood in the middle of the living room. Ariel saw a black piano in the corner, brown furniture, and a big flat-screen TV on top of a bookcase. All the books in the bookcase were organized by the color of their spines, red all the way to black.

"Let me go wake up Jonny. I'm so sorry about all this. No matter how old our children get, they still find a way to keep us up all night worrying about them."

Ariel looked up at Roxanne as she was about to go up the stairs. She said, "Don't be apologizing; I was the one who should apologize, because I was the one who woke you up."

"And for good reason." Then Roxanne was at the top of the stairs and turned down the hallway to go get Jonny. Ariel looked down as she heard her yelling at Jonny to get up. Her mind started to turn. If

Jonny was here without Shade, then where could she be? She lifted her chin, trying not to cry. It is a mother's worst fear to not know where her child is, and Ariel was on the brink of losing her cool.

As she looked down, she saw Jonny's skateboard next to the door where she'd come in. She remembered Shade leaving the house with her skateboard by her side; it wasn't here. Then she looked up at the top of the stairs to see Roxanne and Jonny coming down the stairs.

Once Jonny came into view, Ariel unleashed her words. "Where the hell is my daughter, Jonny?" She raised her voice, and Jonny was immediately awake. He looked at Shade's mom with wide eyes.

Roxanne put her arm in between them as she saw Ariel getting a little closer to him. Jonny immediately took a few steps back onto the stairs. He too was still sleepy and did not know why she was so upset.

"Whoa, whoa. What are you talking about, Mrs. Smith? She never made it home?"

Ariel's jaw dropped at hearing his words. Jonny had his hands up close to his face, thinking that she was going to hit him, but he lowered his hands as she backed away.

"Jonny, what are you talking about, she never made it home?" Roxanne looked at her son as to say, "Tell the whole story, and be honest about it!"—all of what he was now grounded for.

"Well, I took the car without Ma's permission, and I went and picked up Shade, and everything was cool. Then Ma called me to get home—"

Roxanne interrupted. "Yeah, you sure as hell came home. Mrs. Smith, that is primarily my fault, because I was furious with Jonny, and I told him to get back here."

Ariel looked to Jonny to continue his story. She wanted to hear what else had happened on their date.

"So, I told Shade I was gonna drop her off back home, and she insisted she'd walk back. I didn't want to just leave, but she said that she'd be fine and that I should go home, after hearing our phone call. You're telling me she never got home?"

Ariel then started to sweat and she licked her lips after hearing Jonny's story. She couldn't believe that Shade had made Jonny go home and that she would walk back by herself in the middle of the night. She would've thought Shade was a little more responsible than that.

The courage inside of Shade, thinking that nothing would ever harm her, made Ariel proud, but at the same time she couldn't believe how irresponsible she'd been. You couldn't just walk home anymore by yourself at night. Times had changed so much, and there was so much danger in the world.

Ariel said, "No, she didn't get home."

The guilt soon crept into Jonny's conscience. He'd had no idea that this would happen; he'd felt that she would be fine walking home by herself. He hated it that he'd driven off land left her alone, but he'd been totally focused on getting home.

"Oh my God!" He put his hand on his forehead, leaning against the wall and holding onto the railing of the stairs.

"Jonny, honey, what time did you leave the park to go home?" Looking at her son, Roxanne could tell that he felt extremely responsible for Shade.

He looked at the time on his phone, and it said 11:22. Then he looked up at Ariel and said, "That was two hours ago."

Ariel interlocked her hands and put them on top of her head, fearing the worst. She looked up at Jonny, and he wasn't even looking up. He was devastated that he'd let this happen. None of them had any idea where Shade was now.

Roxanne couldn't believe that her son was all of a sudden responsible for someone going missing. Then she, too, started to feel guilty, because if she hadn't gone off on her son on the phone, then he wouldn't have had to come home so quickly. Jonny had only done what he was told, but now Shade was in trouble.

"I'm gonna go look for her." Ariel turned back around, going to the door to leave, and Jonny followed right behind her.

"Wait! I'll come with you." He put on his sneakers that were at the door and went outside with Ariel. She almost didn't want to even look at Jonny's face, but another set of eyes could help, she thought.

Roxanne was left in the house by herself, watching her son rush out of the house to go find his lady friend, whom she had never met. She'd seen the concern in his eyes when Ariel had told him Shade hadn't come home. *I guess I could have let Jonny stay out longer and just return home after his date, so this wouldn't have happened.*

She hated herself for being so vile to him when he'd come home. She was partially responsible for Shade not returning home. She started to breathe uneasily, feeling that she should've gone with them to help look for her. But when she looked out the window they had already pulled out of the driveway.

19

STAY WITH ME

Jonny was in the search for Shade from the passenger seat, looking on the side of the road as Ariel drove a lot slower this time around. He could feel his heart almost beating through his chest; he felt a huge responsibility for Shade not returning home.

Ariel was looking on the opposite side of the street while speaking on the phone again with Aaron. "I'm here with Jonny now." Then she put Aaron on speaker.

Jonny didn't hold back on anything. He spoke his mind freely on Shade. "I'm so sorry! I never should've left Shade by herself. She told me that she could get home okay, and I just drove off. I'm so sorry, sir." Then he buried his face in his sweatshirt, unable to control his emotions.

"Jonny, listen to me. We're gonna find her. It's not your fault."

His eyes poked out of his sweatshirt as Ariel pulled back into a spot facing the skate park. "If my mom just wasn't so damn strict, I wouldn't of had to leave her."

Ariel put her phone on the dashboard as she put the car in park. She got out of the car while Jonny was still talking to Aaron. She left the car door open and heard him ask, "Jonny, did she say that she was going anywhere before she went home?"

"No, she was on her way, walking back to her house. I saw her walking back that way in my rearview mirror as I drove away." Aaron continued to ask Jonny questions, but Jonny had no answers for him. He started to sweat and covered his face again.

Aaron kept talking to him on the phone. "Don't worry. We'll find her, Jonny. It's not your fault."

Jonny became overwhelmed with emotion. What if that was the last time he ever saw her?

Ariel was outside, screaming, "Shade!" and hearing her own voice echo in an empty skate park. The lights started to flicker above the skate park, and she kept screaming her name. Jonny then pulled out his phone from his sweatshirt and called Shade, hoping she would answer while he listened to Ariel screaming at the top of her lungs. But when Ariel yelled she would only hear the wind howling. The lights above the skate park would dim, and then they would return to their original brightness. The skate park had been there for so many years, but the lights above haven't been replaced in a long time.

Jonny's call went right to voice mail, and he started to panic. He jumped out of the car and looked out beyond the skate park, where there were no lights. He scanned along where the skate park ended. If you went farther off that ramp you would enter the woods, but all he could see was dark trees disappearing into total darkness. The lights, which were barely lighting up the park to begin with, continued to flicker, making the distance between Jonny and the woods hard to estimate.

Aaron was still on the phone, but he didn't know that he wasn't talking to Ariel. Her phone was still on the dashboard, but she was no longer in the car.

Ariel continued to scream her daughter's name, outside of the car, screaming so loudly that her face started to turn red. But Ariel felt that yelling wasn't going to do anything. Then she saw some lights on in the houses across the street. It was possible that they had seen Shade. She said, "I'm gonna go across the street to the houses over there and see if they saw her." She looked back to see Jonny worriedly calling Shade over and over and getting the same voice-mail message. Then she turned back to the street, looked both ways before crossing, and ran across to the complex of houses directly across from the skate park. Someone might've seen Shade walking down the street. She had to get some answers as to where her daughter had gone. That would be a good place to start, she thought.

"Come on, Shade—pick up the phone!" Jonny said to himself as he kept re-calling her with still no answer. Aaron was no longer on the phone blabbering and asking a million questions a minute. *He's hung up*, Jonny thought, and he was afraid of what he would do to him when he saw him. Jonny already felt guilty enough for the situation, but he'd have to again explain how he'd managed to leave Shade by herself.

As Jonny returned to looking at the empty skate park, he saw a shadow near the woods. At first he thought it was just his eyes playing a cruel trick on him, but it was a face poking out around a massive forest tree. He stared, trying to see who it was. There were small branches hiding the person's head. Then he got a sense, and he realized it was Shade. He tried to get a better look at the figure. Jonny screamed, "Shade!" and the face he thought was Shade's looked in his direction. It was her!

She immediately started hobbling out of the woods, and Jonny jumped over a skate rail and started sprinting over to her. It appeared that she was hurt; she was walking very slowly. She cried out, "Jonny!" She was holding her stomach and cringing. Jonny could see that she was in a lot of pain, as he could hear her whimper from afar.

Just after Shade exited the forest, a hooded man with knife in hand came out of the opening from the forest and started to charge at her. Jonny saw the man coming up behind Shade and saw that he was close to her. He yelled, "Shade, look out!" as he started to run faster toward her. He ran over and slid down ramps to get to Shade, who was limping and holding her side as she tried to get to him.

Shade heard Jonny scream to her and turned back to see her attacker emerging from the woods to try and get to her again. She dodged his strike as she turned back, the knife almost slicing across her back. Jonny was close enough to see that she had a stab wound; her shirt was now bright red instead of the light-colored shirt he remembered her wearing.

"Stop!" Jonny kept screaming as Shade was pushed backward onto the ground. The attacker was now on top of her. With her forearms, Shade blocked the hand with the knife that was trying to cut her neck.

Shade had been running from this killer for over two hours and had only gotten cut with his knife on her side. He'd thrown a smaller knife in her calf when she'd tried to get away, but she'd pulled it out herself and kept running. Now he was trying to finish her off.

Fighting to get the man up and off her, she kept kicking him, trying to throw him off and escape. Her arms started giving out; his arms were stronger than Shade's. The knife was getting closer to her neck. But before the blade reached her skin, the man was pulled off. It was Jonny.

Jonny then had the knife pointed at him, as they tumbled on the ground. Nick was now on top of him. Shade's vision started to cloud as she saw Jonny trying to force the knife out of the man's hand. Jonny had put himself in harm's way.

Adrenalin pumping through his body, Jonny saw what the man looked like as they struggled for the knife. He saw that the attacker had severe head damage; there was dried blood on his forehead and it was starting to look colorfully bruised. Jonny gritted his teeth and was able to force the knife out of the man's hands. He saw that the knife had Shade's dried blood on it.

Shade got back up and saw them wrestling to grab the knife. Jonny had forced the knife out of the man's hand, and it wasn't too far away for her to try and grab it. Now Nick's hands were around Jonny's throat, and that put him in a trance of pain so he couldn't reach for the knife. Shade tried to grab the knife, but Nick stopped choking Jonny for a split moment to knock her down; he did this by grabbing at her wound on her lower leg.

She screamed as his fingers went straight into the wound, and she fell down again. The wound started to bleed more and more. Shade was too far away to grab the knife, and the pain was too excruciating for her to try and get up again. She cringed as she saw Jonny struggle to get out from underneath him. She desperately wanted to get up and help him, but as she looked down at her leg, she gasped at the sight of so much blood flowing out of her body.

Nick was completely out of his mind. The voices were taking control of all his actions, and they were screaming inside his dark mind: "Finish them!" His force then went back around Jonny's neck. Trying to claw his arms away from him, Jonny was running out of breath.

Struggling to get air, the attacker was extremely set on murdering these two individuals. He was set on Shade, who should bleed out any time, and this young fella who'd gotten in the way. Nick was an insane criminal who had no way out of this one.

For the longest time Nick had wanted to be a normal man, but he was surrounded by demons, and they had truly gotten the better of him. Since he'd woken from his coma his mind hadn't been his own anymore; he had lost control.

Now Jonny couldn't breathe; he started to gag, and he was running out of oxygen. Nick felt that the boy was well out of air supply, and he let up on him slightly to reach for the knife. Just as he did, he heard a loud gunshot.

Nick froze as he heard the sound. Then, looking down at his chest, he saw a bright color red fill his gray sweatshirt, and he started to feel cold. While Jonny started to come to, Nick's grip started to loosen. Nick fell on top of him, his eyes open and his bloody chest falling forward.

Jonny put his hands up, and the man almost fell on top of him as he took his last breath. Jonny pushed him to the side and got from under him. Jonny looked at the attacker, face down in the grass. He got his breathing back under control and then turned and looked up the hill to where the gunshot had come from. A man stood at the top of the hill, holding a gun extended outward. It was Aaron.

Shade looked back to see what Jonny was staring at and let out a breath of relief at seeing her dad. "Dad," she whimpered as Aaron ran down the hill to her. He put the gun onto the ground as he slid onto the grass, holding his daughter in his arms as she cried.

Jonny looked back at the attacker and crawled away from his body. He slowly got up and made his way back to Shade. She looked up from her father to see Jonny as he collapsed right next to her. He saw how she was covered in blood from the wounds in her leg and her stomach. "Shade, you lost so much blood." He looked into her eyes and saw that her face was also severely scratched, probably from running into branches in the woods. Shade then reached over to hug Jonny. Breathing heavily, Jonny held onto her as he brushed her hair on her back.

"Jonny, I thought I was never going to see you again! When I heard Mom's voice—wait! Where is she?" No sooner had Shade said that than Ariel came running back over to the skate park. When she'd been about to knock on the door of the first house in the neighborhood, she'd heard a gunshot. She'd looked back over to see Aaron's car parked next to her car, with the door open. She'd run back across the street and found him standing on top of the hill with a gun.

Shade looked back up toward the hill and saw her mother running toward her. There was no measuring her relief when Ariel saw Shade on the ground. She wrapped her arms around her as she kissed her cheek. "Oh my God, honey, are you all right?"

Aaron answered her. "No, she's gonna need an ambulance." Aaron moved away from Shade as he took his belt off his pants and started wrapping it around her leg. He tightened the belt so she wouldn't lose more blood.

Ariel looked at Jonny and then grabbed his shoulder and looked him in the eyes. "You okay, Jonny?" He nodded and kept hold of Shade's hand as she winced while her dad tightened the belt around her leg.

Ariel stood up from hugging her daughter and called 911. The entire time Shade wouldn't let go of Jonny's hand. Jonny completely caught his breath and looked into Shade's eyes. She sank down onto the grass, unable to sit up anymore. She was flat-out exhausted from running in the woods for over two hours and losing a fair amount of blood. She could barely keep her eyes open, but Jonny made sure she stayed awake with him.

Aaron was at the bottom of the hill, seeing his daughter start to become unconscious, as she looked up at Jonny. Ariel was on the phone with the operator, telling them their location and the need to get here quickly.

Shade had a hard time hearing Jonny, who kept saying, "Shade, stay with me. Stay with me." Then she turned her head to Jonny, crying because she didn't know whether she was going to survive this. She stayed fixated on Jonny as much as she could. Jonny told her, "Keep squeezing my hand, Shade." She did exactly that to keep him ensured that she was very much alive, and Jonny kept telling her whenever her grip started to become weaker.

Ariel couldn't believe that her daughter had been attacked by some stranger. She looked back at the assailant who was lying dead on the grass, face down, some of his blood on the sleeve of his sweatshirt.

"Hold on, Shade, baby, they're coming as fast as they can." Ariel started to cry on the phone as she tried to give a description of what had happened, but her words were not understandable, because she was so shaken up. The operator told her to give the police a report when they got there—which seemed like it was taking forever, Ariel thought. She then looked at Jonny, who was occupied with making sure Shade was conscious.

"Aaron, hun, who's watching the kids?"

"Eric's at the house," he answered.

Ariel tried to compose herself and talk to the operator, but she couldn't help herself. She wiped her face free of tears for only a few moments, and she then started hearing sirens coming their way. Piercing through the trees were blue and red flashing lights. The sound of the sirens continued to grow, along with the lights that were becoming clearer among the trees.

Finally, the ambulance and cop cars filled the skate park parking lot. The bright flashing lights were visible even at the bottom of the hill. Ariel waved them over to where they were, and several people rushed down the hill, where they found a seriously wounded young girl and her dead attacker in the grass near the woods.

Jonny, too, was traumatized by the event. He was shaking when they strapped Shade onto a gurney, and that's when Jonny had no choice but to let go of her hand. She was still alive, he was told by medics, but Jonny released a single tear when he squeezed her hand once more and she didn't respond with a tight grip. Then he watched as she was rolled into the ambulance. The medics checked Jonny out as well.

Aaron called his brother to tell him what had happened. Ariel saw her husband talking to Eric on the phone, brokenhearted about what had happened to Shade. Over by the corner, he sat on a skate ramp, face buried in his hands, while he had Eric on speaker and told him the whole story.

There was honestly no one who felt worse than Jonny did. Ariel stayed right by his side while the medic checked him out and he called his mom and told her what had happened. Jonny kept telling the medical team that Shade was in a lot of pain, and they reassured him that she was in good hands.

Ariel gave the police a statement with everything that had

happened, including the fact that Aaron had shot the attacker as an act of defense for his daughter.

Jonny was a hero, and he made it very clear to his mother that he'd saved Shade's life. If he had not charged at the man when he did, Shade could've easily died at the scene. She couldn't have suffered one more stab wound, the medics had told him.

Once the ambulance pulled away, Ariel and Jonny got in her car and followed it to Mass General. Aaron was not far behind them in his car, and he still had Eric on speaker phone, so Aaron would have his anxiety under control. The time was now 12:49, and on their way to the hospital they were praying that when they got there they wouldn't hear bad news.

Ariel's mind was just consumed on one thing. *Who the hell is this guy, and why did he attack my daughter? At least he's dead, which he deserved*, she thought. She hated the feeling that one of her kids had been hurt and she hadn't been there to protect her.

Jonny had come to Shade's rescue, and Ariel was forever thankful to him, even though she was too distraught to say so. He was now on good terms with his mom, after finally hanging up the phone when they pulled into Mass General. When Jonny had told his mom what had happened in the last hour, Roxanne had found it hard to believe her son, so Ariel had confirmed everything that had happened.

Ariel thanked Roxanne for raising such a courageous young boy. Ariel kept an eye on the ambulance in front of her, and then she looked at Jonny as if to say thank you. She comforted him by saying, "She's gonna be okay, Jonny."

Jonny couldn't bear to look Ariel in the eyes, because deep down he still felt that he was responsible for what had happened to Shade. Ariel could sense that, and she said, "It's not your fault, sweetheart. You can't think like that."

Jonny wiped his face, still on speaker with his mom. Roxanne said, "I'm gonna hop in my car right now, Jonny, okay? You guys are going to Mass General, right?"

"Yes," Ariel answered. Then Roxanne hung up after saying good bye to Jonny, but he had already pressed End Call on the phone. They proceeded to have a quiet walk from the parking lot, into the entrance of Mass General.

Roxanne was on her way to wait with Jonny and the Smiths at the hospital and to hear the doctor's news about Shade. She had not gone back to sleep since she'd heard Ariel banging on her door. She just couldn't believe what had happened, and she felt that it was a bad dream. Ariel and Aaron were living a nightmare as they worried whether Shade was going to pull through and make a full recovery.

Aaron was right behind Ariel's car on the way to the hospital, and he was still on the phone with Eric. Aaron had asked him to stay and watch the kids, while Eric had told Chelsea that he wouldn't be home that night, after what had happened. She was devastated when Eric told her the news, and she wanted Eric to keep Aaron on the phone to keep him from veering into a dark place.

Eric was the last person who would let that happen. Whether Aaron would admit it or not, Eric was his ride-or-die buddy. He didn't love anyone else more in the whole world, but he kept it to himself. Twins have a very special bond together, and oftentimes they are inseparable. Aaron and Eric had been close since they were two feet high. They were each other's life preserver.

Aaron was more shaken up about this event than back when he'd thought he had lost Ariel all those years ago when he'd been away in Germany. Now his daughter's life was at stake, and Eric kept talking to him on the phone, ensuring him that she was going to be okay.

Aaron's anxiety was getting to him, and Eric knew it. He needed to get his brother's blood pressure down while he was talking to him, knowing that he was behind the wheel. Eric just told him to keep taking deep breaths to try and calm him down. "Just breathe, Aaron. Just breathe."

20

WAITING ROOM

Now, at 6:00 a.m., Ariel and Aaron were still waiting to hear word on Shade's condition. After she'd gone in for surgery to repair her stab wounds, they both had fallen asleep in the waiting room. They were anxious to find out whether Shade was going to be all right and make it through the surgery but were so emotionally and mentally drained that they didn't stay awake very long.

Ariel was sitting on the floor, with her back up against Aaron's legs and her head resting back on his lap, while he slept by resting his head on the back of the chair. Next to Aaron was Jonny, curled in a ball on the long waiting-room chair, next to his mom. She was sitting in the chair to his left but still held onto his hand as he slept. Jonny appeared to be sound asleep, but Roxanne was wide awake.

She looked over to Ariel and Aaron to see that they were asleep as well. She was surprised they were even resting. If she was in their shoes, she'd be pacing up and down the hallway of the hospital. Since Ariel had banged on her door last night, she hadn't been able to go back to sleep, and there was no point trying to sleep now, as the sun was starting to shine through the long glass window in the wall of Mass General. Roxanne still had her robe on. She couldn't imagine what the Smiths were going through. She was surprised they'd even dozed off, but it was because they were so exhausted. She didn't want to get out of her chair, because she didn't want to risk waking them up. Sleep was the best thing for them at the moment, and sleep always recharges the mind.

She looked down at her son and couldn't believe that he'd almost sacrificed himself for Shade. Jonny had saved her life, she thought as she skimmed the top of his hand. She was proud of him for performing a courageous act, but at the same time she was very angry at him for putting himself in harm's way.

Roxanne then saw a cluster of people making their way down the long hallway toward her, two individuals with seven kids following them. They spotted the Smiths and walked over two them. A man who looked identical to Aaron bent down to see whether Aaron's eyes were closed. Roxanne said, "I wouldn't wake them; they just dozed off. They had a rough night."

The man looked over to Roxanne and saw Jonny sleeping next to her. He reached out to her. "Oh, you must be Roxanne. I'm Eric, Aaron's brother, and this is my wife, Chelsea. I'm so sorry we had to meet under these circumstances." They shook hands, and then Chelsea said hello and shook her hand too.

Roxanne looked at all the children behind her, who looked rather shy. She said, "Are they all yours?" She kept her voice soft so she wouldn't wake anyone. She then tried to look around Eric to catch a glimpse of the young girl hiding behind him.

Eric turned around and said, "Oh no, these are Aaron and Ariel's kids." He pointed. "Liam, Jack, and Amelia." Liam was resting up against a wall, yawning and scrolling through his phone, while Jack sat in one of the waiting-room chairs. Little Amelia was standing behind Eric, holding a get-well card in her hand. Roxanne thought it was sweet that she had made that for her big sister. She was so shy that Roxanne only saw her head poking out around Eric's thigh and the brightly colored card she had in her hand.

Then Eric said, "And these are our kids—Connor, Evan, Rylie, and Delaney." They were all standing next to Chelsea.

"Nice to meet you all."

Then all of a sudden Aaron awoke to see his kids and his brother all around him. He rubbed his eyes, and said, "Hey, guys." Amelia, seeing her father awake, immediately ran over to him and jumped into his arms. "Hey, sweetheart."

Amelia's movement caused Ariel to wake up and look up from the floor to see her kids. She looked back at Aaron, seeing Amelia in his arms. Liam and Jack came over to her. She stretched before getting up off the hospital floor and then asked, "You guys sleep okay?"

After she stood up, Jack came behind her and said, "Is Shade gonna be okay, Mommy?"

Ariel put her arm around him and replied, "I hope so, honey. We still haven't heard anything."

Liam said, "Why would anyone do this to Shade?"

"I don't know."

Amelia came up from her father's shoulder and showed him the get-well card that she'd made for Shade. Aaron held it and said, "Shade's gonna love it, baby." Then Aaron saw his brother standing with Chelsea and his children. His heart started to ache again, thinking about what had happened to Shade. It was like a terrible dream, but he'd realized it was reality when he'd opened his eyes to see that he was still in the hospital. He was angry at himself that he hadn't been at the skate park sooner to protect his daughter.

Ariel looked down at Jonny and saw that he was also starting to wake up. She said, "Ya hanging in there, kid?"

Jonny shook his head up and down as he rubbed his eyes, sat up, and stretched his arms up to the ceiling. He was taken aback by all the people gathered around Ariel and Aaron. He'd known that Shade had a big family, but he hadn't known it was this big. In Jonny's family, it was pretty much just him and his mother. His dad had died when he was three, and both of Jonny's parents had no siblings. He just got the occasional birthday card from his grandmother and grandfather who lived in Florida.

Eric looked at his brother and could tell that he was still extremely stressed out, even as he was holding Amelia. He said, "Hey, Aaron, why don't we go down to the café and get some coffee? Stretch your legs a little bit." Aaron turned when he heard his brother. His neck hurt from sleeping in a chair for a while. His whole body was incredibly stiff, and he felt a walk would be a good idea.

Aaron said, "Yeah, okay. Amelia, honey, stay with Mommy, and I'll be right back, okay?" She nodded and then slid onto the chair that Ariel was sitting on next to Jack. Aaron got up out of the chair, stretched his back, and attempted to walk. Sitting upward in those waiting-room chairs had done a number on his back, but he'd had no choice but to stay, and he'd been so tired he ended up falling asleep. He straightened his back and then gave his brother a hug. Eric patted his back; he couldn't begin to imagine how Aaron felt after last night. Then they walked down the hallway side by side.

Ariel shouted, "Honey, can ya get me a coffee too?"

"Yeah, sure, hun." Aaron turned back around and continued walking with Eric down to the café. He yawned from lack of sleep as he felt the warmth of the sun coming in through the windows.

"Did you sleep at all last night? I did a little bit, but this won't be the only trip to the café to get coffee today, I'm telling ya." Eric looked at his brother and could feel the pain he was going through. He would be in the same position if something like this happened to one of his daughters.

While Aaron and Eric were in line paying for their coffee, Aaron said, "I just can't believe it, out of all the loonies out there, one of 'em decided to attack my daughter. Like I wanna know who the hell this guy is! He didn't deserve to die—he should have to rot in a cell with all the other people just like him."

They paid for their coffee, and Aaron picked up the tray. One slot held his cup of coffee, and the other slot held Ariel's cup. The two brothers decided to sit down in the café for a quick minute and started to talk about what had happened the previous night, even though Eric had an idea about what had gone down.

Eric hadn't gotten that much sleep either, because Aaron had kept him on the phone to help calm him on the ride to the hospital. Once they'd gotten to the hospital, Aaron had hung up the phone, and that was when Eric had fallen asleep on the couch at Aaron's house. Then, at 5:00 am, he awakened the kids and called Chelsea to come meet him at the house, so they could all go to the hospital together.

"Well, the investigation will play itself out, and whoever this guy was, he's not gonna hurt anyone ever again." Aaron quickly gulped down a sizzling sip of coffee, and then he said, "Well, it's a good thing that guy is dead, because if he wasn't, I would kick the livin' crap outta him."

Eric saw that his brother was still on edge as Aaron continued, "I shoulda been there for her when she needed me. I coulda protected her." His eyes started to fill up with tears, so Eric grabbed his brother's hand across the table. Aaron chose to stare at the ground. Aaron's leg started shaking underneath the table, but he couldn't bear to show his brother that he had become emotional.

"Aaron, listen to me. You did your job. If you didn't show up when you did, neither Shade nor Jonny would be with us now." Eric wanted to see that his words were sinking through into his mind, to make Aaron feel that this was not his fault.

"Aaron, the worst is over." But Aaron still couldn't look up at his brother. He was overwrought with guilt. He hated it that a predator had harmed Shade and he hadn't been there to protect her at first. He imagined Shade being terrified, running in the woods and screaming, and him not there to help. That was one of his worst fears come true, and he hated himself for letting his daughter go out that night.

"Aaron, look at me." He looked up, and Eric saw his brother quivering. He could see the agony he was going through.

"I never would've let her go out if I knew something like this was gonna happen."

Eric responded, "There's no way you could've known." Aaron was in a depressed and worried state; all he wanted was for his daughter to be okay. He still had no word from the surgeon on how things had gone in the OR.

Meanwhile, back in the waiting room, Ariel was surrounded by her kids. Amelia was lying down on her lap, Jack was sitting on her right, and Liam was right behind her, sitting in the next section of chairs, in between Connor and Evan. Chelsea was on her left, talking about the events that had happened, and Rylie and Delaney were playing in the kids' room in the corner of the waiting room. Jonny and his mother were having an intense conversation in the opposite corner, Roxanne with her hands on her hips and Jonny with his arms crossed and leaning up against the wall.

Ariel was saying, "So, I went over to check if anybody had seen her over in the house complex across the street. Jonny stayed over near the car, and by the time I was almost on the doorstep of the first house, I heard a gunshot."

Chelsea was an awe of everything Ariel had been through in the last ten hours. She was resting her chin on her hand, and her elbow was on the arm of the chair. "Oh my God," she replied.

"So I ran as fast as I could back over to the skate park, and I see Aaron with his gun out, and Shade on the ground next to Jonny at the bottom of the hill. I just couldn't believe someone would attack Shade. I knew that Aaron had a gun in the house for protective reasons, but I never thought he would've brought it with 'im out of the house. He knew something was up, and I don't know what would've happened if he didn't have his gun with him."

Chelsea was very focused on Ariel's story. She kept consistent eye contact as Ariel continued speaking. "Aaron always kept a gun in the house for self-defense, and he knew something was up."

Chelsea looked at Ariel and could tell that she was mentally and emotionally drained. Ariel rubbed her forehead with her palm and then pulled the small pieces of hair that were falling out of her ponytail behind her ears. Chelsea had known Ariel for a very long time, and she had never seen her so distraught. "Did you get a chance to look at the person who did this?"

"No, I didn't. I didn't even wanna go near him, and by the time the police arrived the medics had already taken him away. All I saw was he had gray hair, so he was an older guy. I have no idea who he was, but I'm just glad he's dead."

Ariel started stroking Amelia's hair, thinking she was asleep again, but Amelia was really listening to the whole conversation her mom and Chelsea were having. She was frightened that someone had hurt her sister so terribly and tried to hurt Jonny as well. When her mom checked on her, Amelia would quickly close her eyes, so Ariel would continue telling Chelsea about the horrific event, and then she would open her eyes again and listen in.

"Oh, but trust me, soon as I know my daughter is okay, Aaron and I are gonna find out who the hell this guy was and why he did this. Shade didn't deserve this at all." Her face started to crumple as she tried to keep her composure. Chelsea reached over and put her hand on her shoulder. It was certainly hard for Chelsea to comfort someone who had been through what Ariel had. No words could make the pain go away or help her to forget.

Ariel and Chelsea sat in silence and continued to wait for the surgeon's return. All she'd been told was that Shade was going to be moved into the OR as soon as one opened up, and then she'd been told that Shade had gone into the OR a little past 2:00 a.m. Now it was 6:20 when Ariel checked the time on her phone.

A few more minutes went by, and Ariel saw a surgeon emerge from a room down the hall. Still in his scrubs and Crocs, he looked down the hallway toward the waiting room. He lifted his mask off his face as he approached the waiting room.

"Shade Smith's family, I presume." He stood in front of Ariel and looked at how exhausted Shade's family was with the awful events that had taken place. Amelia got up from her mother's lap, and Chelsea and Ariel stood up to talk with the doctor.

"Yes, I'm her mother, and this is her aunt, Chelsea. Is she gonna be okay?" Ariel was stricken with guilt, and all she wanted to hear was that Shade was going to be all right. Fear had haunted Ariel the whole night. She desperately needed to know how it was going to go.

"Your daughter is going to be fine." Ariel gasped, and Chelsea rubbed Ariel's back; she could see the relief on her face. "The surgery went just as planned. I repaired all of her wounds, and if they all heal properly, I don't think there will be much scarring. She lost quiet a lot of blood, but it will be restored in a matter of hours."

Ariel felt that there was going to be a "but" coming in his words, but there wasn't. "I don't know how, but Shade's attacker managed to miss every major organ. Since she did lose a lot of blood, I want to keep her here for a few days under observation, just as a precaution. She is very lucky. A lot of people who have gone through the same circumstance haven't been so lucky. I just finished her up, so the anesthesia should wear off in about an hour. Right now, she needs rest. I have already spoken with the police department, and they want to come down and ask her questions about her attacker. I stressed to them that what Shade needs right now is time to heal—physically and mentally."

Out of the corner of her eye, Ariel saw Aaron and Eric coming back from the café. Aaron was walking at a fast pace, as he didn't want to miss what the doctor had to say. He jumped in on the conversation. "Hey, doc, how is she?"

Aaron then heard the same story the doctor had already told Ariel. In the meantime, she backed away from the conversation to go tell her kids. She looked down at Amelia, who asked, "Mommy, is Shade gonna be okay?"

She squatted down to Amelia's level in the waiting-room chair and said, "Shade's gonna be fine, sweetie."

Jonny overheard Ariel's words from the corner, and overjoyed, he hugged Ariel from the side. Then Amelia got up from her chair to hug her mom. Roxanne came walking over to Ariel and said, "I'm so happy for you folks." Roxanne wasn't much of a warm and fuzzy person, but this was an exception, as she gave Ariel a hug.

Ariel looked at Jonny and saw the relief on his face as he spread the word to Shade's brothers and cousins in the back of the waiting-room area. Roxanne had just grilled Jonny, asking what Shade's family would think of him if she didn't pull through. Jonny had replied with, "If you didn't make me come home early, none of this would have happened." Then Jonny broke up the conversation when he saw the doctor talking to Ariel. "So, did the doctor say when you can see 'er?"

"He said that he just finished surgery, so she should be waking up in about an hour." At that, Roxanne put her hand on Ariel's shoulder and said, "That's so good!" She continued, "I think I'm gonna take Jonny back to the house, and he'll change into some clean clothes, and we'll come right back here." Understanding that Jonny was a wreck worrying about Shade as well, she said, "Oh, ya do whatcha gotta do."

Jonny then rejoined the conversation. "Mrs. Smith, I gotta go back to the house and freshen up. Will you text me when she's awake?" Ariel smiled for the first time in a while when she heard Jonny call her Mrs. Smith. When people called her Mrs. Smith, usually she corrected them and said to call her by her first name, because it made her feel old. But this time she didn't mind.

"Of course I will. Shade will wanna see you. Thank you so much for sticking around, you guys. I really appreciate it."

Jonny smiled; he was so thrilled that Shade's surgery had been a complete success. "No problem. I'll see ya in a little while."

Then Jonny and Roxanne left the hospital. Ariel turned to Aaron and saw that he was still talking with the doctor and holding a tray of coffees. He set down the tray on one of the seats and shook the doctor's hand. "Thanks, doc."

Then the doctor walked away in his scrubs, feeling the accomplishment of yet another day at the job when he'd saved a life. Being a doctor was a very rewarding job when you did good, but sometimes with a patient there was nothing you could do to help save them. He was starting out his day well, bringing good news to a worried family.

"Our baby is gonna be all right." Aaron charged toward Ariel with his arms open wide, and she held onto him for dear life as they embraced. Her bracelet made a jingle as he held onto her and picked her up off the floor. Setting her back down, he kissed her forehead, full of relief at knowing that their daughter was going to make a full recovery.

"Oh my God," Ariel said, now becoming emotional simply because she was thrilled that their daughter was going to be okay. Earlier she'd been crying because she was petrified to hear the news. Since she'd heard the good news, her tears had been of joy.

Eric was happy to see Aaron relieved and smiling like his old self again. He went to hug Chelsea and his kids in the waiting room, happier after hearing the good news. Now all they had to do was wait for Shade to wake up.

21

LITTLE SISTER

As Shade fluttered her eyes, she almost didn't want to open them. She tried to but then closed them again every time because of the bright light above her head. She heard nothing; the room was silent, and she feared that she was no longer on this earth, and she'd gone to heaven. Then she heard a familiar voice and felt someone grasping onto her hand.

"Shade, honey, can you hear me?" She slowly cracked open her eyes again to see her mom sitting close next to her and her dad sitting right next to mom. "There you are." They both smiled, and she realized she was in a hospital room. She couldn't concentrate on anything but one person, the person who saved her life.

As she looked down at her arm, she saw an IV, along with dark bruises, and she started to remember how she'd ended up here. She mumbled in a raspy tone, "Where's Jonny? I need to see him." She scooted upward on the bed so she wasn't lying down any more, and her body hurt all over. As the covers fell down, she saw her whole stomach area concealed with medical wrap.

"Sweetie, Jonny is okay. He just went home to get some fresh clothes. He'll be back later."

Then her dad said, "Shade, honey, take it easy. You just got out of surgery."

She had flashbacks of the face of a man who'd kept chasing her through the woods. Every time he'd caught up to her he'd tried to grab hold of her, but only his knife had attacked her body. She managed to break away from him each time and hide. It had been pitch black, and she'd been so worried that he would come and find her again.

The flashlight he'd been holding had constantly flickered; she'd seen it behind her while she was running. She could still hear the twigs snapping on the cold ground as she tried to maneuver her way around thick tree trunks. The sounds were replaying over and over in her mind. She still felt as if he were there in the darkness. Then she looked at the floral pattern on the hospital curtain and realized that she had finally gotten away from him.

Shade tried to look beyond the curtain of her hospital room, thinking the attacker was just outside. Petrified—traumatized— Shade feared that the man would come back to harm her.

Aaron could see the fear in her eyes. He came to the other side of her bed and squatted down to hold her hand and attempt to calm her down. He saw on the monitor that her heart rate was rising. He hated seeing Shade so distraught. "He's coming! He's coming!" Shade said over and over again, cringing and fluttering her legs up and down.

"Calm down, baby, and look at me." Shade looked at her dad and felt comfort with his words, but the thought was still in the back in her mind that her attacker would come back. Her legs stayed still when she looked at her dad and realized she was no longer in the woods. Shade realized she no longer had to run away, because she was now safe.

"Shade, the man who did this to you is dead. He's not coming back to hurt you."

Shade wiped a tear off her cheek, feeling a sense of security as she looked away from the curtain and back to her dad. She remembered seeing her attacker fall down after the gunshot. "He's not coming back?"

Aaron saw his daughter in the most vulnerable state he had ever seen her. This only added fuel to his fire and hatred toward whoever this guy was. He still hadn't been notified by the police who he was, and the waiting to hear was killing him inside.

"No, Shade, he's not."

Shade quivered as her head slowly slid toward Aaron and he wrapped his arms around her comfortingly. Ariel took in the moment while Aaron embraced her.

Aaron couldn't believe what had happened to his little girl. Even though she was well grown up, he still pictured her as his baby girl. He'd made a vow to himself that he wouldn't let anything hurt her, and he felt that he'd failed as her protector.

"I thought I would never make it out of those woods," Shade whimpered as she rested her chin on her father's shoulder. Aaron let go of Shade and looked at her as she continued to cry while thinking back to the terrifying events. But he wanted to hear her side of the story, and he knew that eventually Shade would have to give a complete statement to the police.

Ariel said, "What happened, and how did he get to you?" Ariel wanted to unleash her wrath on this man for terrorizing her daughter; she thought death wasn't enough of a punishment. He should've endured every hit and stab Shade had felt—and then some.

Shade took a few moments to collect her thoughts, thinking that she would feel better after telling her parents how it had happened. "Jonny had just left, and I was walking back home. Everything was fine, and then I saw a man holding a flashlight, behind me. He said that he was Jonny's uncle and that he wanted to make sure I got home safe."

She cringed, thinking about what had happened next; it made her feel sick. "I soon felt something wasn't right; I knew that Jonny didn't have any uncles. After I brought it up that Jonny had told me he didn't have any aunts or uncles, he lunged at me. I tried to squirm away from him, and I ended up running into the woods. I had nowhere else to turn."

She took a deep breath before she could continue. Ariel and Aaron listened intently to what Shade had gone though. They felt worse and worse to know that they had not been there to protect her. They had done their best as parents, coming to her rescue later in the night. The situation could certainly have taken a turn for the worse if Aaron hadn't shown up when he did.

"So I ran, and he kept catching up with me, because I kept tripping." Shade looked down at her arms and her elbows, remembering how she'd kept falling on the hard ground after tripping over tree roots. The end result was black and blue bruises on her arms, which she used to brace her falls. Shade was rubbing her stomach as if she could still feel the pain from her attacker's knife.

"He got to me a few times, but I kept kicking him off of me, and I got up and ran again. He stabbed me first on my side, and then, when I tried to get away again, he threw his knife at my leg, but I pulled it out, and I kept going. I had no idea where I was or where I was going, but I ran as fast as a could to get away from him.

"I don't know how long I was out there, but I managed to flee away from him. I couldn't see him or anything in front of me. I couldn't see his flashlight anymore, and I decided to hide behind a tree. I had no idea where he was, or where I was, but then I heard you, Mom." Shade looked back at her mom and continued with her story.

"I heard you screaming my name, and I kept moving. Then you were getting louder, and I knew exactly where I was. I don't know how much longer I would've been in the woods if I hadn't heard you. He probably would've caught up to me again. Mom, when I heard your voice, I knew you were somewhere close." Her eyes started to fill up with tears again as she flashed back to how she'd managed to finally get out of the darkness.

Ariel couldn't imagine how her daughter had felt running through the woods with an insane man chasing after her, with a knife. She got up out of her chair and hugged Shade, while Aaron came in on the other side of her.

"You're safe now, honey," Ariel whispered to her. Shade closed her eyes, feeling the comfort from her parents, and when she opened them again she saw her little sister poking her head around the curtain. Ariel sat back down in her chair when she spotted Amelia.

"Amelia." Her parents looked back at the curtain and then saw Chelsea and Eric, along with the rest of the family, wanted to see Shade. Eric pulled open the curtain, and everyone entered and surrounded Shade's hospital bed. People were crowded shoulder to shoulder around Shade's bed.

"Hey, Shade, how ya feelin'?" Eric asked.

"I'm feel okay. I'm better now that all of you are here."

"We're just happy that you're gonna be okay," Chelsea said while looking down at Shade. The dark circles under her eyes indicated that she still had to get some much-needed rest. The recovery time could vary, from what the doctor had said, and Shade would need to heal at her own pace. It could be long or short, physically and emotionally.

Looking to her right, Shade saw Amelia holding a card in her hand. "Whatcha got there, Amelia?"

Amelia made her way past her brothers and father and presented Shade with her get-well card. "I made this for you. I was just worried that I wouldn't be able to give it to you myself."

Shade was so touched that Amelia had made this for her. She smiled, looking at all the different colors and stickers covering the card. She looked back at Amelia and saw that a tear was making its way out of her eye. When she blinked, tears started to flow down her cheeks, as Shade opened her arms and patted the side of her bed for her to lie down with her.

Amelia gently cuddled up next to her sister, as Shade wrapped her arm around her and pulled her in close. Still holding her card in the other hand, she said, "Thank you." Even though there was a big age gap between Amelia and Shade, they were incredibly close. Their bond was something very special that not all siblings have. That connection showed as Amelia and Shade laid together in the hospital bed, while the rest of the family was gathered in the tiny hospital room, so grateful that Shade had survived.

She couldn't believe all her sister had gone through; she heard the conversation between her mom and Aunt Chelsea. Amelia knew how lucky she was to see her sister again after what had happened to her. She whispered, "Don't worry, I'm not goin' anywhere." Shade ran her fingers through Amelia's light-blonde hair, and eventually the two sisters fell asleep. The rest of family thought it would be best for Shade to get some well-needed rest.

As they ventured out of the hospital room, two police officers were waiting in the lobby to question Shade about her attacker. Aaron refused to let them to speak with her, as she'd just gone to sleep and needed more time to rest. She was in no way ready to give a report on what had happened, even though she'd basically summed it up for them. The family felt that Shade's stress level needed to stay moderate; they'd seen her get worked up just thinking about it. The police were kind enough to leave the hospital; they assured Aaron that they would come back the next day to get answers from her.

For hours Shade rested her eyes, until Amelia eventually woke up, watching carefully over her sister while being nestled under her arm. Amelia looked up at Shade, peacefully asleep, and didn't want to wake her, so she chose to stay by her side. As she watched, with the curtain closed all the way, all she could see was the feet of numerous doctors and nurses walking on by; it was busy, like most hospitals. After a while Amelia fell back to sleep again by her sister's side.

When Shade woke up again, she saw Jonny standing over by the curtain, waiting for her to wake up. At his side was Amelia, who must have woken up earlier. Jonny said, "Thank you, Amelia, for keeping Shade company. Can you give me a minute with your sister?"

Amelia nodded her head, opened the curtain, and left the room to join her family in the waiting room. Shade was so happy to see Jonny again, and she smiled at the sight of him. He walked over to her and bent down to give her a hug. He whispered in her ear, "I'm so sorry."

Shade had thought that she would never see Jonny again, and to see him was all she needed to feel better. Shade returned the hug, saying, "Jonny, it's not your fault." He pulled away to look at her as he sat down in the chair next to her bed. He scooted forward to hold her hand as she reached out to him.

"It *is* my fault. I shouldn't of left you." Shade saw that he felt a huge amount of guilt for what had happened to her.

"There's no way you could've known."

Jonny kept stroking her hand and looking into her eyes. The last time he'd seen her, she had been in pretty rough shape. He hadn't been sure that he would ever see her beautiful eyes again.

"You saved me, Jonny. I can't believe you put yourself at risk like that."

"I would do it again if it meant saving you, and I'm never leaving you again."

Shade couldn't believe how much Jonny really cared about her, but after his last remark, she knew deep down that he was telling the truth. They talked for a few more minutes about how thankful Shade was to Jonny and about how they were looking forward to the future.

Soon after that Amelia returned and climbed back up onto the bed under Shade's arm.

"Well, I'll let you get some more rest." Jonny kissed Shade's forehead before letting go of her hand. He looked back at her once more before leaving the room. He saw she was comforted by her younger sister and thought it best to leave her be.

Shade watched him with a smile after he closed the curtain

behind him. She took a deep breath, released it, and pushed her head back into the pillow. She was happy that she had such a loving family, as she looked down at Amelia. She'd almost felt that she was dreaming when Jonny had told her that he would never leave her. For years she had daydreamed about him saying those exact words. Today she had finally heard them.

She started to relax again with the comfort of Amelia by her side, and soon her eyes closed. Hearing the sound of footsteps outside her room, she kept waking up in fear of being harmed again. She felt that she was back in those dark woods, but then she would look down at her baby sister and know that she was safe.

Every once in a while Ariel would check on them, and every time she did she saw both her girls asleep together in the bed. Then she would go back to the waiting room with the rest of her family and be comforted by her loving husband.

22

THE TRUTH

Six days later, Ariel and Aaron were called down to the Boston Police station regarding Shade's attacker. As parents, they wanted to know who the person was that had attacked their daughter. After multiple interviews with the police, it was ruled that Aaron had used his gun for self-defense in saving his daughter. The investigation had revealed that the man who attacked Shade was behind two other unsolved cases in Boston.

Down at the police station, Ariel and Aaron were anxiously waiting to speak with the detective who had been following Shade's case from the beginning. Ariel's leg was tapping up and down; she could barely wait any longer. Aaron was sitting on her right, and he was looking up at the ceiling fan. He watched it revolve around and around, and then his eyes turned to his phone to see what time it was. He thought to himself, *How much longer are we gonna have to sit here?*

The station was completely empty, except for officers at their desks typing away, and no one had paid attention to them since they sat down. They were in a small waiting room in a corner near the entrance. The atmosphere was calm, but inside, Ariel's mind was enraged.

Ariel and Aaron had finally gotten some sleep over the last couple of days. Their main concern was Shade's well-being, because the first night she'd come home from the hospital she'd had intense night terrors, fearing that her attacker was going to come back and harm her again.

Awakened by the screams in her room across the hall, they'd both rushed to in wake her up from her terrifying dream. Those night terrors had continued through the next couple of days, but the previous night Shade had slept all the way through, and Ariel hadn't heard her daughter screaming for the first time since she had come home.

Ariel hoped that Shade had finally conquered her thoughts, not letting her fear haunt her at night. Ariel's hatred toward the attacker had grown each night, and she desperately wanted to know who had done this to her daughter.

Aaron saw how annoyed his wife was. He placed his hand on her thigh to stop her leg from twitching and held onto her hand.

Ariel could not stand being ignored any longer; she was going to take a stand. They had been waiting for what seemed like forever. Just as she was going to get out of her chair, at the opposite end of the room a door opened, and an officer emerged from what it appeared to be his office. With a gun secured on his hip, and dressed in all black, he made his way over to the Smiths. He looked at Ariel, noting the anger through her body language and her facial expressions. He was close enough to see that her leg was shaking like a leaf.

"Mr. and Mrs. Smith, I am Detective Rodgers. I'm so incredibly sorry for the wait. I'm sure this is the last thing you wanted to wait to find out." He shook both of their hands firmly as they stood up from their chairs. Aaron was a head taller than Rodgers; he looked down at him when he shook his hand.

"No, we understand, Detective. Did you identify who attacked our daughter?"

"Come in my office; we have a lot to discuss." Rodgers then led

Ariel and Aaron toward his office. They walked by a man in hand-cuffs being escorted by a police officer to a holding cell, and then they entered his office.

Again there were two chairs sitting in front of a desk. Ariel eyed the folder on top of the desk, thinking that what was contained in the folder would finally give her the answers she'd been looking for.

"Please sit," Rodgers said, closing the door behind him. When Ariel looked around, she couldn't believe all the file cabinets in the office. There were dozens, and some files were stacked high on top of the file cabinets. The window blinds were opened slightly, so a small amount of sun crept into the room.

"First off, how is Shade doing?" Rodgers asked as he sat in the chair behind his desk.

Aaron raised his eyebrows and sighed, thinking about how much longer she had to go, with physical healing as much as emotional healing. "Well … uh … she's getting better each day. Her wounds were all repaired, and she will make a full recovery. She just came home a couple days ago from the hospital, and she's still pretty shaken up by the whole ordeal."

Rodgers grinned at hearing that Shade was going to make a full recovery. After seeing her six nights ago at the skate park, he hadn't been sure that she was going to make it through the night. Then his smile weakened as he heard that she was still traumatized by the event. "Yes, I can't even begin to imagine what you both have gone through the past few days, and I thank you for your cooperation. Everyone is different after they go through something like this."

"Yes, and she actually slept through the whole night last night for the first time, so we're going through a healing process, just as she is. Each day she's getting better," Aaron said.

"Well, that's great to hear. We don't know why things like this happen, but it's something we can't always prevent." Then he put his forearms on top of the desk, looking straight at Ariel and Aaron. He could sense the eagerness in the room; these two parents just wanted to find answers to who had hurt their daughter and possibly traumatized her for life.

"Our team examined the body, and we identified your daughter's attacker. His name is Nick Williams. Williams has been working at a local fish-bait shop in the city, but had recently just retired keeping a low profile, and apparently this was not the only crime that he committed." Ariel took in a deep breath and exhaled when she heard him say the man's name.

Rodgers opened the file on the desk and took out the first picture that was inside. It showed a man with a hat, holding a large box of some sort in front of an apartment building.

Ariel and Aaron examined the picture closely and recognized where he was exactly. "Is this in front of our old apartment building?" Aaron looked up from the picture and at the detective.

"Yes, I'm afraid so. You see, during that time when Williams entered and exited the apartment building, we had no idea who he was; he looked like just a normal delivery guy. When the apartment burnt down, we could not identify who this man was. He had no social media whatsoever in his real name, and our detectives labeled the case as a propane tank accident, that was we thought caused the building to burn down. A few days after the case was labeled, we found evidence in a nearby dumpster that had not burned entirely. In that dumpster was a gas container that was covered with fingerprints. We had no idea whether it was thrown in there a few weeks prior or if it had been in there for a while, but the fingerprints on that gas container didn't match the fingerprints of anyone who lived in the building."

Rodgers took a breath and kept eye contact with the Smiths to see whether he should go any further. After all they had gone through in the past few days, he was afraid that more news could put them over the edge.

Aaron uncrossed his legs and leaned forward, elbows on knees and hands interlocked.

Ariel felt that she was going to throw up. She was sitting straight up with her legs close together. She looked around the room and saw a bucket next to the desk. She thought it would be close enough for her to use if she was going to vomit. That feeling subsided, and she listened back in to what Rodgers had to say.

"When Williams was pronounced dead, our team went to security cameras all around the city, trying to spot him and to see what he'd been doing the last few days. Luckily, one of our older team members who had worked on the case of the apartment building firm was assigned to this case, and he has an eidetic memory. He recognized Williams immediately and proved he was responsible for that fire, over two decades later. We showed him pictures of what he looked like, and then he showed us footage back decades ago of a restaurant near the apartment building, where the camera captured his facial features not too long after the fire broke out."

"Everything clicked once we matched the fingerprints on the gas container from the dumpster to Williams's fingerprints. That was all we needed to show that he was responsible for the fire—the fingerprints were a match. He probably thought that the empty container would be burnt in the fire, but it was the one piece of evidence we found. Now, decades later, we've finally found out who was responsible. Not everyone can hide from their crimes for decades, but he deluded everybody for all that time. We even interviewed some of Williams's next-door neighbors, and they said that he did nothing out of the ordinary; he seemed to be just a normal guy that went to work every day."

He paused, seeing whether the information was really sinking in to the Smiths, before he started speaking again. Rodgers could read the stress on their faces. He didn't know how much more they could take, but he decided to continue.

"Our team did some digging, and myself and a fellow officer then went down to where Williams worked. We interviewed his co-workers and boss to see if Williams ever did anything out of the ordinary over the past few weeks. The news came to a complete shock to his co-workers, and especially his boss. Mark said that Williams had been with the company for over forty years, and he was the most hardworking person he'd ever met. He couldn't recall any time he was unlike himself. Mark was very cooperative with answering all our questions, and he then said that Williams would at times act shaky, or be easily distracted, but he didn't think it was anything to worry about at the time. It appears Williams was a psychopath, who basically lived a double life.

"When we interviewed some of his neighbors, they spoke very highly of his mother and how her passing away really affected him. They were very close before she lost a battle with cancer. We also found a UPS delivery uniform when we searched his home, under his bed. It was the same uniform he'd been wearing on the day of the apartment fire. He obviously was trying to hide it, and it was another piece of evidence to prove that he was the prime suspect we'd been looking for all along."

Aaron thought about his parents every day, knowing they would be proud of the man he'd come to be. Hearing that this person was responsible for his parents' deaths as well as the attack on his daughter made him fume inside. He gasped at seeing the blurry picture on the desk. He couldn't believe that this guy had never been caught until now. He'd been roaming the streets for years—his earliest crime dated back to 1999.

Rodgers continued. "That's not all. We went back in his medical records and family history. It was documented that he was in a coma for four years, and his mother died from cancer shortly after he got out of the hospital. Also, when we searched his home, we found some very interesting pictures inside a chest in his bedroom. Ariel, I'm going to show you some pictures, and I want you to see if you know this person." Ariel nodded while he reached back into the file. He spoke again. "We unlocked the chest with the key that we found in his pocket, and we found these."

Ariel looked down at the desk and then at him, biting her lip as she watched him start to pull more photos out of the file. She didn't understand why he was asked her to identify someone who was in a picture.

The picture that he slid across the table was of a younger version of Nick Williams—and her mother, Amy! A light bulb went off in Ariel's mind as she recognized him—and realized he'd been watching her all this time. Her heart began to race. She couldn't believe what she was gazing upon.

He was the older fellow she'd often seen walking around her old college campus. He would always be there when she went to her favorite coffee shop. After not seeing him for a while, she would sometimes get a sense that someone was watching her when she went food shopping. Every time she turned around, she would see an older man with a hat and scarf. All she could see was his eyes, and then only his back as he turned away from her. Looking back now, she realized that he'd been watching over her whenever she went out of the house.

"Now going back to the Elm Street case, when your parents were killed, we found traces of DNA in the residence, but we had no one to pair it to. It was different than the two victims'. He was our prime suspect all along. He did a terrific job, hiding all these years, thinking that he would get away with what he'd done.

"I can now rule these cases as solved, the killings and the apartment building fire. It looks like Williams and your mother knew each other when they were younger, but we have no answer for you, Ariel, as to why he did these things. I'm really sorry."

Ariel trembled as she looked at the picture of her mother. She couldn't understand how this man had known her mother all those years ago, and she was so frustrated and disgusted that he'd walked a free man for so many decades.

Aaron looked over at his wife, surprised that she was keeping her cool. He knew that the gears were turning in her mind, trying to connect the dots and make sense of how this all had happened.

She grazed the picture with her fingertips, looking at her mother's smile and knowing that she'd finally found out who'd murdered her parents. Aaron grabbed her other hand; he was thinking that both of them had had their parents taken away by the same person—a malicious, evil, person who'd gotten what he deserved. If he'd only been caught all those years ago, he never could have harmed Shade.

Ariel thought about the pain that her parents had suffered and the horror they'd gone through before they'd died. It sent a chill down her spine when she thought about how this guy had known her mother and then had turned around and murdered her and her husband.

The room was silent, until Ariel broke her peace. Not looking up, she said, "Is that all, Detective? I need to go home and spend time with my children."

Aaron was also stunned by the news. He didn't understand why Ariel was so eager to leave after hearing the truth. She was also being very courteous to Mr. Rodgers, which was very unlike her after such an unthinkable thing had been revealed.

Ariel just wanted to get out of the police station as quickly as possible so no one could see her causing a scene. She stared right at Mr. Rodgers, waiting for him to say she could go. Her legs started to twitch again, and the feeling in her stomach returned, as she gulped.

"Yes, I believe that's it. My heart goes out to the both of you. You don't have to think or worry about him hurting your family anymore."

Before he could say more, Ariel got up out of the chair so quickly that the chair was pushed backward and tipped over. She stormed out of the office, letting the door fly wide open. The other officers stared after the upset woman fleeing the building.

Meanwhile, Aaron was still processing everything. He shook his head and said, "Thanks, sir, for your time." Then he got up from his chair, stood up the one that Ariel had knocked over, and pushed it back close to the desk. Then he went after Ariel.

Rodgers felt a breeze as Aaron shut his office door. He picked up the pictures and placed them neatly back into the folder, and closed it. Rodgers got up from his chair and opened one of the file cabinets in the corner behind his desk. He put the folder in the cabinet and pushed the drawer shut. He couldn't believe that three unspeakable crimes had been committed by one sinister person. He felt a sense of accomplishment. The city was now safer with that man not freely roaming the streets anymore. He'd gotten what he deserved. As of right now, his lifeless body was decaying in a morgue.

"Ariel, Ariel wait up!" Aaron yelled across the room as he saw her walking out the front entrance.

Ariel's mind was occupied and consumed by what she had just heard and nothing else at all. She was so furious at how Williams had never been caught after the horrible things he had done. With wind blowing back her hair as she exited the building, she proceeded to march straight ahead. She got a few steps away from the doors, and then Aaron busted through them and caught up with her.

"Ariel, will you slow down!" He tried to grab her hand, but she pulled away from him. She turned around and dropped to her knees, weeping, as Aaron caught her. He knew that she couldn't keep everything bottled up forever and that her emotions would have to come to the surface.

She was thinking that if this man had been caught back when he'd committed the murders on Elm Street, he wouldn't have killed Aaron's parents, and he wouldn't have harmed Shade. Her true emotions came out. She kept screaming, "Why! Why! Why!"

Aaron had no answer for her, but all he could say was, "He's gone, okay! He's not hurtin' this family anymore, all right? He gone for good, and no one else is gonna hurt my family ever again, not on my watch!"

Ariel looked up at Aaron and saw fury in his eyes. She realized that he, too, had found out who was to blame for his parents' deaths.

Wind revolved around them as they continued to hold each

other in the parking lot. Waves of emotion pulled them to the ground. Aaron always put on a tough attitude of a man who never cried, but this news hit his breaking point. He couldn't hold in his tears anymore, so he just let it all out. He and Ariel were both so distraught that they couldn't stand up. The news had literally crushed them.

Minutes went by, and they finally stood up together, looking at the bright sun peeking around the clouds. Aaron wiped the tears from around Ariel's eyes. He hated seeing her so emotional. The wind blew in their paths once more. They looked at each other and realized that they'd finally gotten justice for the deaths of both of their parents.

The warm summer sun beamed down on the city of Boston, and Ariel felt her parents' spirits close by. She knew that they'd been looking down on her and her children all this time. She held onto Aaron and didn't want to let go. She felt that while she had him in her life nothing else bad was going to happen, not ever again. She looked down at the bracelet on her wrist. Ariel realized that her childhood would've been different if she'd been raised by her real parents. She might've not married Aaron, who had been there for her through all the tough times.

The two of them looked up to see three bluebirds fly by and then land on some wires at the end of the parking lot. As they chirped about, Ariel thought of those three bluebirds as herself, Aaron, and Eric. They had gone through a lot together, and they were each very strong, but they were stronger when they were all together.

Then the three bluebirds flew off the wire and away from the parking lot, off deeper into the city. They soared together, one following the other, as another strong gust of wind blew, and then the birds vanished behind a building.

Ever since they were teenagers, Ariel and Aaron had endured a lot of tragedies in their life together. She realized that she had to find the good in this piece of news, and for a short moment she felt relieved that she didn't have to look over her shoulder any more or have that terrible feeling in her stomach.

Ariel and Aaron made a consecutive decision to not tell Shade about her attacker's past. It would only cause her to feel worse about what had happened and feel more upset about the situation. They thought that they needed to be strong for their daughter to start her healing process.

When Shade was born, they'd both made the decision that their kids would not know about their parents' past and what had happened to them. Normally, a kid would have two sets of grandparents, but instead Shade and her siblings just had one amazing aunt and uncle, along with Chelsea's parents.

On the drive home, Ariel was quiet. She kept thinking about all the other times she'd felt that someone was watching her. Either walking down the street or in a store, she would get a weird sense that she should turn around, but she would see no one. Aaron tried to lighten the mood with a joke about the traffic, but Ariel didn't even smile. He asked her if she wanted to listen to some music to try and get her mind off the subject, but she replied, "I just need to collect my thoughts right now, Aaron." He respected that request, and the rest of the ride home was completely silent.

Aaron turned onto Elm Street and saw his sons playing basketball in their driveway. He saw Jonny's car parked on the street in front of the house. Aaron beeped the horn playfully to get the kids to move so he could pull in the driveway. Liam and Jack moved out of the way so he could pull in.

Ariel and Aaron were still struck by the recent news about Shade's attacker, but they had to be strong for their kids. As much as they wanted to break down as they had in the parking lot, they wanted to teach their kids to be strong and to not let anything break you.

Aaron got out of the car and was immediately run into by Jack. "Hey, bud." Aaron hugged him, and he said, "Dad, can you help me beat Liam!"

Liam overheard what his brother had said to his dad and replied, "You can try and help Jack all you want, Dad, but it's not gonna work. You're old!" Then he returned to shooting his basketball.

Aaron looked down at Jack and saw in his eyes how badly he wanted to beat his older brother. He answered, "Well, Jack, it's a long summer. We can get you scoring more by the time you go back to school. In the meantime, I think I'll take on both of ya, because apparently I'm too old, huh?"

He then ran out to Liam and blocked his next shot. Liam screamed, "Hey, Dad!" Aaron then grabbed the ball and started dribbling in between his legs as Jack tried to steal it. He spun away from Jack, only to be met by Liam, but Aaron shot over him, and the ball swished through the net.

"Hey, come on. That wasn't fair! I wasn't ready!"

Aaron replied, "Hey, well, I wasn't the one out here already putting up shots. You should be the one who's making shots, not me. I may be old, but I can still beat ya." Aaron then continued to play basketball with his two sons. Even though his body had aged over the years, he'd never stopped loving the game of basketball. Now he would get to inspire his two sons and show them how to love the game as well.

Ariel looked back as she walked on the porch. She saw how much of a loving father Aaron was. She couldn't believe how much Liam had grown in the last year. He was almost up to Aaron's shoulders, just passing six feet. She had a feeling that he would be the tallest out of all her children. As much as Aaron hated to admit it, he was at the point in his life where he was going to start shrinking.

When she went inside, Ariel saw Amelia sitting on the floor, watching TV and holding her doll. Her face turned happy as she saw her mom standing by the doorway. She dropped her doll and ran over to give her a hug. Ariel returned the hug, saying, "Hey, honey."

She saw Jonny in the kitchen and Shade lying on the couch, wrapped up in a fuzzy blanket. Shade said, "Hey, what did the detective say?" She shut the TV off to hear what her mom had to say.

"Amelia, honey, why don't you go watch your brothers play outside." Amelia looked up at her mom, and Ariel combed her hair with her fingers. "Okay." She picked her doll up off the floor and went out the front door. After she'd shut the door, Jonny came out from the kitchen.

"Hey, Mrs. Smith, how are ya?" Jonny then passed Shade the glass of water he'd brought for her.

"I'm fine, Jonny, thank you. And please call me Ariel." He nodded before sitting down on the section of couch across from Shade.

Shade slightly turned her body so that she could look at her mom. The pain had subsided the last couple days, and she could almost lie on her side entirely without pain, but not for long. Every night she had to sleep on her back. Normally she would sleep on her side, but she had to wait until her body was fully healed. Shade took a sip of water as her mother spoke.

"Well, the man who attacked you was someone who the police have been looking for quite some time. He was involved with a lot of crimes throughout Boston, and he never got caught until now."

She heard how her mother seemed to speak in sections, as if not fully sure what to say next. The truth was that she didn't want to focus on what had happened in her past. Shade had a long journey ahead of her as it was. "But that doesn't matter anymore, because I won't let anyone hurt you ever again." Ariel put her hand on Shade's cheek, and she smiled up at her mom. "Did you sleep a little better last night?"

"Yeah, I did. It feels so good to be back in my own bed again."

Ariel understood that. She then changed the subject. "Jonny, how's your mother?"

"Oh, she's doing good. I hope you don't mind me being here—" Just as he was about to say Mrs. Smith, he corrected himself by calling her Ariel.

"No, of course not, Jonny. It's great that you're here to help out with Shade. I really appreciate it." She slipped off her shoes and left them near the door. "Now, who's hungry for some lunch?" She walked into the kitchen to start preparing some sandwiches for everybody.

Ariel was happy to see that Jonny brought her daughter so much happiness. She looked up from what she was doing in the kitchen and saw them both laughing on the couch. The way she'd seen Shade a few nights ago, she'd thought she would never hear that laugh again. She and Jonny had turned the TV back on and were watching a movie. Ariel saw that Jonny had a soft spot in his heart for Shade. Every single day that summer Jonny came by to check up on her. Their connection was unique, one that not all couples have.

Then she thought about the connection she and Aaron had, and she smiled brightly. As she was getting the bread out of the fridge, she heard Liam say, "Okay, no dunking allowed, Dad!" The kitchen window was cracked open slightly, so Ariel could hear Liam screaming from the front of the house.

It was hard for Aaron to get up high enough to dunk the ball nowadays. He loved spending time with his kids and couldn't wait to watch his boys play ball when they get older. They had just started getting the fundamentals down but still had lots to learn, and much room to grow as players. Aaron was already a proud papa who cheered on the sidelines at every game, and he wouldn't trade those games for the world.

23

FULL CIRCLE

After a long, hot summer and cool fall in Boston, the weather almanac predicted that a nor'easter was going to submerge the city of Boston in snow and ice one January day. The forecast was that the storm would not stop until the following evening.

The storm was just moving in, and the whole city was as quiet as it usually was just after the holiday season, at the beginning of January. Not many people were out; everyone was inside, preparing for the storm and expecting to lose power. The streets were deserted, as inches of snow were coming down every hour. But inside the TD Garden, a crowd was cheering on their favorite basketball organization. Thousands of people were screaming and cheering on their Boston Celtics. With music playing during the timeouts and cheerleaders down on the court, the TD Garden was always a roaring place on a Friday night.

The Smiths still stuck to their tradition, after all these years, of going to a Celtics game as a family. It had all started back when Ariel and Aaron were kids, and now they took their kids along to the TD Garden every January. They got tickets in their stockings every Christmas, something that everybody in the Smith family could enjoy.

As a father, Aaron loved seeing their faces on Christmas morning, when they would empty their stockings first. Peeking out of the tops of the stockings would be the white-and-green tickets, and they would rejoice, excited to go to the game the next month.

Aaron's family was in row twelve, and Eric's family was in row thirteen. Aaron high-fived his brother behind him after a three pointer was made. Standing next to Aaron was Jack, wearing a green curly wig and with signature green clovers painted on his cheeks.

Next to Jack was Liam, wearing his flashing bling necklaces and Celtics sweatshirt. As he'd predicted since the summer, he did make varsity, and it boosted his confidence. Shade was holding up Amelia around her waist so she could see better. Shade had made a full recovery since the last summer and was so much more family oriented than she'd been before the incident. Even though she was physically healed, her thoughts often brought her back to that dark night when she'd been walking home. But the night terrors had left her dreams for good.

Jonny was still with Shade, but he followed her dad's rule: No boyfriend on Celts night. She obeyed him and was having a lot more fun than she'd thought she would with her family. She knew that if she did bring Jonny, her dad would just end up sitting in between them during the game.

Ariel was cheering along and looking backward to talk to Chelsea while watching the game. Aaron felt emotional, knowing that he'd made the right decision to not play overseas in Germany. If he had, he never would've married Ariel and had these four beautiful kids. He was over the moon that Shade was fully recovered. The Smiths had finally come full circle.

Since Jonny was still in Shade's life, Aaron made it his job to annoy her in any way possible, as he had when Ariel had been dating Jordan in college, but not to that extreme. Ariel demanded that he not spy on Shade when she was out with Jonny.

Aaron wasn't the kind of dad that was embarrassing or strict, he would only be protective and sometimes childlike out in public. He might embarrass her, but Shade wouldn't trade her dad for the world. The same went for her mom; she'd grown a lot closer to her parents after the incident.

It was extremely hard for Aaron to let Shade go out of the house after she'd been attacked. Now that the attacker was no longer alive, the Smiths could finally live in peace. Aaron bought Shade a Mace Spray to bring with her at all times, just as a precaution.

As the game went on, boisterous cheering continued through the arena. The Celtics were down by two, and the visiting team had possession of the basketball. The Bulls point guard was handling the ball up the court, being defended by a scrappy Celtic guard.

The twenty-four-second shot clock was turned off, and all the guard had to do was run out the clock. As his focus went to looking at how much time was left, he made a costly mistake, leaving the ball unprotected as he stood up from his athletic stance to see the clock.

As the defender saw an opportunity to snatch the ball, he took action, tipping the ball out of the man's hands and into the back court. The man who had the ball in his possession now became the defender, and he was trying to catch up to him. The Smith family stood up from their seats and witnessed the incredible steal.

The Celtic point guard felt the defender on his hip and immediately went up for the layup after taking his last dribble inside the three-point line. As the ball left his hand, the defender behind him pushed him in the back, causing the referee to blow his whistle.

A common shooting foul, it was then labeled as an and one, as the ball fell through the hoop. The score was then tied. As fellow teammates helped him up, as he was surrounded by loud cheering and electric clapping.

There was sixteen seconds left on the clock, and he had to make his free throw to put Boston up by one. It had been a physical game throughout the entire night, and he wanted to finish the game; an overtime was the last option. If he made this, then the Bulls would have no time-outs left, and they would have to get a fast-break point to win.

Players lined up at the free-throw line, and the ref bounced the ball to him. Trying to zone everything out, he went back to when he was a little kid shooting around in open gym and thinking: I want to be remembered, not as good player but as a great player.

In the hushed arena, he bounced the ball three times and took a deep breath before shooting. He bent his knees and extended his arms high as the ball shot into the air. With all eyes watching in the TD Garden and at home on TV, the ball neatly swished through the net, putting the Celtics up by one point. The arena came to life again as the ball sailed through the net. The center passed the ball in quickly to the point guard.

He was looking up court and saw a power forward running the floor hard, with no one on him. He threw the ball up-court, only to have it intercepted by the same Celtics point guard that had just made the free throw. If he hadn't sprinted back the way he did, the Bulls would've had a wide-open layup.

Back-to-back steals, and the crowd continued to stand on their feet while he dribbled the ball and the clock ticked down. When the buzzer went off, the Celtics had pulled off a one-point win against the Bulls. The steal had been sensational, and the entire game had been neck and neck, but Boston had pulled it out at the very end.

Outside of the TD Garden, thick fluffy snowflakes fell from the night sky, amid loud car horns and lights shining through the thick snow all over the city. High up in the sky the Zakim Bridge could be seen, glowing as if full of wonder. It glistens, in all its glory, among the rest of the city lights.

When some people come and visit Boston for the first time, they end up buying an "I *heart* Boston" sweatshirt or T-shirt. When they return home, they realize that Boston has become a part of them and will remain in their hearts forever.

About the Author

Syd Sullivan writes edge-of-your-seat thrillers from a small town in New Hampshire. *Prime Suspect* is the exciting sequel to *Unsolved Case*.